TRUTH AND
CONSEQUENCES

"You said that you love me," he said. "And always will. Tell the truth now."

"How can I love you?" Grace answered. "I hate you. No, not that. I am indifferent to you."

His face was angry, she saw in the moonlight. "Liar!" he said. "We will have the truth spoken, Grace. You hate me, perhaps. I will accept that. You are not indifferent to me."

She cried suddenly, her eyes excited. "I hate you. I hate you. I hate you!" She raised both fists and pummeled at his chest.

"Now we are getting somewhere," he said, and he took her by the upper arms and lowered his head and kissed her, and she felt her knees weaken. . . .

A
PROMISE
OF SPRING

by

Mary Balogh

A SIGNET BOOK

NEW AMERICAN LIBRARY

A DIVISION OF PENGUIN BOOKS USA INC.

NAL BOOKS ARE AVAILABLE AT QUANTITY DISCOUNTS WHEN USED TO
PROMOTE PRODUCTS OR SERVICES. FOR INFORMATION PLEASE WRITE
TO PREMIUM MARKETING DIVISION, NEW AMERICAN LIBRARY,
1633 BROADWAY, NEW YORK, NEW YORK 10019

SIGNET TRADEMARK REG. U.S. PAT. OFF. AND FOREIGN COUNTRIES
REGISTERED TRADEMARK—MARCA REGISTRADA
HECHO EN DRESDEN, TN., U.S.A.

SIGNET, SIGNET CLASSIC, MENTOR, ONYX, PLUME, MERIDIAN
and NAL BOOKS are published by New American Library, a division of
Penguin Books USA Inc., 1633 Broadway, New York 10019

First Printing, February, 1990

1 2 3 4 5 6 7 8 9

PRINTED IN THE UNITED STATES OF AMERICA

To
Maryann Vincze
A neighbor and friend

1

When the Reverend Paul Howard, rector at the village of Abbotsford in Hampshire, died at the age of two-and-thirty years, his death caused considerably more stir than his life had ever done. He had been a gentle, studious man, revered as a saint, honored as a guest, coveted as visitor to the sick, and largely ignored as a preacher. It was the least of their troubles, the older Miss Stanhope had once remarked to Mrs. Cartwright, to be forced to sit through the hour-long sermon each Sunday when one had only to look at the reverend's face to know that the Almighty had sent them one of his blessed angels in disguise.

In death the rector was lifted once and for all beyond the ordinary. Mrs. Cartwright told several of her acquaintances in some awe that Miss Stanhope's words had been prophetic. The Reverend Howard was walking home after visiting one of the cottages beyond the village, his nose in a book as usual, when the screaming of children had penetrated his consciousness and he had looked up to see one small child in a forbidden field, cornered by a bull that someone had obviously been annoying.

The rector hurled his precious book to the dust, roared with greater ferocity than anyone would have guessed him capable of, vaulted over the wooden fence with more agility than he would have thought possible, picked up the child and lowered him gently over the fence to join the other screaming youngsters, and turned to face the bull—for all the world

like David about to take on Goliath, Mr. Watson, the farmer
poet, said afterward, though Mr. Watson had not been
present to witness the incident. Only the children had.

Unfortunately, the Reverend Howard did not possess a
slingshot as David had done. He was dead probably even
before the terrified children turned and ran screaming toward
the village and help. He became an instant martyr, a man
who had given his life for a child. The poor bull survived
him by only a few hours.

But the people of Abbotsford and the surrounding countryside were not allowed to bask in the glory of such a sen-
sational tragedy. They were faced with a very practical
problem. Their rector had left behind him an unmarried
sister. A destitute sister, as far as anyone knew. She had come
with her brother five years before to live at the rectory as
his housekeeper. Neither had ever spoken of any other family
members. It was assumed that there were none. And the
Reverend Howard had not been a wealthy man. He had been
in the habit of giving away almost more than he possessed,
so that Mrs. Courtney and Mrs. Cartwright were agreed that
it was a wonder Miss Howard found anything in the rectory
kitchen to cook. Perhaps like angels the two of them lived
on air.

In the days following the death of her brother, Grace
Howard seemed unaware of the unenviable position in which
his heroism had placed her. Always quiet and dignified, she
seemed now wholly turned to marble. Paul had been all she
had left. Now she had nothing. No one. She could not think
beyond that deadening fact to consider also that she now had
nowhere to go and no means by which to live.

But the people about her were by no means so unaware
or so apathetic. Miss Howard's brother had died in order
to save one of their children. Miss Howard must be looked
after.

"She could come to live with us," Miss Stanhope said
to a small gathering of ladies in her parlor the day before
the funeral. "Letitia and I are all alone here since Mama
and Papa died and dear Bertie moved away. There is plenty

of room for all three of us. But will she be willing to come? Or will she see our offer as charity?"

Most of the ladies nodded to indicate that, yes, indeed, Miss Howard might be too proud to accept such a generous offer.

"She is a dear lady," Miss Letitia Stanhope added in support of her older sister, "and would not at all upset our routine, I am sure."

"Mr. Courtney has said that I might ask her to be governess to our Susan," Mrs. Courtney said. "But Susan is fifteen already and not much longer for the schoolroom. And what is to happen to Miss Howard then? The other four are all boys." She added absently, "And they are all older than Susan anyway."

The poorer people of the village, those who worked as laborers for the Earl of Amberley, took up a collection of food and money, which they planned to present to Miss Howard after the funeral. But they knew that such a gift, although a sacrifice to them, would not solve her problem for longer than a week or two at most.

The Countess of Amberley broached the subject to her son the earl as he sat with her in the conservatory at Amberley Court after they had returned from a visit to the rectory.

"The poor lady," she said. "One can clearly see, Edmund, that she has not yet quite comprehended either what has happened or what her predicament now is. She is in a daze. And Doctor Hanson swears that she has not even cried yet. I am so glad, dear, that you thought to offer to send Mrs. Oats and a couple of the other servants over tomorrow to help when the bishop arrives for the funeral."

The Earl of Amberley sighed. "We are very privileged, Mama, are we not?" he said. "We know very well that no matter what disaster befalls us, materially we may live still with great comfort. I shall have to find a situation for Miss Howard. I don't suppose she will accept a pension from me, will she?"

"It is unlikely," his mother replied. "Perhaps the bishop will have the inspiration to appoint a new rector who will need a housekeeper. But perhaps she would not choose to stay at the rectory, with her brother gone. I have been thinking of offering her the position of companion. What do you think, Edmund?''

"Companion?" he said with a frown. "You mean to you, Mama? You would hate to have such an employee, would you not?''

"Oh, dear," the countess said, "I am afraid I would, Edmund. But what else is one to do? I feel very deeply for Miss Howard. I know just how it feels to lose someone who is everything to one. I ache with memories of Papa at a time like this.''

The Earl of Amberley reached out and touched his mother's hand. "Let me talk to her first, Mama," he said. "Perhaps she has some idea of what she would like to do. Perhaps you will not have to make the sacrifice of burdening yourself with a companion.''

"It would not be a burden, Edmund," she said. "Miss Howard is a sensible lady.''

The earl smiled fleetingly. "Perry is taking this death hard," he said. "He was a very close friend of Howard's, you know. I was even somewhat jealous of the fact until I realized that being a friend of one person does not exclude one from being another's too. Perry and I have been friends for as long as I can remember.''

Sir Peregrine Lampman did not consult with anyone on what should be done about his friend's sister. He paid a call on her the morning after the funeral, after the bishop had left and before his neighbors and friends could put into effect any of their less-than-satisfactory suggestions for Miss Howard's future. And he asked her to marry him.

Sir Peregrine Lampman was the owner, since his father's demise three years before, of Reardon Park, a modest estate when compared with the lands of Amberley that adjoined it, but nevertheless large enough and prosperous enough to set him in the forefront of social life in the county. He lived in a neat eighteenth-century house of gray stone, built by his grandfather; the house was unimposing when compared to Amberley Court which was set in a picturesque valley close to the sea, but it nevertheless contained no fewer than ten guest bedchambers.

Sir Peregrine was a man of sunny nature and considerable charm, a man who seemed always to be smiling. He was not particularly tall, but he was slender and graceful. His friends and neighbors were in the habit of thinking him handsome. Yet there was nothing in his appearance to set him above the ordinary. His hair was neither dark nor blond, neither straight nor curly, neither short nor long. His eyes were neither blue, nor gray, nor green, but a mixture of all three. His clothes were fashionable, yet there was no suggestion of the dandy about his person.

It was his charm and his friendliness that probably gave the impression of handsomeness. Women especially were wont to admire him. He always had a teasing word, and even sometimes a wink, for the older ladies. Miss Stanhope was in the habit of calling his behavior "outrageous," yet she was clearly pleased by his attention. Miss Letitia Stanhope frequently simpered when "dear Sir Perry" commented on how becoming her new cap looked on her. He always thought, or pretended to think, that her cap was new.

He liked to flirt with the younger ladies and girls, yet always in just the right way so that none of them would ever mistake his intentions and consider them serious. For Peregrine had never been in love, despite his five-and-twenty years, and had never thought to be. It was too enjoyable to be free to let one's eye rove, to set a blush to glowing in this one's cheek, a sparkle in that one's eye. And as for his real needs, he could satisfy those with no trouble at all during his not infrequent though never lengthy visits to London.

He particularly liked to flirt with Lady Madeline Raine, the sister of the Earl of Amberley, who was five years his junior. He had teased her and indulged her all through her girlhood when she had tried desperately to keep up with the energetic and frequently dangerous exploits of Lord Eden, her twin brother. For the past two years, since she had made her come-out, he had flirted with her. She knew the game and played it as skillfully as he. One could smile very directly into Madeline's dancing eyes, pay her the most outrageous compliments, kiss the tips of her fingers, and know that the next moment she would tap one sharply on the shoulder with her fan, laugh back into one's eyes, and whisk herself off to some other admirer.

With men Peregrine was more serious. He looked for more than amusement and light conversation from his male friends. He read a great deal and thought a great deal and liked nothing more than to have another mind against which to sound his own ideas.

He had been friendly with Edmund Raine, the Earl of Amberley, for as far back as he could remember. And they were still close friends, despite Amberley's increasing tendency since inheriting the title to withdraw into himself. Amberley had been loaded down with responsibility too early, his own father having died when he was but nineteen, his twin brother and sister only twelve, and his mother close to nervous collapse for a year or more. And Amberley spent several months of each year with his family in London. The friendship of the two men was still firm, but they were not nearly as inseparable as they had been as boys.

The Reverend Paul Howard had filled the gap left in Peregrine's life. Quiet, gentle, and saintly as he appeared to his parishioners, he was a man of fiery intellect when confronted by someone who could match him in knowledge and understanding. Together the two men explored the worlds of literature and art and science and religion and philosophy and politics, frequently disagreeing, often arguing with rising, excited voices, but never quarreling. They learned to respect each other's minds.

Peregrine was a frequent visitor at the rectory. Almost daily he was in Grace Howard's company for at least a few minutes. He rarely spoke with her at any length as she was contained and always busy about some task. She seemed content to fade into the background behind her brother, never putting herself forward. Her large gray eyes looked on the world with great calm. Yet there was about her lovely face a certain tautness, most noticeable in the set of her lips, that occasionally made Peregrine wonder about her, about her

life, about what went on behind the quiet, neat exterior that
was Miss Howard.

Certainly she was capable of creating extraordinary beauty.
He liked to watch her as she embroidered, the flowers and
other designs creating themselves beneath her fingers so that
one almost felt that if one held the linen close one would
be able to smell their fragrance. And the flower garden
behind the rectory over which she toiled sometimes for hours
rioted with color and heady perfumes from early spring to
late autumn.

Peregrine was shocked and numbed by the sudden and
seemingly pointless death of his brilliant friend. For a whole
day he could think of nothing but his own loss and that empty
ache left inside. It was only when he went to the rectory to
pay his respects to Miss Howard that he became suddenly
aware of her plight. There were six other visitors crowded
into the little parlor, all talking in muted voices, as if afraid
of wakening the rector, who lay in his coffin in the dining
room next door.

Miss Howard sat in the middle of them, no different from
usual, except that to the eyes of Peregrine, who had seen
her almost daily for the past five years, there was perhaps
a little more tautness about her mouth and a little more
emptiness in her eyes than usual. She sat straight and serene
in her black mourning dress, her hands, usually so busy,
folded quietly in her lap, her eyes moving from speaker to
speaker, her control never for one moment slipping.

What would she do? Where would she go? Strangely,
despite the closeness of the friendship that had existed
between Peregrine and the rector, they had never talked about
personal matters. Peregrine had been very familiar indeed
with the Reverend Howard's mind. He knew almost nothing
about him as a person. He knew even less about his sister.

She would not be able to stay at the rectory. She would
be destitute. As far as Peregrine knew, brother and sister
had had no income apart from his pay as rector. And the
rector had been generous, even careless, with his money.
There would be no more money for Miss Howard.

He sat looking at her as the other callers talked and

commiserated with her. And he saw a brave and a lonely woman, one whose face and bearing denoted dignity and depth of character. He saw the quiet attractive woman who had made his friend's life comfortable and his home a place of some beauty. He saw a woman he had admired for years almost without realizing it. He saw a mysterious woman, one he had known for five years without knowing her at all.

He saw someone whom, belatedly, he wished to know.

Yet she would surely now disappear from Abbotsford to some unknown destination and to a life of dreariness or drudgery. Perhaps with her brother dead no one would ever again know Grace Howard.

Peregrine wanted to know her.

Even before he rose to his feet at the end of twenty minutes, took her cold hand in his and bowed over it, and left the stuffy, oppressive atmosphere of death and stunned grief, he knew what he must do. He returned to the rectory the morning after the funeral, before it was likely that there would be any other visitors, and asked Miss Grace Howard to marry him.

Grace moved across the parlor to stand at the window that looked out on her flower garden. She stood very straight, her hands clasped in front of her. Her black mourning dress, with its unfashionable natural waistline and full skirt, its plain, high-necked bodice, and its straight long sleeves accentuated her slimness. Her dark hair was dressed in its usual style, parted at the center, looped smoothly over her ears, and coiled at the back. She wore a small black lace cap.

"I cannot," she said, "though I must be sensible of the extreme kindness of your offer, sir. Paul would be pleased by your thoughtfulness. He valued your friendship more than I can say. But then you must know that."

"I wish you would reconsider, Miss Howard," Sir Peregrine said, standing in the middle of the parlor, his hands clasped behind him, watching her face in profile. It was, he realized for perhaps the first time, a rather handsome profile. "I believe you are in need of a home, and I am both free and willing to offer you one. But I will make it more secure than this one has been for you. I will make sure that an independence will be settled upon you in the event of my predeceasing you.''

She turned her head to look fully at him with her large, calm eyes. ''How very kind you are,'' she said in some wonder. ''I have always liked you, Sir Peregrine. You have been the friend that Paul always needed and never had before we moved here. Now I can respect you for my own sake too. But my answer must remain no. There are far too many reasons for our not marrying.''

Peregrine hesitated. ''You refer to our age difference?'' he asked.

A fleeting smile crossed her face before she turned back to the window. ''I am five-and-thirty years old,'' she said. ''Did you know that? I have never gone to any pains to make myself seem younger than I am. Paul was my younger brother.''

''And yet,'' he said, ''ten years is not seen as such an insurmountable gap when the man is the older.''

''Men do not bear children,'' she said quietly.

''I have never considered children essential to the fulfillment of my happiness,'' he said. ''If that is your only concern, Miss Howard, I beg you again to reconsider. I truly wish to have you as my wife.''

''For Paul's sake?'' she asked. ''You wish to look after the sister he left behind? It is a kind gesture, sir, but hardly one that will carry you through a lifetime. I am more grateful than I can say, but no. You would quickly tire of a wife ten years your senior, and one who is no match for you in either charm or intellect.''

''No,'' he said, ''it is not just on account of my friendship with Paul that I offer you marriage. It is on your account. It is true that we have scarcely conversed together in the five years since you have been living here. But I have seen a great deal of you in that time and have absorbed impressions of you that I was largely unaware of myself until I have given them deliberate thought in the last few days. I like you, Miss Howard, and believe I could be happy married to you.''

She turned fully to face him. Her face, he saw, was paler

and more tense than usual, though she looked at him with eyes whose calm was undisturbed. "Oh," she said, "you know nothing about me, Sir Peregrine. Nothing whatsoever. I have lived for thirty-five years. And despite the tranquillity of the life you have seen me lead here, they have not been uneventful years. Not by any means. If you knew but half of what there is to know about me, you would be thankful for my refusal, sir, believe me."

Peregrine shifted the weight on his feet but did not move or withdraw his eyes from hers. "Tell me, then," he said, smiling slowly at her. "Tell me what is so dreadful in your past."

She looked away from him suddenly, up to one corner of the ceiling behind his head. "Do you know?" she said. "Did Paul ever tell you that our father is Lord Pawley? Baron Pawley of Leicestershire. Prosperous and well-respected. No, I can see that he did not tell you. Paul quarreled with our father, broke with him, on my account. And took me with him wherever he went after that. For four years while he was a curate and for five years here—nine years during which there has been no communication between our father and our older brother and us. I was sitting in here before you came, wrestling with the question I have pondered for the last several days. Should I inform my father of the death of his youngest child? The one I took away from him."

She was still gazing upward at the ceiling behind his head, but Peregrine could see even so that her eyes were bright with unshed tears. And her lips began to tremble. He took a couple of steps forward and stretched out a hand to her.

"Ma'am?" he said. "Has my question caused you pain? Forgive me, please."

She did not move or respond to his words. "I have not cried," she said, "since . . . I have not cried for more than nine years. I did not expect to do so ever again. I did not think any tears were left inside me."

But she was clearly crying now. Her facial muscles were working beyond her control. Two tears spilled from her eyes, rolled down her upturned face, and dripped onto her dress. "Paul," she said as Peregrine took one more step toward her and gripped her shoulder with one strong hand. "Paul. Oh, Paul."

And then she was crying with racking sobs that seemed to be tearing her in two, her forehead on Peregrine's shoulder, his two arms about her, holding her loosely and comfortingly.

"Do you believe in heaven?" she asked a few minutes later, having dried her eyes and blown her nose on Peregrine's handkerchief. "Do you believe Paul is in heaven? I used to believe in such a place. But how can I continue to do so when I cannot believe in God, or at least not in a good God? Do you think he is in heaven? Has something good come out of all this?"

Peregrine smiled and absently reached out to put a fallen lock of hair back from her face. "I know how Paul would answer your question," he said. "And on this occasion I think I agree with him, though we never could agree on very many ideas. Even if heaven is not a place that exists for eternity, it can be a moment in time. I know how Paul must have felt when he knew he was about to be gored by that bull. He had saved the life of a child. He had with his own hands robbed death of one victory. I suppose he had no time for clear thought. I suppose he might have known a moment of terror seeing what was facing him. But I believe too that he felt exultant, happy. He was in heaven."

Grace reached up and pushed the stray lock of hair more firmly into the rest. "Thank you," she said. "Yes, that is just what Paul would have said. I was often angry in those first years, often rebellious. But Paul could always calm me. His logic was always irrefutable. His sermons were dull, Sir Peregrine—yes, I know they were—because he worked so hard on them. But when he spoke from the heart—and it took him only a few moments, not a whole hour—he could convince me that perhaps there is a God after all and perhaps He is even good. Who knows?"

"Are you better now?" Peregrine asked. "Do you wish to sit down?"

"I need a cup of tea," she said. "And I owe you an explanation. I have not explained what happened to sever

Paul and me from the rest of our family. Will you excuse
me for a few minutes while I boil the kettle?''

"If I may," Peregrine said, "I shall come with you and
watch you make the tea.''

He perched on the corner of the kitchen table, his arms
folded across his chest as she busied herself filling the kettle
and setting it on the fire to boil, measuring tea into the teapot,
taking two cups and saucers from a cupboard, and setting
out milk and sugar. She talked as she worked, her eyes on
what she was doing, not on him at all.

"I had a child," she said abruptly. "A son. He died. He
drowned.''

Peregrine had to swallow before he could find his voice.
"I did not know you had been married," he said.

"I have never been married," she said quietly and
deliberately. "My son was the child of my lover.''

"I see." Why did the room suddenly seem very small and
very quiet? Peregrine wondered.

"I am sure you do not," she said. "I will explain." She
sat down on a wooden chair close to where he sat on the
table, and watched the kettle as it began to hiss and hum.

"I did not mean to pry into your life," Peregrine said.
"You need say no more if you would rather not.''

"Paul and I never talked about it," she said. "Never once,
even though he gave up our father and our brother for me.
I must talk about it now, if you please. I grew up with Gareth.
He was not even a year older than I. We were playmates,
friends. We were going to be married. And then he decided
quite suddenly that he must buy a pair of colors and go off
to the wars. His country became more important to him than
any of the plans for his life and ours. We would resume those
plans when he came home, he said. We would marry, have
children, live happily ever after. We became lovers for a
few days before he left. And he left me with Jeremy. My
son.''

Peregrine could feel her pain, though she sat quietly at the
table, her hands folded together. There was something in
her voice, a certain throbbing that he had not heard there
before. "He died?" he asked gently. "Your l—Gareth?''

She stared into the fire for a long time. He thought she would not answer. "Yes," she said, one corner of her mouth twisting into a parody of a smile. "Yes, he died. And I was left to face the fury of my father, the contempt of my brother and sister-in-law. After Jeremy was born, I had to accustom myself to hearing him called bastard more often than Jeremy. And always he had to take a distant third place behind his two cousins. A very distant third place."

She rose to lift the boiling kettle off the fire and pour the water into the teapot. She fitted the cosy very carefully over the pot. "So distant," she said, "that the governess who was entrusted with their care when they went swimming at the lake did not even notice when Jeremy's clothes became entangled in some undergrowth and dragged him down. She did not even distinguish his cries from the shrieks of the other children playing. He was four years old. And then I had to endure hearing people tell one another that that was the best fate for a bastard: death before he could realize fully the awkwardness of his situation."

Peregrine got to his feet and poured the tea.

"Paul came home from university," she said. "He was the only one to show me sympathy, the only one to stand up against all those who thought of Jeremy as of little worth because he was born out of wedlock. He had a dreadful row with Pap—with my father and my older brother. And then he told me he would take me away, that I need not live any longer with the insults and the daily reminders of my son. I could be at peace, he said. And I was so broken with the pain of it all that I let him take me away. I hope I did not spoil his life. But I do not believe he ever wished to marry and have his own family. I think I was able to provide his life with some comfort."

Peregrine leaned forward from the chair he had taken and covered her hand with his own. "I am sure of it," he said. "There is no doubt whatsoever in my mind."

She looked up at him suddenly out of her large eyes and down at the cup that was set before her. "Oh," she said. "Did you pour? So you see, Sir Peregrine, the skeleton in my closet is a very large and a very sordid one indeed. I am not by any means the person you must have thought me all these years. Not quiet, demure Miss Howard, the rector's housekeeper, but a fallen woman, mother of a bastard son, mercifully dead.''

His hand was still over hers. ''Will you marry me?'' he asked.

She looked at him incredulously.

''I have always admired you as a woman of character,'' he said, ''someone very much in command of her own emotions and her own life. Now I am sure that my impression was correct. Will you do me the honor of becoming my wife?''

''You ask me at the wrong time,'' she said, frowning. ''At entirely the wrong time, sir. I am raw with the pain of my memories and the loss of my brother. I am very vulnerable.''

He clasped her hand more firmly in his own. ''Will you marry me?'' he asked.

''Don't,'' she whispered. ''For your own sake, don't.''

''Marry me,'' he said. ''Please. Give me the chance to put some joy into your life.''

She shook her head. ''I will take the joy from yours,'' she said.

Peregrine smiled. ''Give me a chance to prove you wrong,'' he said. ''Say you will marry me. Say it. One little word. Please?''

Grace drew a breath that shuddered out of her again. ''Yes, then,'' she said. ''Yes. Oh, God forgive me. Yes.''

2

The Misses Stanhope called on Grace immediately after luncheon, laden with fruit and vegetables, freshly baked currant cakes, and a chicken, for the purpose of inviting her to stay with them until she got settled elsewhere. It was better not to invite her to live with them, Miss Stanhope had explained to Miss Letitia, as she might feel beholden to them; better to make it seem that she was to be their guest and to let the term of her stay drift on indefinitely until she forgot about leaving them. But when they called upon Grace, it was only to have their invitation denied with gracious thanks. Miss Howard had that morning accepted Sir Peregrine Lampman's offer of marriage.

Well, Miss Stanhope declared later that afternoon to Mrs. Cartwright and later still to both Mrs. Courtney and Mrs. Morton while Miss Letitia nodded her agreement, she might easily have been knocked down with a feather if anyone had cared to try. And she was very much afraid that her mouth had dropped open and she had gaped. No, Miss Letitia assured her sister, nothing so ungenteel had happened, but she could vouch for the fact that her sister had turned several shades paler as had she.

Miss Howard was to marry Sir Perry, that handsome, sunny-natured young man they had known from childhood. And such a mischievous young boy he had been for sure. Did anyone remember the time when old Mr. Watson—God rest his soul—had been sleeping peacefully through the old

rector's sermon and young Perry in the pew behind had
begun to snore gently? A good thrashing he had probably
got for that prank if his father's frown had been any indication
of what was awaiting the boy when they arrived home.

And did anyone remember, Miss Letitia added, the time
when young Perry and the young earl—not that he was earl
at the time of course—had climbed the steepest part of the
cliff from the beach and Perry had got stuck almost at the
top? Young Lord Edmund had had to run back to Amberley
for help. Both lads had probably been thrashed for that one
too.

All the ladies appealed to remembered well and laughed
and nodded and added their own reminiscences.

And now Sir Perry was going to marry Miss Howard when
they had scarcely realized that he was old enough to marry
anyone at all. And Miss Howard must be . . . Surely she
must be . . . Well, she was older than he by at least ten
years, surely. And so quiet and prim and correct. Had anyone
ever seen her smile? No, no one had. A kind and gracious
lady, of course. They had all grown to love her, though no
one had really got to know her. Did anyone feel they knew
Miss Howard? No, no one did. But surely she was not suitable as a bride for Sir Perry, who was so young and so handsome and so full of fun.

"But it is just like him to do something so noble," Mrs.
Courtney suggested. "How very kind of him, for sure. Miss
Howard must be very gratified indeed."

"But she is so old for a young man's bride," Mrs. Morton
said. And forgetting her audience, "She is rather old to be
only just starting to present him with children, you know."

Both the Misses Stanhope blushed scarlet and avoided each
other's eyes. They did not know, or at least they had been
too refined to think about such a delicate matter.

Everyone paid a call at the rectory to congratulate Grace
and wish her well. And there was no spite or hypocrisy in
their wishes. They genuinely respected her, though they
admitted that they did not know her, and they were happy
that her future had been settled in such a fortunate way. They
genuinely wished her well.

If most of them believed that the marriage could not possibly be successful and that it must bring unhappiness to Sir Peregrine at least, then they also wished they might be proved wrong. Peregrine was a definite favorite in the neighborhood, and Grace had been accepted as one of them both for her own sake and for the sake of her brother, who had died so that one of their children might live.

The men doubtless had their own opinions on the betrothal too and doubtless expressed them to one another over their port when they had a chance. Some of them probably shared those opinions with their wives. Mr. William Carrington, brother of the Countess of Amberley and uncle of the earl, certainly did.

"It's as likely to succeed as any other marriage," he said when quizzed on the matter by his wife.

"Oh, William," she said scornfully, "she is ten years or more older than he. How can it possibly work?"

"Well, my dear," he said, pinching her ample bottom so that she shrieked and slapped at his hand, "I am almost ten years older than you, but it seems to me that we get along tolerably well together. Except when you are slapping out at me, of course."

"William! Do behave yourself," she said. "What if any of the children should see?"

"They are not allowed into our bedchamber unannounced, my love," he said reasonably. "And if they saw, they would only discover that their papa still fancies their mama after eighteen years of marriage."

"William," she said. "But this betrothal is a different matter. She is older than he. That is unheard-of. And Perry such a happy-go-lucky young man."

"Who is to know what couples will suit?" he said. "Who would believe that a careless, teasing sort of fellow like me would still be pinching a scold of a wife like you after almost twenty years, Viola, and getting away with only a slapped hand? They will work things out between them, never fear. Leave it to them, my love. You come on over here. That pinch has whetted my appetite."

"I hope you are right about Miss Howard and dear Perry,"

his wife said, wandering toward him almost absentmindedly. "Oh, William, what are you about now? And in broad daylight too. Anyone would think I was still a spring chicken. Oh, dear, I really think I am old enough now that this should be done only in darkness. Oh, very well, then. Are you sure the door is locked?"

The Earl of Amberley paid a call on his friend when he heard the news.

"It is really true, then, Perry?" he said when they had walked out behind the stables and stood looking out over the fields of Reardon Park.

"I assume you refer to my betrothal," Peregrine said. "I have heard that tone of voice from several others in the last day. I did not look for it from you, Edmund. Yes, it is true. Miss Grace Howard has consented to honor me with her hand. She is going to be my wife."

Lord Amberley was silent for a while. "She needs help," he said. "She is quite destitute, as far as anyone seems to know. But she is older than you, Perry, and although I will admit that she is a handsome woman, she seems to be quite lacking in openness and charm. Is your gesture not just too noble? Are you prepared to ruin the whole of your life for the sake of doing a kindness?"

Peregrine allowed his friend to reach the end of his speech before throwing the whole of his weight behind the fist that connected painfully with the earl's nose.

"Damn you, Edmund," he said between his teeth, glaring as the other staggered on his feet and lifted a hand to the blood that was spurting from his nose. "Damn you to hell. You will apologize if you expect me ever to speak to you again."

The earl took a handkerchief from his pocket and mopped at his bleeding nose with a slightly shaking hand before looking at his friend again. "I am sorry," he said from among the folds of the linen. "I do apologize, Perry. What I said was unforgiveable. The lady is your betrothed, and of course you must defend her honor." He withdrew the handkerchief, glanced down at it with a grimace, and raised a tentative hand to his reddening nose.

"I shouldn't have hit you," Peregrine said, turning sharply away to look out over the fields again.

"Yes, indeed you should," Lord Amberley said, checking the bridge of his nose to see if it were broken. "I could be happier without this pain, of course, but I am glad you did hit me, Perry. It proves something to me. Forgive me, please." He held out his right hand.

Peregrine took it and the friends smiled ruefully at each other. "It's not quite what you think, Edmund," Peregrine said. "It's not just because she is destitute, and it's not just because Paul was my friend. I care for her. I know that most people will never believe that. And I suppose it does not matter to me a great deal as long as she believes me. But I would like you to believe it. You are my oldest friend, Edmund, and probably the nicest person I know."

Lord Amberley squeezed his friend's hand. "It seems strange to think of you married, Perry," he said. "Somehow I have never thought of you settling down. I thought I would race you to the altar, though I have no thought of marrying before I am thirty. Three years to go yet! I wish you well. I really do. All the young ladies around here will be wearing the willow for you, you know."

Peregrine grinned. "Why would they miss me when they have you to angle after?" he said. "And Dominic twenty already and as tall and handsome as they come. And the Eden title and an estate in Wiltshire to boot. That nose of yours is shining like a beacon, Edmund. And still bleeding a little. We had better go back to the house and get some cold water for it."

The bishop had told Grace before he left late on the day of the funeral that he would send a new rector in one month's time and that she might stay at the rectory until then. Peregrine arranged it that the new man should marry them on the day after his arrival. Grace spent the night before her wedding with the Misses Stanhope, who preened themselves indeed on the distinction of having a bride married from their house. Even dear Bertie had not been wed at home.

Grace spent the month cleaning the rectory from top to bottom and sorting through Paul's effects. His books, his most valued possessions, she gave to her betrothed. His other few belongings, including his vestments, his sermons, his watch, and pitifully few other items, she put together into a box inside her own trunk, which was by no means overflowing when it was finally packed.

Sir Peregrine Lampman and Grace Howard were married on a gray and chilly morning in spring with all their friends and neighbors in attendance. It was a quiet celebration. Both bride and groom wore deep mourning. The Earl of Amberley and his mother, as well as his sister and brother, Lady Madeline Raine and Dominic, Lord Eden, had postponed their removal to London for the Season in order to provide a wedding breakfast in the state apartments at Amberley Court.

The gathering was a large and a quietly cheerful one. If the warm affection and hearty good wishes of a community could ensure the happiness of a marriage, then this one must prove to be one of the happiest. If any of those present still felt dismay at the age difference between bride and groom and at the disparity of their personalities, then they hid those feelings well and in all probability pretended even to themselves that they felt no such misgivings.

Peregrine took his bride home late in the afternoon and showed her the house and the garden and the stables. She had been to Reardon Park only once, several years ago when Peregrine's father had still been alive and his mother still at home.

Grace looked quietly at the long lawns and few trees behind the house and felt her husband smiling at her.

"I have an unimaginative gardener and am no better myself," he said. "If you wish to work your magic here, Grace, please feel free to do so. I have always been an admirer of your garden at the rectory."

"There is room for a rose garden here," she said. "I have always longed for a separate rose arbor. There was not enough space behind the rectory. And there should be daffodils and primroses among the trees. And flower beds.'' She gazed about her, obviously seeing in her mind far more than the bare green expanses that surrounded them. "There is room for a splendid orchard over there.'' She pointed to another stretch of lawn to the east of the house.

Peregrine laughed. "My gardener will be handing in his notice,'' he said. "I shall have to hire others. And I will learn from you, Grace. I have always wanted a beautiful garden, but I am afraid I gaze about me and cannot picture what can be done. You shall convert me into a devoted and domesticated gardener.''

Grace looked at him seriously. "You must not curtail your activities on my account,'' she said. "I will be content just to be here. You must not change your life.''

He smiled. "But my life has changed,'' he said. "Today. I am a married man now, my dear.''

It seemed strange to Grace after nine years to have a maid again to help her change her dress for dinner and brush out and coil her hair. It seemed strange to go down to a dinner that someone else had planned and prepared and to have it served by a butler and a footman. Strange to have someone else clear away the food and the dishes, and to know that someone else would wash the dishes in the kitchen.

And it was strange and somewhat embarrassing to discover that, although she had her own dressing room and sitting room, she was to share a bedchamber with her husband. She had not been at all sure during the past month exactly what kind of a marriage it was that Peregrine planned.

"I thought that perhaps you were offering me a marriage in name only, Peregrine,'' she said when he came to her after she had dismissed her maid and stood in the middle of the bedroom, her nightgown covering her decently, her hair brushed out and lying smoothly down her back. Her one concession to vanity was the absence of a nightcap.

"Perry, if you please,'' he said, coming to stand close to her. "I love my mother dearly and loved my father, but I have always been appalled by the lack of sensibility they showed when they named me.'' He grinned. "Grace, I have

married you. You are my wife. I would have offered you
the position of housekeeper here if I had not wanted more
of you. And I have always thought rather strange the frequent
custom of a husband and wife occupying separate rooms.
I will want to make love to you frequently. It is far more
convenient for us to share the same bed. Is it not to your
liking?''

She raised her large calm eyes to his. Her thin face was
pale. ''Yes,'' she said. ''Yes, I will be the wife you want
me to be, Perry.''

''You have beautiful hair,'' he said, reaching up both hands
and smoothing them lightly over it. ''You are a beautiful
woman, Grace.'' He bent his head and kissed her pale lips.
''Come to bed. I will see to the candles.''

As so often happened after a gloomy day, the clouds had
moved off during the evening, and the night was brightly
illuminated by an almost full moon and myriad stars.

Lady Grace Lampman lay with her head turned to one side,
watching her husband sleeping beside her. He looked
absurdly young in the repose of sleep, his fair hair rumpled,
his usually smiling face relaxed. She felt an ache of
tenderness for him. Perhaps there was an end to punishment,
after all. For her, that was. Only time would tell what her
marrying him would do to Perry.

She had not expected to come alive again. She had given
up life nine years before. Because she could never, even in
her worst moments, contemplate suicide, she had been forced
to keep on breathing and eating and sleeping and filling in
the time until she could stop living indeed. And she had
always been thankful for the small but infinitely precious gift
of Paul's love and for his need of her time, that commodity
that hung most heavily on her hands. But she had never
expected more than that, had never felt the need of more.

Until Perry had tempted her and in her weakness she had
given in to that temptation. And even then she had hoped
not to be forced back into life again. She had hoped that what
he wanted of her would be no different from what Paul had

accepted for nine years. She had hoped to be no more than his housekeeper, to share no more than his name.

She had always liked Perry, had always brightened at his knock on the rectory door, at his sunny smile, his frequent inquiries after her health, his praise of her embroidery and her garden. She had loved him for the brightness he had brought into Paul's life. Paul had always been different: small, gentle, studious, misunderstood and reviled by would-be friends as a boy, alienated by a family who would have liked him to be more aggressive, more ambitious as a clergyman. Perry had been not only a friend of the intellect to Paul; he had brought laughter and some gaiety into her brother's life for the first time ever.

She had liked to look at him, slender and graceful, handsome in his own very special, sunny-natured way. Yet she had never looked at him in the way a woman looks at a man to whom she is attracted. He was so much younger than she, a boy almost, though he was in fact well past boyhood. It amused her at church, and at the social gatherings she sometimes attended with Paul, to see the young girls look at him with admiration and some longing and to see him smile back and flirt with them. Yet never in a cruel manner. They knew perfectly well that he merely flirted. He did so even with the older ladies, though never with her.

She had always thought that perhaps he would end up marrying Lady Madeline Raine, a young lady of equally sunny nature and equal ability to flirt quite inoffensively. They would make a handsome and a glittering couple, Grace had thought. They could not fail to be happy together. Lady Madeline was twenty years old. But he had married a thirty-five-year-old woman instead.

Grace lifted her head from her husband's arm, on which it had been resting. His arm would be horribly cramped if he left it there. She eased it slowly down to his side. He grumbled slightly in his sleep, but did not wake. He turned over onto his side, facing toward her.

Her own youth seemed such a very long time ago, Grace thought. It could have been another lifetime altogether. She had always been restless and headstrong, stubborn, the spoiled daughter of a father who had only two sons beside her. Her mother had died soon after Paul's birth. And she had been the close friend of Gareth, only son of the Viscount Sandersford, for as far back as she could remember. Gareth, as headstrong and as stubborn as she, arrogant, intelligent, vibrant with life, yet with a streak of cruelty that often showed itself on weaker playmates, especially Paul.

She had played with him, defended him, argued with him, fought with him, and ultimately loved him. And she had given herself to him during those final days before he left for the wars, heedless to the consequences that she must have known were a strong possibility. She must have known. She had been one-and-twenty already. She could even remember feeling a stubborn, frightened sort of pride when she first suspected that she was with child, though Gareth had no longer been there to scorn with her the opinion of the world.

It had been a love with a cruel ending. A love and an ending that could only deaden anyone who survived it. And she had been dead to all intents and purposes for nine years since Jeremy had left her, and only painfully alive for more than four years before that, knowing when it was far too late to acquire such wisdom that her own selfish heedlessness of the moral code would ultimately bring more suffering to her innocent son than it would to her. She was half-dead anyway with Gareth gone. Jeremy was the only light in her life. Yet she had doomed Jeremy from the moment of his conception.

And was she to come alive again now? It was far more peaceful to live in the shadowed land of the half-dead. There was no pain there. She had fought off the pain of Paul's death, fought desperately, allowing it to force itself past the barriers she had built around her emotions only on the morning after his funeral when Perry had come to her, and put outside the barriers again immediately after.

But Perry had married her in good faith, with every intention of making her his wife indeed. And he had made her his wife, in the quiet ceremony that morning, with a strange rector taking Paul's place, and in this bed an hour before. And though she had not made the comparisons at

the time, she could not help making them now. Gareth and
Perry.

She had allowed Gareth numerous intimacies in those few
days, because she knew she was losing him perhaps forever
and because she did not care what her father or her stuffy
brother and despised sister-in-law might say, and because
she was young and very, very foolish. It had always happened
outdoors, almost always on the hard ground, Gareth heavy
on her so that sometimes she had almost screamed with the
pain of stones or hard earth pressing into her back. She had
loved what he did to her because it was forbidden and daring
and dangerous. He had always done what he did quickly and
lustily, intent on his own pleasure. But then she had assumed
that that was what sexual relations were supposed to be like.

Perry had not been like that at all. Perry had called her
beautiful and he had made her feel beautiful in what he had
done to her very unhurriedly on the bed before he had fallen
asleep. She had been embarrassed and tense at first because
she was a woman approaching her middle age and he little
more than a boy, and because it had been fourteen years since
she had last been with a man, but he had made her feel like
a woman again, like someone of worth, someone desirable
before he had lain on her and come into her.

And the barriers had come crashing down under the gentle
caress of his hands, the warm touch of his mouth, the
soothing murmurings of his voice. She had come alive again.
All her feelings had come slowly and painfully and achingly
alive for him, so that when he had come inside her finally,
she had been unable to present herself to him as a dutiful
wife. She had become a woman opening to her lover. And
if there had been any chance that she might have recollected
herself before he finished, he had destroyed that chance by
working slowly and rhythmically in her even at that cul-
minating stage of his lovemaking. And so she had given
herself openly to her husband and had received his gift of
pleasure.

She had said nothing. She had held him with her arms,
but she had kept her inner trembling in check. And she had
closed her eyes and turned her face into his shoulder when

he had moved to her side and put his arm beneath her. So, when he had kissed her cheek and pulled the blankets up around her shoulders, he had assumed she was asleep already and had fallen asleep himself. She did not know if he knew. She did not know if she wished him to know.

But she knew that he was a man with far greater depths of kindness and gentleness and love than she had ever suspected. She knew that he was a man in a thousand. A man who deserved the very best that life could give him. A man who should have love and laughter in his home. And children.

And she knew that she was alive again and so full of pain that she did not know quite how she could lie still so as not to disturb him. She must not allow it. She dared not allow it. It was too late now for her to come alive and be the wife Perry needed and deserved. If she came too much alive, she would become too terribly aware of the injustice she had done him, and she would not even be able to be a good wife to him. She would come to watch for signs of discontent in him. She would come to watch him with other, younger women, watching for signs of longing and restlessness. And she would come ultimately to hate him for having reminded her that life could be for living if only one had not misused one's youth so very badly.

But the tautness of her body must have disturbed him after all. His eyes were open when she looked across at him again. He was smiling, as he usually was.

"Still awake, Lady Grace?" he asked, running one knuckle down the length of her nose. "Is this very strange to you, dear? It is to me too, I do assure you. I am not accustomed to waking up to find a wife on the pillow beside me."

"Yes," she said, "it is a little strange."

His smile faded. "I did not hurt you, Grace? Or outrage you? Or embarrass you?"

She shook her head. "I am your wife," she said.

"Yes, you are." He gazed at her in silence for a while. "Grace, I know you have a great many memories. I know that you have loved. And tonight especially the memories must be painful. I cannot compete against the father of your child. I do not wish to compete. I do not wish you to try to suppress those memories or put me in his place. I just want to give you some comfort, dear, some security. Some affection. Don't feel guilty if you are remembering him tonight.''

Grace could only gaze mutely back into his eyes.

He smiled and closed the distance between their mouths. ''But I do like waking to find a wife here,'' he said before kissing her.

He should not have woken when he had, Grace thought. She had not had time to come to terms with her very live feelings. And perhaps she never would again, living with him by day as she must, sleeping beside him and with him by night. Perhaps she would never be able to die inside again for as long as they were wed. Perhaps she must step out into the world again and learn again how to live, how to love, how to enjoy, and how to suffer.

She found herself wanting more than the warm kiss. She wanted to know if it would always be as it had been the first time, if he would always be her lover as well as her husband. It was only when his mouth moved to her throat and his hands found their way beneath her nightgown and his weight bore down on her and his manhood came into her that she let go of her anxieties and allowed herself to become a woman beneath him again, made beautiful by the gentle force of his lovemaking.

3

Spring was coming fast. There was no time to be wasted indoors. Not when a large and barren garden cried out for an artist's touch. Grace could no more resist the call than a painter could resist a large bare canvas, or a pianist a new and priceless pianoforte, or a writer a block of blank paper.

Peregrine's old gardener and two new lads hired from the village began the heavy work under her directions, but it was Grace herself who did all of the planning and much of the planting, kneeling on the newly turned soil in an old black dress she had had since Jeremy's passing, an equally old straw hat shielding her neck and face from the early spring sunshine, a pair of gloves protecting her hands.

Much of the time she stood gazing about her, seeing with narrowed eyes her dream begin to take shape, seeing with her mind the fruit trees and blooms that would make their home beautiful later in the year and in the years to come.

And Peregrine as often as not knelt or stood at her side, planting bulbs and seedlings under her directions, laughing as she reached over to turn a bulb he had planted upside down ("Would it bloom in China, do you suppose?" he asked her), teasing her when she stood silent, with her narrow-eyed gaze, that she was just too weary to do more work and was merely pretending to concentrate on other matters.

Yet he admitted as he looked about him after a few weeks that already, even with much bare earth and a only few frail plants pushing their way toward the sun and rows of trees that looked impossibly fragile, his house and its surrounds were looking more like a home. It would all be a showpiece within a few years, he was convinced. And he glanced in some wonder at his wife, who was working the miracle.

They went about a great deal together in the afternoons and sometimes in the evenings, visiting their friends and neighbors, attending the few assemblies and social gatherings with which the families of the area entertained themselves. Grace was a little less withdrawn than she had been as the rector's housekeeper, recognizing that more was expected of Lady Grace Lampman than had been of Miss Grace Howard. She discovered that her neighbors were quite prepared to accept her in her new status. She had been afraid that they might resent her rise to social prominence and her taking away of their favorite.

Peregrine was as charming and as sunny-natured as ever and every bit as willing as he had ever been to converse with the ladies and compliment them on a new cap or lace collar or a recovery from illness. But he no longer flirted.

The young ladies accepted reality with perhaps a sigh of resignation and wondered when they might expect the Earl of Amberley to return from London. Several were agreed that he was without a doubt the most handsome gentleman in the county even if his manner was a little more reserved than they might have wished and even if his title and wealth and property did set him somewhat beyond their touch. Others, especially the very young, protested that his younger brother, Lord Eden, was by far the more handsome. And so tall. And with such open, pleasing manners. And would he come home to Amberley for the summer, or would he take himself off to his own estate in Wiltshire?

Peregrine went about very little on his own, a fact that somewhat disturbed Grace at first. Not that she minded having him near her. It was a pleasing novelty to have company in her gardening, and a constant amusement to discover the vast extent of his ignorance about plants and landscape gardening. But she had not wanted to tie him down. She had not wanted to kill the joy in his life. She relaxed more as time went on and he seemed to be quite happy to

spend his days with her and to see his garden being transformed before his very eyes.

When they were not out of doors and not visiting or
entertaining, Peregrine sat reading as often as not. It had
always been his favorite hobby. He enjoyed it even more
now after discovering that he could share interesting facts
from his books with Grace without either boring or
mystifying her. Indeed, he realized soon, Grace was an
intelligent and a well-informed woman. He thought of all
the times he and Paul must have talked in her silent presence
and he had never suspected that her mind was as active and
as interesting as his friend's had been, even if not perhaps
quite as knowledgeable.

Sometimes he read aloud to her as she stitched at her
embroidery. And he never tired of watching the design grow
from the blank linen beneath her long, slim fingers. On
occasion he did nothing else but sit and watch her, her black-
clad figure slim and shapely, her hair sleek, the black lace
cap that she wore indoors hardly distinguishable from the
color of her hair, her dark eyelashes fanning her pale cheeks
as she bent to her work.

She would look up at him eventually with her large gray
eyes and sometimes a fleeting smile, and he would resume
his reading, not wishing to embarrass or to make self-
conscious the grace of her movements. If his parents had
made a disaster of naming him, Grace's parents could not
have picked a more perfect name for her.

He was never sure how happy or unhappy she was. She
went about her work with quiet energy and created beauty
wherever she went. She had taken quiet control of his household and won the ungrudging respect of a housekeeper and
servants who had gone largely their own way since his mother
had left three years before to live with his aunt, her sister,
in Scotland. And he had noticed that she was taking her
rightful place among their associates as his wife. She was
no longer the silent presence in company that she had always
been when Paul was alive.

He was not sure, either, how she felt about sharing his

bed each night. She never complained or showed any sign of distaste or reluctance, even when he awoke her in the middle of the night or in the early morning, as he very frequently did. He could not leave her alone. He had never consciously found her attractive when Paul was alive, even though he could look back now and remember that his eyes had rested on her often and found her pleasing to look at. She was not beautiful in any universally accepted sense. And yet he had found her so since his marriage to her.

He never tired of looking at her narrow, rather pale face, her dark hair, her slim, graceful figure. And he never tired of touching her with his hands and his mouth and his body. There was a woman's maturity to her body that excited and aroused him to loving her over and over again. And she was not entirely indifferent, he thought at times. She never openly participated in their lovemaking, never by word or sound showed any emotion.

But her body betrayed some enjoyment. There was a tautness to her breasts, which he occasionally touched beneath her nightgown, a welcoming wetness when he came to her, a certain tightening of her inner muscles as he worked toward his unhurried climax, a tilting of her hips to allow his deeper penetration. And her arms always held him when he lay on her and in her.

He hoped he did not misread the signs. He would hate to discover that the nights of their marriage, which were becoming more and more magical to him, were something only to be endured for her. He knew that she did not love him, that he could never expect her to do so. She had done so much more living than he. Her eyes showed that she had lived and suffered and survived. And she had loved. He could not forget the look of agony on her face and the sounds of anguish in her voice as she had told him about her lover and her son. He could not fight against the past, against the dead. He had accepted both, had accepted her just as she was at the particular moment when he had found her, had decided that he would take just and only what she had to give.

But he did not want her to give out of reluctant duty. He

wanted her life to be tranquil, secure, peaceful. She could never be happy again, perhaps. But he wanted to bring her contentment, as she was bringing it to him.

It was not at all clear to Peregrine why he demanded so little for himself from his marriage when he was a young man who had always loved life and who had seen for several years past that it was possible to attract the interest of almost any female he cared to have. He might have married almost any beautiful young girl he wished to choose. He might have commanded her admiration and love. Yet he had chosen an aging woman of questionable beauty and charm, whose love had long ago been given elsewhere and from whom the most he could hope for was respect and affection.

However it was, Peregrine grew content, even if not wildly happy, during the first year of his marriage. Perhaps he did not realize fully the extent to which he loved his wife. But he did know that she mattered to him, that he cared for her, that seeing to her contentment gave meaning and shape to his days, that her presence in his life gave pleasure to his days and joy to his nights.

And Grace was content. She had a home on which to lavish her energies and her creative talents. And she had a husband whose almost constant presence in her company took away the long loneliness and emptiness of nine years, even though she had had Paul during those years. She was very conscious of the selfishness of her feelings. It was all very well for her at her age to feel contentment with the quiet routine of their life. Perry, she felt sometimes, should have more of excitement and gaiety. And yet he seemed not to be unhappy. The laughter had not gone from him. It played about his eyes almost constantly when they were in company and when he worked with her in their garden. And even in repose, when he was reading or sleeping, his lips had a good-humored curve.

She knew that she was capable of giving him actual pleasure, and she consoled herself with the knowledge. She knew that he admired the orchard and the rose arbor and the flower gardens she was creating around his home. And she knew that he liked to watch her at her embroidery, though she tried not to lift her head to reveal that she knew herself being observed. And she knew that he liked the quiet efficiency with which she ran his household. And strange as it seemed to her, she knew that he enjoyed making love to her at night.

And so there was a measure of contentment in her life. She lived for each day as it came, knowing from past experience and from the strange nature of their marriage that good times could not be expected to last. Although at unguarded moments, particularly at night if she lay awake as he slept beside her, she knew that she loved him, she kept the knowledge from her full consciousness. It would be easier to bear the pain in the future if she never admitted to herself that he was more to her than a kind and fun-loving and lovable boy.

And there would be pain in the future. For both of them. He could not continue contented forever with the kind of life they had established during their first year together. He was still only six-and-twenty at the end of it. Sooner or later, however kind his nature and sincere his intentions, he must realize how much of life and happiness and pleasure was passing him by while he was tied to an aging wife.

The knowledge, the discontent, the eventual misery would be painful to him. For Perry was a good and honorable man. And it would be painful to her. But not unbearably so. Not unless she began to listen too closely to the whisperings of her treacherous heart. Not unless she lost the daily battle to keep herself at least partly dead. She loved Perry as one friend loves another, as a mother loves her child, as any human being must love someone full of goodness and kindness and laughter. Not as a woman loves the other half of her being. No, never that. The whisperings were very rarely allowed to reach her hearing.

Soon after her marriage, Grace wrote to her father, on the advice of her husband, to inform him of the death of his son and of her marriage. It was a difficult letter to write. She had had no communication with her father for nine years. Indeed, she did not know for sure that he still lived.

But he was still alive. He answered her after a month, in a brief, stiff letter that gave almost no indication of his feelings on either of the events she had announced. The only clue perhaps was in his request that she send to him any of Paul's effects that still remained.

Peregrine took the box from her and undertook the painful task of sending away all that remained to her of her brother except for his books, which were in their library. Afterward he brought Paul's vestments to her in her sitting room, where she sat with her embroidery, and laid them beside her on the chaise longue. And he bent and kissed her on the mouth, something he rarely did during the daytime.

"You must keep something of him, Grace, as I do," he said. "And I know that you would not have chosen his most valuable possession, his watch. That and everything else have been sent on their way."

And she wrapped her arms up around his neck—something she did very rarely—and looked earnestly into his eyes. "Thank you, Perry," she said.

It was not until well into the autumn that another letter came, from her sister-in-law this time, Grace saw with a lift of her eyebrows. It was too bad that Paul had been stubborn and had consequently never seen his father again after their quarrel, Ethel wrote. The same thing must not happen with Grace. She must come home while there was still time. The need for reconciliation was long overdue. She must come with her husband for Christmas.

It was a strange letter. Grace showed it to Peregrine at the breakfast table and read it again over his shoulder. Was she being invited now as an equal? Was she being offered forgiveness and was therefore still being viewed as the lost sheep of the family? Was she being blamed for the fact that they had not seen Paul before his death? Did her father want her to go? Her brother? Was her father sick? And should they go?

Peregrine handed the letter back to her after reading it through twice, and looked searchingly into her eyes. "What do you want to do, Grace?" he asked. "That is all that matters. You cannot know their attitude toward you unless

you go there, and you can always leave again if you find
it intolerable, you know. Besides, I am invited too, and I
would be there to protect you from insult. It will be as you
wish, dear. Exactly as you wish.''

She sat staring at the letter for several silent moments. "I
was a different person," she said. "You would not know
me if you could meet me as I was then, Perry. I think perhaps
I deserved much of the treatment I received. I no longer
blame them entirely, as I used to do. Perhaps it is time to
forgive and forget.''

"You want to go, then?" he asked.

"But there was Jeremy," she said. "He did not deserve
any of it. And they would not welcome him back if he were
still with me.''

He touched the back of her hand with his fingertips.

"But he is there," she said. "I do not even know if anyone
has tended his grave in nine years.''

She made no decision that morning before going to confer
with the cook on the day's menu. But her eyes were troubled,
Peregrine saw, and she chose to go out walking alone when
he sat down with a book after young Walter and Anna
Carrington had called on them in the afternoon to invite them
to an evening of charades the following evening.

"Tell me about your father and your brother, Grace,"
Peregrine said to her that night before he made love to her,
easing his arm beneath her head on the pillow and pulling
the blankets warmly up around her. "And about your childhood.''

And she turned her cheek onto his arm and began to talk.
She remembered her father as a tall and handsome man, strict
even to the point of oppressiveness with his boys, generous
and indulgent with her. She had loved him with all a child's
mindless and uncritical faculties. And he had never seen any
fault in her, despite the repeated complaints of a string of
governesses, despite the accusations of a jealous older
brother. But he had turned on her when she had told him—
in his office one morning, her feet planted firmly on the
Turkish carpet before his desk, her head thrown defiantly
back, her color high—that she was going to have a child.

He had raged and stormed and ultimately—since there was nothing he could do about the matter at that late date—turned cold and acted almost as if she did not exist. In the four years when Jeremy had lived in his home, she did not believe he had once looked directly at his grandson or ever spoken his name.

"I suppose now I can see there was some leftover feeling, some grudging sort of love in the fact that he did not turn us off," she said, "and in the fact that he never once questioned the bills for either my clothes or my son's. Or for his toys and books. And I did not spare the expenses. I did not want my son to have any less than his two cousins had."

And she told him about her older brother, Martin, with whom she had never enjoyed a close relationship, and about Ethel, his wife, who had resented her when she had first been brought to the house as Martin's wife, and who had not failed to make the most of her sister-in-law's disgrace afterward.

"But perhaps she had some reason to hate me," Grace said. "I was a headstrong arrogant girl who did not want to share the position of privileged female in my father's home. You would not have liked me, Perry. I do not like myself in memory."

He kissed her. "You are harsh on yourself," he said. "I do not believe you can have changed so much. And I like you very well now."

But it was difficult to imagine another Grace, he thought, and a family and a life that were wholly unknown to him. Difficult to know what ghosts haunted her, what might be accomplished by bringing them to life again, what harm might be done. He closed his arm around her and kissed her more deeply.

He drew her arm more closely against his side the next morning when they were out walking along the leaf-strewn lane that passed Reardon Park, their feet crunching on the dried leaves. "You are very quiet this morning," he said. "No laments for the bare branches and the death of the leaves?"

"No," she said. "Spring will come again. It always does.

That is one lovely certainty of the seasons. And there is a certain beauty in bare branches, Perry. Look at the clouds scudding along behind them. We would not even be able to see them so clearly if all the leaves were still there.''

Peregrine laughed. ''That is what I call making the most of a bad situation. What were you thinking about before I spoke, Grace? Your letter?''

She nodded.

''We will do what you wish, as I said yesterday,'' he said. ''But if you want my opinion, I would say that I think you need to go back. I think you need to see your father again, and your brother and your sister-in-law too. And their children who were growing up with your son. I think you need to come to terms with your past.''

''I believe you are right,'' she said, reaching up with her free hand to grasp his arm through which her other one was linked. ''I dread going, Perry. I don't know how I can face the people or the memories. But I think I must. Not at Christmastime, though. Oh, not at Christmas, Perry. We are going to go caroling with the Carringtons and the Mortons. And the earl has invited everyone to Amberley for the evening. And I want us to celebrate Christmas Eve at the church here with our friends and to have our goose and our Yule log and mince pies at our own home here. And everything.''

''My mother and my aunt are going to London during the spring,'' Peregrine said. ''And I have been thinking to suggest to you, Grace, that we go for a few weeks too. I would like to show you the sights and take you to some of the theaters and assemblies and have you meet my mother again. And Edmund and the countess and the twins are always there too for the Season. Why do we not go to your father's home in the early spring for a while and then move on to London? And we can be home in time to enjoy our summer garden.'' He grinned. ''Do you notice how I said 'our?' ''

''Yes,'' she said. ''We will do that, if you please, Perry. London? I have always wanted to see London.''

''Only for a few weeks, though,'' he said. ''I have never

been very happy away from home for any great length of time. Now more than ever I find that I am content here. Are you, Grace?''

''Yes,'' she said, gazing up through the bare branches above her head to the blue sky and the racing clouds, ''I am content.''

It was with considerable misgiving that Grace leaned forward for her last glimpse of Reardon Park through the carriage window at the end of the following February. She had not been away from it for one night or even one full day since Perry had brought her there on their wedding day. They would miss the coming of spring there, though they had discovered a small clump of snowdrops and three separate crocuses in the grass among the trees just the day before.

Perry was holding her hand suddenly, she found, at the same moment as she realized that she could no longer see the house. He was smiling his usual cheerful, comforting smile when she turned to him.

''It will still be there when we come back,'' he said. ''And much as I love my home when I am living there, Grace, I find that I love it even more when I am returning to it after an absence.''

''Yes,'' she said, returning his smile and settling her shoulders back against the squabs. She was glad that he did not relinquish his hold of her hand, though he did lean over her to tuck the fur-lined rug more snugly around her legs.

Yes, Reardon Park would doubtless still be there when they returned. But would they be the same? Would everything be spoiled by the time they came back? Was this the end of their contentment, here and right now?

They were journeying back into her past. She did not know what her reception would be at home, what her relationship with her relatives. And she did not know how strong or painful the memories of Gareth and Jeremy would be when she was once more in the places where it had all happened a lifetime ago. She wanted to see her father. She wanted to see Martin. And she wanted to be close to Jeremy again.

But she could not picture Perry in such a setting. Perry was everything in her present and perhaps a little of her future. She did not want him mixed up with her past. And yet she could not even contemplate going back there without him. She might become trapped there. She might never be free.

She had made no mention in her letter to her father or in the two letters she had written to Ethel of the age of her husband. She felt something of the old stubborn defiance when she thought of the look that might well be on all of their faces when they saw and looked at him. She would not care what they thought. They might look and think and say what they pleased. She did not care.

Ah, but she cared every bit as deeply as she ever had. They would think that she had made a selfish grab for Perry. And they would think he had pitied her. They would not know that there was a contentment, a certain tenderness in their marriage. And they would have her doubting again. They would revive the feelings of guilt and inadequacy that she had ignored for almost a year.

And then they were to go to London, and she must face the same ordeal when they met Perry's mother. What would she think when she met her daughter-in-law? They had met, of course, when Grace had been Paul's housekeeper. And what would others think, all the members of the *beau monde* to whom she would be persented? And what would it be like for Perry to be surrounded by people—women—younger and more vibrant and more lovely than she?

Grace let her hand lie in the warmth of her husband's and her shoulder rest just below the level of his as she gazed out of the window at the faded greens and browns of the fields and the bare branches of the trees. Spring would come soon to the land and clothe everything in bright beauty again. But not to her life. Her life was heading into autumn and perhaps even winter. A cold and stark winter.

It might well be winter when they came home again even if all the fruit trees and flowers were blooming and the air was heavy with the scent of her roses and Perry's.

4

No one came out into the cobbled courtyard before the main doors of Pangam Manor when their carriage pulled up there, Grace noticed, except for a groom and two footmen. But then it was a cold and blustery February day. Both Martin and Ethel were waiting in the hall, however, both looking remarkably unchanged since she had last seen them.

Martin's fair hair was perhaps a little thinner on top, his figure a little stouter, his complexion a little more florid. But there was still that air of importance about him, and still the line between his eyes that had always denoted impatience with the slowness and lack of understanding of others and a general dissatisfaction with his life. Ethel was still thin and pale. And still unsmiling.

But they were there, Grace thought, moving forward to hug her sister-in-law and rest her cold cheek against Ethel's for a moment and turning to place her hands on her brother's shoulders and stretch up to kiss him on the cheek.

"You are looking well, Grace," Martin said, resting his hands on her waist for a brief moment in acknowledgement of her embrace.

"You must be very cold," Ethel said. "I have ordered tea to be brought up to the drawing room. Perhaps you would like some before I have you shown to your rooms."

Grace turned back to Peregrine, who stood silently behind her. She took his arm and watched her brother and sister-in-

law as she presented him to them. Not one flicker on the
face of either showed surprise or any other emotion. They
were all civil politeness.

"Where is Pa—? Where is Father?" Grace asked.

"He keeps to his rooms a great deal through the winter,"
Ethel said, taking Grace's arm and leading her in the direction
of the stairs. "But he will come down for tea when we send
to let him know that you have arrived."

"He is unwell?" Grace asked.

Ethel shrugged. "He has slowed down," she said. "He
is getting older, as we all are."

There seemed to be no double meaning in the words, Grace
decided. And she would not look for snubs where perhaps
none was meant. She was no longer Grace Howard, headstrong daughter of the house. She was Grace Lampman, and
she recognized the necessity of being civil and expecting
civility from those with whom she must associate.

"How are the children?" she asked.

"The children?" Ethel gave her a strange look as she led
Grace into the drawing room. "Oswald is away at school.
He is almost sixteen. Perhaps you had forgotten that so much
time has passed. Priscilla will be down for tea. We will be
taking her to town for the Season this spring. She is nearly
eighteen, you know."

"Yes, of course," Grace said. "It is amazing to think that
they are quite grown up already." Jeremy would have been
fourteen.

Miss Priscilla Howard arrived in the drawing room at
almost the same moment as the tea tray. She was a younger
version of her mother, Grace saw as she rose to her feet.
She was slender and fair-haired and wore a frilly pink dress
that had obviously been donned for the occasion though the
color did not quite suit her. Yet she was pretty enough, with
a mass of ringlets bouncing against the sides of her head and
the color high in her cheeks, her gray eyes sparkling with
mingled shyness and excitement.

"Hello, Aunt Grace," the girl said, curtsying low. "I
remember you. You really look very little different from the

way you used to be. Do you wear mourning for Uncle Paul? Grandpapa does too, though Mama and Papa left theirs off at Christmas.''

"You talk too much, child," her father said. "Make your curtsy to your Uncle Peregrine."

Priscilla turned her eyes on him and her blush deepened as she curtsied. "Sir," she said. And her eyes continued to scrutinize him curiously.

Perry's eyes were laughing at his niece-by-marriage, Grace saw. He bowed elegantly. "I have just overheard your mother say that you are to make your come-out this Season," he said. "I can warn her now that all the young bucks will be lined up at your door, Priscilla. And we will make that Uncle Perry if you please."

Priscilla smiled. "Yes, Uncle Perry," she said. "Though I think you are too young to be my uncle. Have you been much in London? Mama and Papa have not been there since they were young. I am sure much has changed in all that time."

Peregrine grinned. "I daresay people went to parties and balls and assemblies and theaters and picnics and what not in those long ago days just as they do now," he said. "And danced and flirted and otherwise amused themselves. And your mama would have been presented to the same queen as you are like to make your curtsy to. Grace and I will be going to London too, you know."

"Will you?" she said. "How splendid! Did you hear that, Mama?"

The girl plied Peregrine with eager questions about London for the next few minutes while Martin and Ethel made polite inquiries of Grace about the journey.

But they were interrupted before they could finish their tea by the arrival of Lord Pawley. He left his valet in the doorway and proceeded into the room alone, leaning heavily on a cane. He was still tall and thin, Grace saw as she rose to her feet. Still severe and distinguished-looking. But the gray hair she remembered had turned to pure white, and the lines running from his nose to his chin had deepened. His eyes sought her out and looked into hers with quite as much bright keenness as ever. He was dressed in deep mourning.

"Well, Grace," he said, stopping a short distance from her, "you have come home."

"Yes, Father," she said. "How are you?"

"Well," he said. "I am glad to see that you appreciated your brother enough still to wear mourning for him."

"I loved Paul, Father," she said.

He nodded. "I suppose I did not," he said. "Present me to your husband."

Her father looked long and hard at Peregrine, Grace saw in some discomfort after she had made the introductions. She found she was holding her breath.

"I am grateful to you, sir, for taking care of my daughter at a difficult time for her," the baron said eventually before seating himself and turning to take a cup of tea from his daughter-in-law.

Peregrine was smiling, apparently quite unperturbed by the long and steady scrutiny he had just been subjected to. "Thank you, sir," he said. "But Grace and I did not wed merely because she was in need, you know. And may I express my belated sympathies on the passing of your son? Paul was a particular friend of mine. I wear mourning for him still on my own account as well as out of respect for my wife."

The baron nodded curtly and the conversation became general.

It had been very stiff and very difficult, Grace thought half an hour later as she and Peregrine followed Ethel upstairs to the bedrooms. And much, much easier than she had anticipated. If she looked back on the bitterness of her departure ten years before, it was amazing enough that they had all been able to behave civilly over tea in the drawing room.

Ethel showed Peregrine to his room, in which his valet was already unpacking his things and laying out his shaving gear, before taking Grace across the hallway to her old room.

"Do you want this room?" Ethel asked hesitantly. "I did not know. But it is still thought of and spoken of as yours." She flushed.

"Yes," Grace said, wandering across it and looking about

her. "And it is just the same. The Chinese wallpaper, the green curtains and bed hangings. Why did I expect everything and everyone to be so different?"

"You look no older, Grace," her sister-in-law said. "Indeed, you look a great deal better than you did when . . ."

Grace had crossed to the window to see that, yes, she could still see along the elm grove to the summer house, where she had sat so often as a girl with a book or talking with Gareth. She turned to look back at Ethel. "Yes," she said. "I am feeling a great deal better."

"I am glad you have come," Ethel said. "Papa needs you, I believe. But he would never have asked for you, of course."

Grace turned completely from the window. "How did he take the news of Paul's death?" she asked.

Ethel's lips tightened. "He showed Martin your letter, ordered mourning for himself and the servants, straightened his shoulders, which were becoming stooped, and said no more about the matter," she said. "Does that answer your question?"

"Yes," Grace said. "He took it hard. I think I am glad, both for his sake and Paul's."

Perry was standing in the doorway, she saw suddenly, his face smiling, his very presence lightening the atmosphere.

"This is where you are," he said. "What a lovely room. And don't tell me." He held up a hand. "This was your room when you lived here, was it not, Grace? And you planned it and chose the wallpaper and the colors of the paint and the bed hangings and the carpet. I could walk into this room anywhere in the kingdom and say without any hesitation at all that it is the handiwork of Grace Lampman." He grinned and turned to Ethel. "Now, tell me that I am wrong and make me feel very foolish."

Ethel was smiling, Grace was surprised to see. "No," she said. "You are quite right."

Peregrine laughed and strolled right into the room. "An indoor garden," he said. "That is a thumb of the nose to English weather. I was going to suggest that you move your things to my room, Grace, but now I think I must beg to be allowed to bring mine here.'' He turned to Ethel, still smiling. ''Grace and I share a room always. You will not mind?''

''Did she mind?'' he asked Grace a few minutes later when they had been left alone. ''She certainly turned pink and left in some haste. But I would feel foolish to be observed creeping across here to you each night, Grace, as if I were up to no good. Better for everyone to know that we sleep together.''

''Yes,'' she said, strangely pleased.

''You do not mind, Grace?'' he asked. ''Perhaps you would prefer to have your room to yourself again? Perhaps you need some time alone? I am remarkably selfish, am I not, thinking only of my own comfort.''

''No,'' she said sharply. ''I would prefer to have you here, Perry.''

He came closer to her and touched her cheek with the backs of his fingers. ''This is all very hard for you, dear. Do you think I do not know that? But you have done the right thing to come. Your family wants you back again. Perhaps you are too involved in your own emotions to see that clearly. I can see more objectively. And it is so, Grace. You are loved here. And I can see just as clearly that you want them too. You have never stopped loving them. It will be hard for you, the next week or so, but it is right to force yourself to live through it. It is what you need to do.''

She clasped his wrist and turned her head to kiss it briefly. ''Yes,'' she said. ''I am only sorry that you have to be involved in the discomfort, Perry.''

He smiled at her. ''I think you may need an arm or a shoulder to lean on from time to time,'' he said, ''though of course you could do it alone if I were not with you. But since I am here, it will be my arm and my shoulder, Grace. And I must confess to some curiosity to know the people and places that figured so largely in your life before I even knew you. I must go back to my dressing room to shave. Perkins had gone for the water before I came across here,

and there is nothing more terrifying to behold than the wrath
of Perkins when he has just been forced to watch my shaving
water grow cold." He bent and kissed her cheek.

Grace was surprised and somewhat gratified to find in the
following days that Ethel was making an effort to be friendly.
They spent some time together, sitting over their embroidery,
wandering through the orangery, examining the shooting
plants in the garden, which would be transformed into
daffodils and tulips within a very few weeks.

"I am glad you have come, Grace," Ethel said on more
than one occasion. "The cloud of your leaving has hung over
Papa and Martin for a long time. They never mentioned either
you or Paul in all those years, of course, but I know them
both well enough to understand that that meant only that they
were hurting deeply."

Grace looked at her sister-in-law curiously. She had never
liked Ethel, had never tried to like her, perhaps. She had
not wanted another young woman in the house when Martin
had first brought his bride home. And she had been jealous
when the births of her niece and nephew had diverted some
of her father's attention from herself. Then, of course, for
the last five years she had been at home, pregnant during
the first, with Jeremy for the remaining four, Ethel had been
the favored lady of the house.

And Ethel had gloated. She had made the most of her triumph, both for herself and for her very legitimate children.
Grace had hated her, if the truth were known. But Ethel was
a person like any other, she saw now. And she was clearly a
person who knew and understood her husband and her father-
in-law. And cared. And now she was holding out an olive
branch to the sister-in-law who had treated her badly for
several years and to whom she had finally returned the
compliment.

"I did not even write about Paul's death until six weeks
after it happened," Grace said. "I did not know if they would
wish to know."

"You are as stubborn and as blind as they are, Grace,"
Ethel said. "You are all so similar, you know, the three of
you.. Only Paul was different."

Grace looked up again in surprise.

"Martin cried," Ethel said. "I was frightened, as you may
well imagine. I had never expected to see him cry. And he
talked on and on about how he had always ridiculed and
mistreated Paul as a boy. And about how he had let him go
and had never even tried to communicate with him after."

Grace pointed to a bunch of primroses, almost hidden in
the grass. "Was it Martin's idea to invite me for Christmas?"
she asked.

"It was mine," Ethel admitted. "But I know it was what
Martin wanted, Grace, and Papa too, though they would
never have said so in a thousand years. I know both of them
rather well after almost twenty years of marriage."

With her brother Grace did not talk a great deal. They
never had had a close relationship. Martin was five years
her senior. He had always been a rather slow, plodding boy,
who worked with dogged perseverance to be worthy of being
his father's oldest child. And he had watched his younger
sister, willful, heedless, frequently disobedient, engrossing
all their father's love, though she made no effort whatsoever to ingratiate herself with him.

They had despised each other, even hated each other
through most of their life. Or had they? Had they not always
watched each other for the smallest sign that the other would
be willing to be loved? Grace wondered now. It was strange
to be back, to be involved again in the emotions she had
thought long dead, and yet to be able to see her family more
objectively than she had ever done, and her own part in it.

"I have seen the new enclosures and the land that was
drained five or six years ago," she said to her brother one
day after driving out with Ethel and Peregrine. "And Ethel
says that the estate is prospering more than ever, Martin.
You have worked hard."

He looked at her sharply as if to detect some sarcasm.
"Yes, I have," he said. "Papa has lost interest in the land

these last few years, you know. And there was no one but me to see to things.''

"You have done well," she said, and reached out to touch his hand lightly with her fingertips. She and Martin had never touched each other often.

He withdrew his hand uneasily but looked at her. "The news of your marriage took us by surprise," he said. "Are you happy, Grace?"

"Yes," she said. "Yes, I am."

"He is younger than you," he said rather jerkily.

"Yes," she said. "Ten years younger."

"Ten?" He looked away from her in some embarrassment. "Well, as long as you are happy."

"Yes," she said.

Lord Pawley did not come out of his rooms very often. But Grace made a point of visiting him there twice each day, alone in the mornings, with Peregrine later in the day.

"You have come home, then," he said to her almost every morning.

"Yes, Father," she said. "I have come home. For a visit."

"Did he suffer?" he asked abruptly on one occasion. "Was it instant?"

"Yes," she said. "It was instant, the doctor said." She hesitated. "His neck was broken when the bull tossed him. He is remembered as a great hero in Abbotsford, you know. He saved the life of the son of one of the Earl of Amberley's laborers."

Her father grunted. "Young fool," he said after an interval.

"He would like that description," Grace said gently. "Paul liked to be a fool. A fool for Christ, as his namesake said in the Bible."

Her father grunted again and said nothing more.

"You have changed," he said on another occasion.

"Have I, Father?" she asked. "I am ten years older."

He looked at her broodingly. "You have learned what I should have taught you when you were growing up, I daresay," he surprised her by saying. "I spoiled you. Gave you no training at all. It was all my fault. Everything that happened.''

''No,'' she said. ''That is not true. No one is ever entirely to blame for what happens to another. I was an adult. I had a mind and intelligence of my own. I made my own choices, my own mistakes. I blame no one else. And I do not even like the words 'mistakes' and 'blame.' Because they imply that Jeremy was all wrong. And he was not wrong. He was my son. Despite his death, I would not have my life any different from the way it has been. Perhaps that is something I have learned in ten years. Everything that happens in life happens for a purpose. I would not be the person I am if there had not been Jeremy. And I would not wish to be different even if I could be.''

Her father continued to watch her broodingly, though he clearly had nothing more to say. She left him after a few minutes, hesitating a moment before deciding not to stoop down to kiss his head. She had not touched him since her return home.

Her niece was inclined to be friendly with the aunt she remembered as something of a favorite, probably, Grace thought, because she had spent more time with the children than any of the other adults during the four years of Jeremy's life. And Priscilla was clearly charmed by Peregrine's good looks and by his easy humor and teasing. She introduced her two special friends to him, and the three girls, giggling, dragged him off walking with them on more than one occasion, pretending to quarrel over how they were to divide his two arms among the three of them.

Grace found that she spent very little time alone with her husband during the daytime. She was happy to see him occupied and in his usual good humor—she had been very afraid that he would be oppressed by the atmosphere of her home and by the old, still-unresolved quarrels. And she was glad that her time was taken up so agreeably with her relatives, even if they had still not conversed on any matters

that really concerned their relationships and even though there
was much awkwardness still among them.

But it was strange not to have Perry's continual companionship, strange not to be alone with him for large segments
of the day. She found herself, as she viewed Ethel's garden
with her, looking back with a great deal of nostalgia on the
previous spring when she and Perry had worked side by side
in their own garden, often for long hours. And she often
thought with some longing of their quiet afternoons and
evenings, sometimes both of them reading, sometimes just
Perry doing so while she sewed.

But there were still the nights, she consoled herself. There
was something especially comforting about having Perry
sharing the room that had been hers until she was six-and-
twenty years old. She had always loved to leave the curtains
back at night so that she might see the garden on her walls
picked out by the moonlight. She liked to see it still, her head
against his arm, just the two of them silent together.

She often lay awake long after he slept—and had done so
even when they were at home—but she never minded, never
fretted over what might have been called insomnia. She very
consciously enjoyed every moment of their closeness. It could
not last forever. There would come the time when he would
tire of her, when he would want the greater freedom of a
separate room. Kind as he was, the time would come, and
she would let him slip away from her gradually so that he
would not dream that she knew, that she was reluctant to
accept the new arrangement.

Until that time came, she was happy to lie awake and enjoy
the nights. And happier still when he woke, as he sometimes
did, to turn to her with a sleepy smile and a gradually
rekindled desire for her. He often apologized for troubling
her when he took her for the second time in a night, and
she would smile secretly to herself as she held him in her
arms again.

At the end of the first week at Pangam Manor, there was
only one thing Grace had not done that she fully intended
to do. But the opportunity came finally when Martin had

borne Perry off one afternoon to see something on the estate, Priscilla in tow, and Ethel had begged to be excused from any outdoor exertion as she had a headache. Grace assured her that she would leave her alone so that she would not feel obliged to make conversation. And she took herself off to the east end of the lake, where the private family burial ground was situated.

No one had objected to her having Jeremy buried there. No one had offered an opinion on the matter either way. But she had not wanted to have him put in the churchyard. The graves there were so close together, the tombs so elaborate. It was a place of death, heavy and black death. Jeremy was dead, of course. She had realized that. She had never, from the moment when Priscilla had come shrieking back from the lake with the news that Jeremy was drowned, been able to doubt the fact. But she had not wanted him in a place of death. She had wanted him in a place where he could become part of nature, part of the wild beauty of the universe.

There were no elaborate tombs in the family burial plot. Only neat headstones announcing essential information for the eyes of the living. And neatly mown grass and a neat wooden fence to keep out grazing animals.

The grass was short on Jeremy's grave, as on the others, Grace saw at a glance, kneeling down on it and touching the marble headstone with its legend: "Jeremy Howard. Beloved son of Grace Howard. 1796–1800. R.I.P."

Jeremy. She took her hand away from the cold stone and closed her eyes. Jeremy. A thin, wiry little boy. His father's dark curls and dark eyes. Bright, eager eyes. Her own rather long, thin face. Small white baby teeth. A dimpled chin, another legacy from his father. A surprisingly low-pitched chuckle that could quickly give place to a shrieking laugh after a little tickling. Warm, soft clinging arms. A wet baby kiss. Wet, muddy hair and a dead face. She closed her eyes more tightly and clung to the grass on either side of her.

She was lying facedown on the grass when Peregrine found her half an hour later. He had guessed where she had gone when he had returned to the house with Martin to find Ethel sitting alone in a darkened parlor. He had been expecting it since their arrival. He asked directions to the graveyard of Martin, and declined his company, with thanks.

He stood at the fence watching her for a few minutes before climbing over it, ignoring the gate, and approaching her. She was not crying. He did not think she was sleeping, though she had not moved since she had first come into his sight.

She seemed to sense his presence. She turned her head, though she did not look up.

"Do you want to be alone, Grace?" he asked. "Would you prefer that I went away?"

There was no response.

"I shall wait for you over by the trees, out of sight, shall I?" he asked, stooping down and laying a light hand on her head. She was not wearing a hat.

She shook her head. "Don't go." Her voice was muffled by her arms, on which her face rested.

He sat on the ground cross-legged beside her, his hand still on her head, and waited for her. She moved eventually and sat beside him. She did not look up.

"I don't know who it was who dragged me away from here after the funeral," she said. "I cannot remember if it was Martin or Paul. It was not my father because he did not come. But someone took me away, very much against my will. And I did not come again. Not until now. It was terrible to leave him all alone here. He was only four years old."

He took her hand and held it in a firm clasp.

She laid her head on his shoulder. "I loved him, Perry," she said. "For four years he was my life. No, for five. I loved him every moment I carried him."

"I know," he said. "You must not feel guilty, dear."

"Do I?" she said. "Do I feel guilty? For letting someone else care for him when I should have been with him? But he was an independent little lad. He wanted to be with his older cousins. A mere mother was a nuisance when they were there to be played with."

"For having him," he said. "You feel guilty for having him, Grace. Don't. It is never wrong to give life, dear. And love."

"Isn't it?" she said. "That is a dangerous moral

statement, Perry. It is not wrong to bear a bastard?''

"Don't use that word," he said. "Don't punish yourself with it. Children die every day, Grace. It is no judgment of God on the parents when they do. Your son was one of the fortunates of this world. He was dearly loved from the moment of his conception to the moment of his death. Not all children are so loved, not even those born in wedlock. Forgive yourself, dear. If you committed a sin, you have also atoned for it a thousandfold. And you have suffered for it. Let him rest in peace now. And let yourself live in peace.''

Grace sat for many minutes with her eyes closed, her head resting on her husband's shoulder. She was letting Jeremy go again and wishing and wishing one thing. She was wishing that Perry had been his father.

Perry, who had been twelve years old when Jeremy was born! She sat up and smiled wearily at him.

"I am ready to go now," she said. "Thank you for coming, Perry. It must have been a dreary afternoon for you. And thank you for your words. I am not sure I can quite accept them. It is far easier to forgive others than oneself, you know. But thank you. Paul would have disagreed with you. Paul forgave me and never mentioned my sin to me after we left here. But his very silence told me that he thought it a very great sin, nevertheless.''

"Yes.'' He smiled as he got to his feet and pulled her to hers. "Paul and I disagreed most noisily on the nature of sin. You were oppressed by his forgiveness, weren't you? You were so very quiet and withdrawn during those years, Grace. You need not fear my forgiveness. You gave love—to a man and to a child. I can only honor you for doing so, dear, and feel sad for the pain that those loves still cause you.''

What had she ever done to deserve Perry? Grace wondered as he drew her arm through his and began to walk back with her to her father's house. But she could not forgive herself for all that. She never would, despite what she had said to her father. Jeremy would not have drowned if she had not lain with Gareth.

5

A few of her former acquaintances called upon Grace during the first week. She returned some of those calls with Ethel and Peregrine and sometimes Priscilla. But she had not expected the invitation to attend a dinner and evening party at the home of Viscount Sandersford. Gareth's father had ignored her very existence after his son had gone away. He had never acknowledged his grandson by any sign whatsoever.

"Perhaps the invitation is really for you and Martin and Priscilla," Grace said uneasily to Ethel when the latter told her of the card that had arrived that morning. "Perhaps he does not know that I am here. Or perhaps he does not recognize my name and believes himself to be inviting two unknown guests."

"No," Ethel said, looking at her sister-in-law briefly but searchingly, "he specifically named you in the invitation. I can refuse for all of us if you would prefer it, Grace. We are not on intimate terms with him ourselves, as you may imagine."

Grace thought for a moment. "No," she said, "don't refuse. We will go."

After all, she thought, she had come home in order to confront her past. She might as well face all of it. There had been a time when she had liked the viscount, who had indulged Gareth as much as her father had her. She told Peregrine of the invitation. She did not explain that their host was Gareth's father. She had meant to, but did not add the information when the time came. Perry must be tired of hearing of her former lover and her son. It seemed almost an insult to his good nature to be constantly referring to them.

Peregrine was in his usual good humor when he crossed from his dressing room to join Grace in hers before they left on the evening of the dinner.

"Perkins' chest has just swelled by a good two inches," he said, grinning at Grace's image in the mirror. "He has finally succeeded in tying a mathematical. You see?" He indicated his neckcloth. "Don't you think the folds quite magnificent, Grace? I feel I should be on my way to St. James's or Carlton House at the very least."

"Quite splendid," she agreed.

"Ah," he said, "you are wearing a blue gown. I think you are right that it is time to leave off our mourning gradually. You look delightful in color again. Did you enjoy your walk with Ethel this afternoon?"

"Yes," she said. "We called on two of the sick cottagers. I remember them well. It was good to see them again."

Peregrine grinned. "How delightfully silly young girls can be," he said. "I swear those three did not stop giggling all the time I was with them this afternoon. One of them had to purchase ribbons and another lace. And they all had to try on a dozen bonnets each at the milliner's, though they did not buy one between them. And they found the eating of ices and cakes at the confectioner's an enormous joke. The new curate saw us through the window and came inside to pay his respects. And they all blushed and giggled behind their hands. The curate didn't giggle, by the way, but he did blush to the tips of his ears."

Grace smiled at him in the mirror and dismissed her maid. "Priscilla and Miss Stebbins will be going to London soon," she said. "And there they will join dozens of other giggling girls, Perry. It is the Season, the marriage mart."

He was laughing, she saw, his eyes dancing in merriment, his teeth very white and even. "Life there will certainly not be dull," he said.

Their group were not to be the only dinner guests. That

was clear as soon as they approached Lord Sandersford's drawing room behind the straight back of a footman and heard the buzz of voices coming from inside the room. Grace was nervous. She drew Peregrine back behind Martin and Ethel and Priscilla—her father had declined to come—and tried to calm her thumping heart. The viscount was greeting two other guests, who stood between him and her view.

But finally he was able to turn to greet the new arrivals. He bowed to Ethel and Priscilla, shook Martin's hand, and turned to Grace and Peregrine. He was a tall man of military bearing, fit and well-muscled, extraordinarily handsome. His hair was dark and wavy, rather long, his face tanned even though March had scarcely begun. A slight cleft in his chin added to his attractive appearance. He regarded his guests with keen, rather mocking eyes.

"Ah, Lady Lampman," he said, taking her cold hand and bending over it as he raised it to his lips. "As lovely as ever, I see. Sir Peregrine Lampman, I assume?" He took Peregrine's hand in a firm clasp and stood exchanging pleasantries with him for a couple of minutes.

But Miss Stebbins and her mama attracted Peregrine's attention and beckoned him away. He must, it seemed, admire the ribbons that he had witnessed the girl purchase just that afternoon.

"Well, Grace," the viscount said when they were relatively alone, "are you going to faint, or are you going to scorn to do anything so weakly feminine?"

"Your father is dead, then, Gareth?" she asked, her voice sounding far away to her own ears.

He laughed. "Had you not heard?" he said. "Did you not know it was I you were to meet tonight? How famous! My father died six years ago."

"I did not know," she said. "I had not heard. Or that you had come home. Where is your wife?"

"Dead too," he said. "She was a poor thing, Grace. Weak. Following the drum was just too much for her constitution. She died in childbed more than nine years ago. And even the child did not survive."

"I am sorry," she said.

"You need not be." He shrugged. "It was all a long time ago. Come. My butler is summoning us to dinner, I see. I will lead you in. Take my arm, Grace. You are not going to faint, are you?"

"No." By sheer effort of will Grace dragged herself back along the dark tunnel that had been sucking her toward oblivion for the past several minutes, and lifted a hand that felt as if it were not quite part of her to rest on Lord Sandersford's arm. She looked around for Perry and saw him across the room offering his arm to Miss Stebbins and saying something that had both the girl and her mother laughing merrily.

Peregrine was rather enjoying himself. It had amused him since his arrival at his father-in-law's to find that he had been adopted as a favorite by three very young ladies, his wife's niece among them. It had always been so, he thought entirely without conceit, ever since he had grown past boyhood. He had never had to make any effort at all to attract the attention of young ladies or the liking of their mothers and older female relatives.

He had never been able quite to explain to himself his success with the ladies. And perhaps it was not any great success either, he thought. Very rarely, if ever, had he felt that one of his admirers was languishing with love for him. They merely seemed to enjoy his company and do a great deal of giggling and flirting when he was by.

Perhaps they sensed that he liked women a great deal. He had always found it a good foil to his more serious and introspective side to amuse the ladies and devise new ways to draw their laughter and their blushes.

And it was amusing to find that he could still surround himself with giggling girls and their smiling mamas even though he was a staid married man. It amused him even further to note that the same girls who derived great merriment from his company tended to blush and sigh over the thin and romantic figure of the young curate, who looked as if he could do with a good square meal. Doubtless they all dreamed of feeding his stomach and finding a way into his heart. None of them seemed at all smitten by the very handsome figure of the evening's host, who was apparently widowed and therefore perfectly eligible. But then they were very young ladies and Sandersford must be close to forty.

Peregrine stood patiently and good-humoredly behind the pianoforte stool turning pages of music as his regular trio of young girls each in turn tried to impress both him and the rest of the company with her musical talents. And he grinned across the room at Grace, who was seated with some of her former acquaintances. She looked so very suited to her name and so very lovely without the usual black mourning gown that he gazed rather too long at her and missed his cue to turn a page.

A few minutes later a delegation of young ladies asked the viscount if they might dance, and the servants came in to roll up the carpet, and a plump matron took the stool in order to play for those eager to exert themselves. And Peregrine found that he had hardly a moment even to think of his wife. He laughed and danced his way through one vigorous set after another, assuring two young ladies that, yes, their dancing skills would be quite up to the standards of Almack's and a third that, yes, dancing in Lord Sandersford's drawing room was every bit as splendid as dancing in the grandest ballroom in London.

Peregrine was enjoying the whole experience of meeting his in-laws and the other people who had been a part of Grace's past. He liked the rather dull and plodding but solid and respectable Martin, and the serious, dutiful, and shrewd Ethel. And he was intrigued by his father-in-law, who spent most of his days shut up in his own rooms, rather like a volcano that one was never quite sure was dormant. There was a great deal of resentment and guilt and love and other muddled emotions locked up inside the old man, Peregrine was sure. He only hoped that Grace's father would not die before he had come to some sort of peace with himself.

And Grace. Peregrine, standing beside a panting Miss

Horlick, sipping lemonade with her, looked fondly at his wife, who was not dancing at that moment, though she had accepted a few partners. This was a hard time for her. She was looking rather as she had looked at the rectory for five years: withdrawn, rather tight about the lips, only her eyes calm. It was only now that he realized that in the last year since their marriage her expression had relaxed, softened, and that she had bloomed into a mature beauty.

She was looking severe again. Perhaps a little less than beautiful, though it was hard for him to tell. He knew her so well, was so familiar with her every mood and expression, that he could not possibly say any longer if she was beautiful or not. He could only say that, to him, she always was. She was Grace, his wife. She was the only woman, perhaps, on whom he looked not with his customary indulgent amusement, but with something of an ache. He could make other women happy without any conscious effort. He wanted so very badly to make Grace happy, and he was not at all sure that he did so.

This time was hard for her. But it was also good for her. He was sure of that. Her life would never be complete if she could not be reconciled with her family. And that reconciliation was coming slowly, inch by cautious inch. And she could never be at peace until she was reconciled with herself, until she could forgive herself. She must have this time, agonizing as it might be for her now, to learn that there had been no connection whatsoever between the death of her child and her sin in conceiving him out of wedlock. She must learn to see that death as the tragic accident it had been.

She was looking particularly drawn tonight, Peregrine thought. It must be more than usually hard on her to be in a gathering such as this, surrounded by all the people who had known her when she lived through her five-year ordeal. His eyes twinkled down at Miss Horlick as he took the empty glass from her hand and assured her that she would doubtless survive even if Mr. Piper, her next partner, did choose to swirl her down the set as he liked to do. And his heart ached for his wife.

There was only so much he could do to help her. She must live alone through the torment of her memories. She must find her own peace. He could only be there to smile at her, to hold her hand during the worst moments, to leave her alone to find room for her memories, to hold her and love her with slow tenderness at night.

He caught her eye across the room and smiled warmly as he came toward her.

"Are you enjoying yourself?" he asked, knowing very well that she was not. "Will you dance this next one with me, Grace?"

"I have promised it to his lordship," she said, looking up at him with her large, calm eyes and setting her hand in his without seeming to realize that she did so.

"Grace?" Peregrine frowned and lowered his voice so as not to attract the attention of anyone else. "You are not going to faint, are you?"

"No, of course not." Her eyes appeared to grow larger. "Only it is hot in here, Perry. And I have been dancing. Of course I am not going to faint."

And of course being overheated did not turn one as pale as any ghost, Peregrine thought, squeezing her hand and turning his attention and his smile on the lady seated beside her.

Grace had told only one conscious lie in her relationship with her husband. She had told him on the day he had offered her marriage—or, rather, she had agreed with his assumption —that Gareth was dead. And yet at the time it had not seemed like a lie. Gareth was dead to her, had been since his final letter to her when she had already been increasing for six months, explaining that circumstances had forced him to marry a girl she had never heard of.

That was all. He had not explained what the circumstances were or what made them more important than returning home to marry the woman he had claimed to love for the past four years, the woman who was bearing his child. There were the usual protestations of undying love and a few enthusiastic details about life as an officer in the Guards.

He was dead. As far as Grace was concerned, he was dead. Except that she had not grieved or worn mourning for him. She had merely died a little inside and grown up a great deal and turned all her thoughts and her passion inward to the child she had so selfishly and so carelessly conceived.

The lie to Perry should be easy to correct. It had been a fairly innocent lie, and Perry was not a hard man to deal with. She should have been able to turn to him when he came from his dressing room later that night, put down her hairbrush, and simply tell him. Tell him that Gareth was still alive, that Gareth was the Lord Sandersford who had been their host that evening. It should have been easy. And it was certainly essential.

"Let me do that," Peregrine said, reaching for the brush. "You have such lovely hair, Grace. Did you send Effie to bed?"

"She was yawning rather loudly," Grace said. "Effie is quite an expert at dropping not so subtle hints."

"She is very young," he said.

"I know." Grace smiled at him in the mirror. "And very smitten with that blond-haired footman of Martin's. Have you noticed?"

He grinned back at her. "It was a pleasant evening, wasn't it?" he said. "We haven't danced since Christmas."

"Yes," Grace said, "it was pleasant." She closed her eyes. He was drawing the brush gently through her hair. Her heart was thumping uncomfortably.

"Was Sandersford ever a soldier?" he asked. "He certainly bears himself like a military man."

Grace kept her eyes closed. He had provided her with the perfect lead-in to what she must say. "Yes," she said. "The Guards. He sold out, I believe, when his father died six years ago. He . . . we . . . they have always been neighbors of ours."

"A pleasant man," he said. He laughed suddenly. "Who do you think is going to get the curate, Grace? Would you care to place a wager?"

"I think that to a young girl he must appear remarkably handsome," Grace said.

"With the added attraction of being far too thin and underfed," he added with a grin. "All those girls are just bursting with maternal concern. The only problem, as I see it, is that the poor man may never get up his courage to ask any of them. I think he can outdo any one of the girls in the matter of blushes."

"You ought not to laugh, Perry," she said, turning and taking the brush from his hand, "just because you find it so easy to converse with the ladies."

"Laugh?" he said. "When the man is in the enviable position of having at least five young female hearts beating for him? I am not guilty, Grace, I swear. He has nothing but my admiration. You did not enjoy yourself a great deal, dear." He set his hands on her shoulders and looked into her eyes. The smile had disappeared from his face.

"Yes, I did," she said. "Of course I did, Perry."

"Is it difficult for you to be with all these people again?" he asked. "Did they treat you badly before you left here?"

"No," she said. "They treated me with amazing courtesy. I was never made to feel like a pariah."

He framed her face with his hands. "The viscount too?" he asked. "And his father? They received you?"

Grace had never been suffocated by her husband's nearness before. She swallowed awkwardly and could not look away from his eyes. "I was never received there," she said, "after Jeremy."

"Ah," he said. "But this viscount wants to make amends. He seated you beside him at dinner, Grace. Was he a friend of your Gareth? A relative, perhaps?"

It should have been so easy. It was easy. He was making it as easy for her as it could possibly be. "A friend," she said jerkily, removing her eyes from his at last and lifting her hands to the lapels of his dressing gown.

"Ah," he said again. "I guessed as much. But the pain can be allowed to recede now, Grace. He wants to make a friend of you again. That was very clear. Forgive him, dear. Let it all go, the bitterness. People do behave badly, you know. We all do on occasion. We owe it to one another to give a second chance, and sometimes even a third and fourth.''

"Yes," she said, running her palms along the smooth silk of his lapels. She looked up into his eyes, gathering resolution, gathering courage from the kindliness she saw there. "Perry . . ."

"Hush now," he said, lowering his head and kissing her lips. "Let's forget it all for tonight and go to bed. It is late."

"But, Perry . . ."

"Sh," he murmured against her lips. "Come and let me make love to you. Does it relax you to make love? Or is it a trouble to you?" He raised his head enough to smile into her eyes.

"You know it is not a trouble," she said. "You know that, Perry."

"Sometimes I need reassuring," he said with his old boyish grin. "You get into bed, Grace. I'll see to the candles."

She would tell him afterward, Grace decided as she got into bed. She would tell him later when they were lying quiet and relaxed, her head on his arm. Or tomorrow morning, perhaps . . .

But she did not tell him. The moment had passed. She had told the lie, and she had clung to it when the only thing to have done was to tell the truth simply and directly. And immediately. She would just have to see to it, she decided the next day, that they did not cross paths with Gareth again during the two weeks that remained of their stay before they went to London.

"You did not tell me that Lord Sandersford died," she said to Ethel when the two of them were alone, gazing down at a daffodil bud that was about to brave the brisk air of early spring. "Or that Gareth was home."

Ethel looked stricken. Her hand flew to her mouth. "You did not know?" she said. "But he has been back home for years. Oh, Grace, I am so sorry. But of course you would not have known. You have been gone for ten years. I am sorry."

Grace touched the bud gently.

"I wondered that you were willing to go last night," Ethel said. "I wondered that you did not beg me to refuse the invitation. It must have been a dreadful shock for you. Does Peregrine know?"

"No," Grace said abruptly, and moved on.

But her hope of staying clear of Gareth for the remainder of their stay was not to be realized, as she might have known.

"We ran into Sandersford," Peregrine said late one afternoon after he and Martin had ridden into the village on some business. "He took us back with him to look at his stables. He has enough horses to mount a whole hunt, Grace, and still have enough left for the ladies' carriages. Some impressive horseflesh too. He made himself very agreeable."

"Did he?" Grace looked at him in some unease, but he did not elaborate on what topics the viscount had made himself agreeable about.

"And I bought you a length of blue ribbon," he said, removing it from his pocket and presenting it to her with a bow and a grin, "to replace the black one on your straw bonnet. I wish I might have brought you a more valuable gift, but village shops do not offer much beyond the purely practical."

"Thank you, Perry," she said. "It is a lovely shade. And quite as valuable as diamonds, you know."

And she could not avoid Gareth on her own account either, Grace was to discover. She was walking with Ethel one afternoon along the bank of the stream that flowed into the lake, looking for wild spring flowers, when he came riding along the road that ran parallel to the water. The road led directly from his house to the village. He stopped to hail them, and Grace reluctantly followed Ethel to the fence to exchange civilities.

"Well met," he called. "Are you ladies just out for a stroll?"

"Yes," Ethel said. "The weather is so lovely suddenly and the wild flowers blooming."

"I feel tempted to join you," he said while Grace examined the small bunch of primroses she held in her hand.

"Please do." Ethel's words, to do her justice, Grace thought, came rather stiffly and after a slight pause.

"I wonder," Lord Sandersford said, dismounting from his horse and looping the reins over the fence, "if I might beg the indulgence of a few minutes alone with Grace, ma'am?" He smiled at Ethel.

Ethel looked inquiringly at her sister-in-law while Grace said nothing, but smoothed a finger lightly over the petals of a primrose. "Grace?" she said.

Grace looked up tight-lipped into Gareth's face. "Yes," she said. "I shall follow you home later, Ethel." She resumed the absorbing task of smoothing the flower petals until the other woman had walked beyond earshot.

"Well, Grace . . ." Gareth said.

He had changed. He had always been handsome, attractive, confident of his power to charm. He had been tall and slim when he had left her. He still had all those qualities. But now he was a man, powerfully built, exuding a seductive and assured sexuality. He was the sort of man no woman would be able to resist if he set his mind on attracting her. Not that that was anything very new either.

"You have changed," he said, echoing her own thoughts.

"I am six-and-thirty years old," she said, looking finally into his dark eyes. "No longer a girl, Gareth. Time is not always kind."

"Oh," he said, "I would not say it has been unkind to you. You had the grace of a girl when I knew you. Now you have the mature beauty of a woman. But you have lost your proud look, your defiance."

"I grew up," she said.

He swung his long legs one at a time over the fence that divided them and offered his arm so that they could stroll along in the direction of the lake.

Grace shook her head, but fell into step beside him.

"You wear mourning?" he said. "You did not a few evenings ago."

"We wear it in the daytime here still out of respect for my father," she said. "We will leave it off altogether when we go to London."

"Ah, yes, Paul," he said. "He died in predictably heroic manner, I heard. Saving a child?"

"Yes," she said.

"And cut himself off from his family in equally heroic defense of your honor, I gather," he said.

"Yes."

"I would have thought the gesture unnecessary," he said. "I did not think you would run away, Grace. You used not to be a coward."

"Some things are too hurtful to be borne," she said, "especially when they concern someone one has harmed irrevocably."

"The child," he said. "Did you care about him, Grace? My father once told me that he looked like me. Did he? Did you think of me when you looked at him?" He smiled.

"I loved him," she said. "He was my son. And, no, I did not see you when I looked at him. Or myself. I saw Jeremy. He was a quite separate person. He was not either you or me, I thank God. He was an innocent child."

"You are bitter," he said, "and I suppose that is understandable. The child was a nasty mistake, and unfortunately you had to bear the consequences. Are you still bitter that I did not come home to marry you?"

Grace's voice shook with fury when she finally answered. "Jeremy was not a nasty mistake," she said. "He was not a mistake at all. He was the most precious thing that has happened in my life, except perhaps . . ."

"For me?" he completed. One eyebrow was raised. His mouth was drawn into the ironic half-smile that she had always found so attractive. "Did I let you down very badly, Grace?"

"It was a long time ago," she said, looking away from him and walking on. "A lifetime ago."

"She was just too wealthy, you know," he said. "Martha, I mean. And Papa was in debt and my pockets to let and an officer's pay just too small a pittance for my needs. I could not have offered you much of a life, Grace. Or the child. But it was you I loved all the same. You never doubted that, did you?"

"Strangely, yes," she said.

"And did you stop loving me?" he asked.

"Very soon," she said. "Long before Jeremy was born."

"Well," he said, "my feelings are not so fickle, Grace. And I am not sure you tell the truth. There has always been something between you and me. We both knew it fifteen years ago and more. And you felt it when we met again a few evenings ago, did you not? And you feel it now, Grace, as I do. Fifteen years cannot erase a love like that we shared."

"And yet," she said, "you seem to have lived very well without me in all that time, Gareth."

He shrugged. "And what is this marriage you have contracted, Grace? What is he like, the beautiful boy? I would guess he is not much of a man."

Grace was smoothing the petals of her flowers again. "It depends upon your definition of manhood, Gareth," she said. "I daresay he would not be long on his feet in a mill against you. But there is more to a man than fists and muscles."

He laughed. "Well said," he said. "And don't tell me that that part is good with him, Grace. You need more of a man to give you that, my love. I know. I have had you, remember?"

Grace examined her flowers, her jaw set in a hard line.

"Why did you marry him?" he asked. "To spite me?"

She laughed. "You are not in my life, Gareth," she said, "and have not been for fifteen years. It is a long time. You have no part in my life any longer."

"Why, then?" he asked. "Tell me, Grace. I am curious to know."

She looked up at him. They had stopped walking. "My reasons for marrying Perry and my whole relationship with him are private matters between me and him," she said. "They are none of your concern, Gareth."

"Ah, but I believe they are, Grace," he said, "or soon will be. Will you not admit that your interest in me has been rekindled in the last few days? Come, Grace, I know you of old. You cannot lie to me."

"You are wrong," she said. "All connection between you

and me is buried at the end of the lake with Jeremy. All feeling between us was dead before that. Have you ever been there? Have you ever seen your son's grave?''

''Yes,'' he said. ''Once.'' He lifted a hand and laid one finger beneath her chin. ''The child is buried there, Grace. Not you and I. Despite your protestations to the contrary, you know that nothing is ended between us. Just dormant. This day has been coming. We have both known it.''

His eyes had that intense, passionate look that had always mesmerized her. In years past she had invariably ended in his arms when he had looked at her like that. She felt a twinge of fear. ''You are my past, Gareth,'' she said. ''Not my present and not my future. My past.''

''You think that boy is your future?'' he said. ''Poor Grace. He is a ladies' man. Have you not seen that? His head is already turned by the admiration of those silly girls. Imagine what will happen when you reach London and all the new little butterflies of the Season. Grace, my love! He is far too young to appreciate your mature attractions. You will lose him, you know. I would give your marriage perhaps another year. Then he will be lost to you.''

''That is not your concern, and never will be,'' she said.

''Well,'' he said, ''I am a patient man, Grace. We will see in a year's time. Do you wish me to walk all the way home with you?'' They had been strolling back the way they had come.

''No,'' she said. ''No, that is unnecessary.''

''I shall leave you here, then,'' he said, patting the neck of his horse over the fence. ''Is this all a secret from the estimable Peregrine, by the way? Does he know of the child? Of me? Does he know who I am?''

Grace buried her nose in her flowers. ''He does not know who you are,'' she said. ''The rest he does know, and has done since before our marriage.''

''I see,'' he said, smiling down mockingly at her. ''Then I am to make sure that the secret does not slip out, am I?''

''I am not asking anything of you,'' she said.

''You leave yourself very much in my power, do you not?''

he said, crossing the fence again and disentangling the reins of his horse.

"No," she said. "I ask nothing of you, Gareth. No favor. You may tell Perry what you will."

Sandersford swung into the saddle and smiled down at her. "Ah," he said, "the old defiant Grace. All that is missing is that dark mane loose down your back as you toss your head. But the spark is back in your eyes. I will not tell your secret, Grace. I would not be so poor-spirited. *Au revoir*, my love. I shall see you again soon." He touched the brim of his hat with his riding whip and turned his horse's head to the roadway again.

"Good-bye, Gareth," she said, lifting her chin and watching him out of sight.

6

Grace and Peregrine were to leave for London five days before her brother and sister-in-law. Priscilla was to go with her aunt and uncle, much to her squealing delight and the envy of Miss Stebbins, whose mama and papa were not leaving for another full fortnight.

"Aunt Grace," Priscilla said after Grace had spoken on her behalf and persuaded Martin to allow her to travel with them, "I will be ever so good, you will see. And I will keep you company in Portland Place while Uncle Perry goes out to his clubs—Papa says that is what gentlemen do with their time in town—and I will not beg at all to be taken about until Mama and Papa come and I remove with them to Cavendish Square."

Peregrine chuckled. "I belong only to White's and Watier's," he said, "and cannot imagine wanting to spend every hour of the twenty-four at one of those, Priscilla. I shall probably drag myself out of them long enough to take Grace about, anyway. She is as new to London as you are. And I will be delighted to have two ladies for whom I might demonstrate my superior knowledge."

"Hyde Park?" Priscilla said with sparkling eyes. "And Kensington Gardens? And St. James's Park?"

"And the Tower and Astley's Amphitheater and one or two other places you might enjoy," he said with a grin.

"Oh, Uncle Perry," Priscilla said, clasping her hands to her bosom and executing a pirouette on the carpet before

him while her father frowned his disapproval, "I don't think
I can wait. I really don't think I can."

"You will be waiting five days longer if you cannot
remember to act more like a lady, miss," Martin said.

Peregrine winked at her as she sank into a chair, her
manner more subdued. He smiled at Grace.

Grace spent much of the day before their departure with
her father. She even persuaded him to take a short walk
outside with her during the afternoon. Peregrine had gone
with Martin and Priscilla to take his leave of the numerous
new acquaintances he had made during the two weeks of his
stay.

"So you are going away again, Grace," Lord Pawley said.

"Perry's mother and aunt are to be in London," she said.
"I have not met his mother since our marriage."

"You will never come again?" he asked.

"I would like to, Father," she said. "I have missed you."

"It was a bungled affair," he said. "All my fault."

"No." Grace drew him to sit on a wrought-iron bench
overlooking a bed of daffodils, most of which were now in
bloom. "It is a mistake always to blame oneself for the past.
And probably a mistake to brood on the past too."

"I wanted everything for you," he said. "Or was it really
for you I wanted it? I wanted everything for myself, I
suppose. And you were the only one with any spirit, although
you were the girl. Or so it seemed at the time. Paul had more
spirit than the lot of us put together when it came to the point,
didn't he? And Martin is one who has stayed loyal to all
this." He gestured with one hand to the house and the gardens
and the land beyond.

Grace took his arm and patted his hand.

"I wanted someone to be proud of, someone to boast of,"
he said. "I wanted you married to Sandersford and lording
it over everyone for miles around. He was a fine figure of
a man. *Is*, rather. Have you seen him, Grace? Yes, you went
there for dinner, did you not? I was angry with both of you
for making a mess of it. But only you were here to vent my
anger on."

"It is all long in the past," she said.

"Hm." He brooded on the flowers for a few minutes. "I should not have taken it out on the lad," he said.

"You were not cruel," Grace said. "You gave him a home. You provided for him."

"I gave him nothing," he said. "Nothing at all. I was punishing you. I did not even attend his funeral."

"No," she said.

"So." He seemed to forget her presence for a while. "I am judged. It is too late now. Too late to give anything to my grandson."

"It is not too late," she said. "It is never too late. There are always other people to whom you can give your love. Some of it might be given to yourself. It is time you came out into the light again, Father. You are not an old man."

"Seventy," he said. "How old would the boy have been, Grace? Jeremy."

"Fourteen," she said.

"Well," he said. "Well. I'm glad you came back, Grace. Can you be content with this husband of yours? Seems like a very young puppy to me. Fond of you, though."

"Yes," she said. "I have been very happy with him for the year of my marriage."

He nodded.

Lord Pawley came downstairs the next morning when the travelers were about to be on their way. He stood leaning on his cane on the cobbles, having rejected the assistance of both his valet and his son. He kissed his granddaughter and shook hands with Peregrine.

"Perhaps you will be well enough to visit us later in the summer or next Christmas, sir," Peregrine said. "You would be very welcome."

The baron nodded. "I would like to see my son's grave before I die," he said.

Grace held out a hand. "Good-bye, Father," she said. "I hope you will come."

He ignored her hand. "I like what you have become, Grace," he said. "I am proud of you, after all."

She lowered her hand and looked into the fierce eyes of

her father. "Papa," she said. She set her hands on his
shoulders. "Oh, Papa, I never meant to disappoint you. But
I was never able to apologize for Jeremy. Maybe what I did
was wrong, but he was not wrong. How can a living being,
a child, be wrong? I can never be sorry for having him,
though I had him for such a short time. But I never stopped
loving you either. I never did, Papa."

She kissed him on the cheek, hugged him quickly, and
turned away to where Ethel and Martin were both simul-
taneously trying to remind an agitated, tearful Priscilla of
the thousand and one rules and pieces of advice they had
drummed into her head the night before and indeed for all
the days since it had been decided that she would travel to
London with her aunt and uncle.

Peregrine, who had been standing close to Grace, looked
searchingly at his father-in-law to see that no assistance was
needed there, then he followed his wife to the waiting
carriage, handed her inside, and climbed in after her to sit
beside her and hold her hand in a very firm clasp while final
farewells were being said outside and Priscilla scrambled in
to take the seat opposite, her father's large linen handkerchief
pressed to her eyes.

He felt Grace's cheek touch his shoulder for a few moments
after the carriage lurched into motion. She did not, as Priscilla
did despite her tears, scramble toward the window for one
final view of her relatives gathered before the doors of
Pangam Manor. He clasped her hand even more tightly.

The presence of Priscilla did not leave the other travelers
with a great deal of time for reflection or any time at all for
private conversation. Even at the inns where they stayed for
two nights they were never alone together. Grace's maid was
with them, riding in the baggage coach with Peregrine's
valet, and could have slept in a room with Priscilla, but both
her uncle and aunt thought it safer and more proper to have
Grace stay with her.

Peregrine spent two restless and lonely nights, tossing and
turning on his bed, wondering how he had ever got a good
night's sleep before his marriage. The bed felt uncomfortably

and coldly large. It was almost disturbing, he thought, how easily one became accustomed to married life, how quickly another person could become quite indispensable to one's comfort and peace of mind.

Accepting on the second night that he probably would not sleep a great deal and that he would merely make matters worse by turning restlessly from side to side and punching his pillows vengefully, Peregrine propped his head on his hands, his fingers laced together, and considered the state of his marriage and his own life.

He had been living now for a year in a marriage that he had contracted rather hurriedly and with little consideration. He had been fond of Paul and had liked Grace and had felt the necessity of looking after her. After hearing the story of her past, he had also felt a deep respect for the woman whose life he would have guessed to have been rather dull and uneventful. He had come to see that her quiet dignity had been won at great cost, that she was a woman of extraordinary strength of character.

Had he given her the comfort he had set out to give? A few weeks before he would have answered with a cautious yes. There had been no great passion in their marriage, and they had reached no high pinnacles of ecstasy. But there had been companionship and affection, mutual friendship with respect, a satisfying sexual relationship—for her as well as for himself, he believed, despite the fact that she never openly showed that satisfaction.

There was no question of the fact that she had brought him far more contentment than he had dreamed of. His house, in which he had always spent a good deal of his time and which he had always loved, had become a home under Grace's quiet and efficient management. And a place of great beauty. Indeed, he lived in far greater comfort than any man had a right to expect.

And his neighbors, of whom he had always been fond and whose company he had always enjoyed, had become friends during the past year. He had, he realized in some surprise, grown during the year from a young man whom other, older adults tended to treat with amused indulgence into a full-grown man whom they accepted as a peer. And he liked the change.

And he liked Grace a great deal better than he had when he married her. He found himself so totally comfortable with her that for much of his days he was almost unaware of her as a separate person. He could talk with her, complain to her, laugh with her, be quiet with her as if she were just another part of himself.

Then, of course, she had become a very important part of his nights. He had always found her pleasing to look at and had certainly not been repelled for even one moment when he decided to offer for her by the knowledge that as his wife she must also be his sexual partner. But he had not expected to find her quite as attractive as he did find her. He made love to her probably far more frequently than was normal after a year of marriage, he thought, ruefully aware again of the emptiness of his bed for the second night in a row.

But it was not just the lovemaking. Just to have her there beside him in his bed was enough to fill him with content-ment and settle his mind for sleep. Even during the fourth week of each month, when he could not make love to her, he could feel happy just to lie with his arm beneath her head talking with her until one or both of them fell asleep.

His marriage had been quietly successful, Peregrine felt. *Had* been. He was not so sure that it still was. He was not at all sure that their few weeks at Pangam Manor had not sent Grace away from him. He did not really want to think the matter through. He felt a little ball of panic in his stomach when his mind touched on the thought. But what else was there to do but think when one was lying awake in a less-than-comfortable inn bed, one's wife not beside one either to love or merely to hold?

He had encouraged the visit. He knew that when Paul had taken Grace from her home, the past had been bottled up. It had not been erased. There was a great deal of unhappiness, pain, anger, grief, misunderstanding, throbbing beneath the surface of her life. He might have lived with Grace for the rest of their lives in mild contentment. It could be a

reasonably happy life. But there would always be that something. Peregrine had learned in his year with his wife that
that calm in her eyes he had always admired was not really
calmness at all. It was death. She had put all feelings of any
intensity to death when she had gone away with Paul.

She had to live again. She needed to do so. And so he had
taken the risk of encouraging the visit they had made. And
he was not at all sure that his hopes had been realized. On
the surface their visit would seem to have been successful.
Her father, Martin, and Ethel had appeared genuinely pleased
to see her again and had made an effort to be more than just
civil to her. And she had responded. But he did not believe
that any of them had talked openly about the painful events
that had led to her leaving. The baron had begun to do so
just before they left, and there seemed to have been something
of a reconciliation in those last few minutes. But was it
enough?

And had it been good or bad for Grace to revisit the grave
of her son? It was impossible to know. She had been
wretchedly unhappy for a few days after doing so, though
perhaps no one but him would have known it. But neither
of them had spoken of the matter since.

And Grace was still unhappy. Withdrawn. Taut as a bow.
Haunted. And with that tightness about her face and about
her mouth that had made one largely unaware of her beauty
for the five years she had spent at the rectory. Perhaps it
was necessary for her to go through that in order to eventually
come to life again. And perhaps she would still be his at the
end of it all. He did not know. But the panic was there inside
him. She was not talking to him.

Oh, she was not silent with him. Had he not been her
almost constant companion for a year, perhaps he would not
have even realized that she was not talking to him. He had
strolled out into the garden with her the evening before their
departure for London. They had talked about trivialities for
several minutes.

"Are you glad you came, Grace?" he had asked at last.
"Yes," she had said. "It has been good to see Father

again. And Martin and Ethel. And Priscilla, of course. It is time that old quarrels were allowed to die."

"I am glad," he had said. "And so you have your family again."

"Yes," she had said.

"Has everything been put quite to rights, Grace?" he had asked.

"Yes." She had looked at him with her calm eyes. "Of course, Perry."

"What is it?" he had asked, stopping in order to look into her eyes. "What is it that is still troubling you?"

She had looked hunted, trapped for several unguarded moments. She had stared back into his eyes, and he had felt her tension, her need to communicate with him, her inability to do so. He had felt failure at that moment. She was unable to tell him about the torment that he clearly saw because he knew her. And he had been unable to do anything but stand there and look back at her as gently as he knew how, telling her with the whole of himself except his voice that he was her husband, her friend, that she might say anything in the world to him and not lose one ounce of his respect or affection.

"Nothing," she had said. "Nothing at all, Perry. Have we done the right thing to allow Priscilla to go with us, do you think? It is a great responsibility to have her in our care."

He had grinned and started to walk again, her arm tucked through his. "I will vouch for it that there will not be a silent or dull moment during the whole journey," he had said.

And so the torment was still there, safely tucked away behind the calmness of Grace's eyes. Perhaps she would never be able to bring it out and fling it from her. Perhaps all the visit had done for her was to open old wounds and scarcely close old ones at all. Perhaps he had made a mistake. Perhaps he should have sheltered her from the past, from life itself, as Paul had done. And perhaps he would lose her now. Perhaps she would find it increasingly impossible to share her inner self with him. And he would lose her.

Peregrine turned against his panic and punched his pillows

with greater than usual venom. How could innkeepers reconcile their consciences with charging poor travelers through the nose for a bed and then providing them with mattresses and pillows that even a dog would not be able to sleep on? He turned onto his side, closed his eyes determinedly, and wanted his wife.

Grace was happy to have Priscilla with them, though she had worried a little about the responsibility of caring for an exuberant young girl for several days in London. But Priscilla was easy company and kept both her and Perry busy and amused. She made it possible for one to keep thought at bay and to keep one's husband's concern at a distance.

It was evening when they arrived at the house on Portland Place that Peregrine had taken for the Season. Far too late to go out to see what was to be seen. Anyway, they were all tired after a three-day journey and eager for a bath and a good meal and a comfortable bed. But for all that and despite her assurances to Grace when she had first been permitted to come with them to London, Priscilla wheedled a promise from Peregrine to take them out the next morning.

And out they went, every day until Martin and Ethel's arrival, and one evening too. They drove and walked in Hyde Park and St. James's, gazed in wonder at Buckingham House, where the king and queen held audiences when in town, at Carlton House, home of the Prince Regent, at the Houses of Parliament, Westminster Abbey, St. Paul's, the Tower. They visited and took out subscriptions at the library, and Peregrine left with an armful of books. He had been loudly lamenting his library at home ever since they had left there.

And they strolled up and down the pavements of Bond Street and Oxford Street, Priscilla exclaiming over all the bonnets and fans and shawls and other finery that she was convinced she could persuade her father into buying when he arrived in town. Peregrine bought her a new ivory fan and chip-straw bonnet over her blushing protests and bore Grace off to a fashionable modiste to be fitted for new gowns and walking dresses now that she had officially left off her mourning.

They went to the King's Theater one evening to see and listen to Signor Tramezani, Signora Collini, and Madame Calderini sing in the opera *Sidagero*. Peregrine and Grace sat enthralled by the music. Priscilla was perhaps more interested in the seven magnificent tiers of boxes, all decorated in gold and azure and hung with brocade curtains. And in the people who sat inside those boxes.

"Oh," she said in something like an agony before the performance began, "do you think that in a few weeks' time, some of these faces will become familiar? Will Mama and Papa be able to procure some invitations?"

"Of course," Grace said reassuringly. "You just need a little patience, Priscilla. You are going to be presented to the queen, you know. Of course there will be so many invitations that you will not know which to accept and which to throw away."

But Priscilla did not have to wait quite so long for some introductions. During the interval there was a knock at the door of their box, and a young lady and gentleman entered.

"Perry," the young lady said. "I was never more surprised in my life than when Mama pointed you out. I thought you were going to rusticate forever. It must be two years at least since you were here."

She was holding out both hands to him, an exquisitely beautiful young lady in an emerald green silk gown, with real emeralds at throat and wrist and flaming red hair and slanting hazel eyes to ensure that the gown and the jewels did not overshadow her person.

"Leila," Peregrine said, surging to his feet and taking her two outstretched hands in his own. "You are here too? And looking quite as lovely as ever. Yes, it is two years. It seems like forever, does it not?"

"And here is Francis too," Leila said, indicating the young man behind her with a slight turn of the head.

Peregrine smiled and shook hands with her companion. "May I present my wife, Grace?" he said. "And Miss

Priscilla Howard? Lady Leila Walsh and Mr. Francis Hartwell, Grace, old friends of mine.''

"You are married, Perry?" Lady Leila asked rhetorically,
turning toward Grace and Priscilla, who were seated side
by side. "How perfectly horrid of you." She smiled impishly
and extended a slim hand to Priscilla. "I am pleased to meet
you, Lady Lampman. Ma'am." She inclined her head to
Grace.

Priscilla giggled. "Oh, you have us mixed up," she said.
"I am Priscilla Howard."

Lady Leila flushed with mortification and looked more
closely at Grace. "I do beg your pardon," she said. "Perry,
what do you think you are about, waving a vague hand in
the direction of two ladies and expecting me to know which
is which?"

Mr. Hartwell bowed to both ladies. "It takes a great deal
to make Leila blush, Lady Lampman," he said. "May I
congratulate you?"

Grace sat in some discomfort while Lady Leila allowed
Peregrine to seat her, and prattled brightly for what remained
of the interval.

"Oh, Perry," the girl said, "life is indescribably dull this
early in the Season, is it not? Absolutely no one is here yet
and not likely to be for perhaps another fortnight. You must
come to the Halstons' rout tomorrow night. I shall see that
an invitation is sent to you in the morning. There is no one
on the guest list below the age of thirty, I would swear, except
for Francis and me and Annabelle Halston, and Christina
Lowe and Humphrey Dawes. And Silas Crawley, of course,
but he does not signify. Say you will be there too. You always
did know how to brighten up even the dullest gathering.''

"I think not," Peregrine said. "Priscilla is not yet out,
you know, and her parents are not due in London for another
two days. It would not do for us to take her into society before
they decide how they want her introduced.''

"How tiresome," Leila said, her eyes resting on Priscilla
for a moment. "But you could come, Perry. Your wife would
not mind staying at home with Miss Howard, I am sure.
Would you, Lady Lampman?''

Grace was saved from having to answer when Peregrine laughed. "Leila hasn't changed, has she?" he said, grinning at Mr. Hartwell. "Perhaps Grace would not mind, Leila, but I am afraid I certainly would. I see your mama looking very pointedly this way. The opera is about to resume, I take it."

Leila sighed and got to her feet. "You have not grown stuffy merely because you are married, have you, Perry?" she said. "Humphrey has not, I do assure you. He has not even brought his wife to town with him. I believe she is in a delicate way, if you understand my meaning. Lady Lampman, you will not allow Perry to become stuffy, will you? It would be a great shame, you know, when he was always the life and soul of any party." She smiled winningly as she got to her feet.

"I think Perry would find it quite impossible to be stuffy," Grace assured her. "It is not in his nature."

Peregrine was still grinning. He laid a hand on his wife's shoulder as the two visitors prepared to take their leave. "You had better listen, Leila," he said. "Grace knows me better than anyone."

"Isn't she just beautiful," Priscilla said, saucer-eyed, when they were alone in their box again. "Are ladies really allowed to wear gowns so low cut, Aunt Grace?" She giggled. "Was not that amusing when she thought I was you? She thought I was your wife, Uncle Perry. I told you that you were too young to be my uncle. How amusing it will be if other people think you are my beau instead of my aunt's husband."

Peregrine sat down, took Grace's hand in his, and set it on his sleeve. He kept his hand over it to warm it. He smiled down at her. "Leila never did have a brain in her head," he said. "I always thought it was fortunate for her that she is so pretty. And wealthy, into the bargain. Can you imagine my going to an evening party without you, Grace?"

Grace said nothing. She was glad to see that the performance on stage was about to resume. Of course it would be natural for Perry—and Priscilla—to be drawn into a young crowd. He had friends here, made during the years when he had regularly come to London for at least a few

weeks of the Season. Friends below the age of thirty, as Lady
Leila Walsh had put it. Friends who would want him to join
them in their various entertainments and whom he would
wish to join.

How had she not realized that London would be the very
worst place to come with Perry? Both he and she could only
become increasingly aware of the age difference between
them there. It would drive a wedge between them and add
an awkwardness to an already strained relationship. She had
still not been able to bring herself to tell him about Gareth
even though seemingly perfect opportunities had presented
themselves more than once. Even as recently as the night
of their arrival in town he had asked her again what troubled
her as she lay nestled in his arms after an achingly slow and
beautiful lovemaking. And again she had protested after a
long and agonized silence that nothing did.

It did not matter now, she told herself. They were away
from Gareth's neighborhood and unlikely to be back there
for a long time. But it did matter. Her former lover, the father
of her dead child, was still alive, and Perry thought him dead.
They had both met him and accepted his hospitality. Perry
had gone with him to view his stables and thought him a
pleasant man. And she had walked alone with him and felt
the unwelcome pull of his powerful personality. She had not
touched him or spoken an encouraging word to him, and yet
she felt as if she had been unfaithful to Perry. She had not
even told Perry that she had walked with Lord Sandersford.
And even if she had, she would have still been deceiving
him. He would still not have known that she had walked with
her lover.

Grace allowed her hand to remain on her husband's sleeve
and felt the warmth of his body seep into the chill of hers.
And there was a dullness inside her. She was going to lose
him. It was all spoiled, their marriage. Partly because he
was young and needed a young man's amusements. And
partly because she had lied to him and could not tell the truth
that might drive him away faster than he would go anyway.

7

By the time Martin and Ethel arrived in Portland Place late on the afternoon of the day they were expected, in order to take their daughter to Cavendish Square with them, Priscilla was in a state of high excitement. She hurled herself first at her mother and then at her father.

"It seems like forever," she said. "I thought you would never come."

"How lovely to see you again and to find you looking so well, dear," Ethel said, holding on to her dignity in the presence of her sister- and brother-in-law.

"You should watch your manners, miss," Martin said. "We have not even had a chance to greet your aunt and uncle yet."

But Priscilla was not to be cowed. There was too much news of their journey and their days' activities to be told, and too many favors by way of new clothes and future entertainments to be discussed, to enable her to act the part of the demure young lady just yet.

Consequently a full half-hour passed before the new arrivals could do more than greet Grace and Peregrine and ask after their health. Only after Priscilla dashed from the room, having suddenly remembered that she had a new bonnet and a new fan to show her mama, although they were packed already in her trunk, was Ethel able to give any news of home.

"Papa is well," she said, "and went out of doors each

day after your leaving. We were very gratified, were we not, Martin? He stays altogether too much inside his rooms. And all the tulips were bursting into bloom. I hated to leave them.''

"Yes," Grace agreed. "We have been lamenting our garden at home too.''

"Spring is altogether a foolish time for the Season in London," Peregrine said with a smile. "Grace and I have been considering lobbying everyone here this year to see if we cannot have it changed to the winter, haven't we, Grace?''

She laughed. "This is the first I have heard about it," she said. "But I do think it a quite brilliant idea, Perry.''

Ethel placed her teacup very carefully back in its saucer and examined the Wedgwood pattern closely. "Lord Sandersford has also decided to spend the Season here," she said. "Martin met him on the road to the village the day before we left. He was planning to leave a few days after us, I believe.''

"Indeed?" Grace said, her voice sounding distant to her own ears. Martin, she noticed, appeared to be studying the tea leaves at the bottom of his cup.

"Splendid," Peregrine said. "And you were afraid that you would know no one here, Grace. Soon London will be filled with our friends and acquaintances and relatives. Edmund and his family should be here soon too. And my mother and aunt some time during April.''

"And the Stebbinses will be bringing Lucinda," Ethel added. "I am pleased that she and Priscilla will be able to keep each other company.''

Grace was thankful for the return to the room of Priscilla and the lively argument that developed between Perry and Martin, who felt he should pay for the fan and the bonnet.

"We must give a dinner for our friends once they have all arrived in town," Peregrine said to Grace later. "And perhaps some music and cards afterward. Even some informal dancing, do you think? We do not boast a ballroom here, but the drawing room is large enough for a dozen couples. Do you think it a good idea?''

"Yes," she said. "Will there not be a great many other

entertainments for it to conflict with, though, Perry?''

"We shall set the date now, then, and let our friends know as we see them," he said. "I am expecting every day to see Edmund at White's. It will be good to see him again and Madeline and Dominic. Sandersford must have made a spur-of-the-moment decision to come. He did not say anything while we were there, did he?''

"Not that I heard," Grace said.

"Perhaps he is thinking of taking a new wife," Peregrine said with a grin. "Did you know his first wife, Grace?''

"No," she said. "He was living from home when they were married.''

He nodded. "Do you suppose Priscilla will get all the finery she has set her heart on in the last week?" he asked.

"I doubt it," Grace said. "Martin did not sound too encouraging even about the few things she mentioned this afternoon.''

"And yet he dotes on her," Peregrine said with a laugh. "And I am sure she understands perfectly well that his bark is many times worse than his bite. It must be very difficult to be strict with a daughter, mustn't it? I would probably spend a fortune on one merely because I could not face her look of disappointment when I said no.''

In the event, it was Lord Sandersford whom Peregrine met at White's, not Lord Amberley. They were both there to read the morning papers, but adjourned to the dining room when they recognized each other.

"I was not even planning to come here this year," Lord Sandersford said. "But one does feel the pull of town amusements when spring comes, does one not? And female company, of course.''

"Yes, although the social rounds can be trying year after year," Peregrine said. "Through one's youth it seems that there is nothing so enjoyable as the Season and that the rest of the year must be spent in dullness waiting for the next spring to arrive. But other interests begin to take priority as the years pass.''

"And is Lady Lampman enjoying being here?" Lord Sandersford asked, looking his companion over with lazy, penetrating eyes. "It is her first time in town, I believe?"

"Yes," Peregrine said. "She has been suitably impressed with all one is supposed to be impressed with. And she is constantly busy. She is out shopping this morning with her sister-in-law and Priscilla. I think Grace is just as happy, though, at home in the country with her garden."

"Is she?" The viscount raised his eyebrows. "Then she must have changed. I cannot imagine Grace pottering around in a garden."

"No?" Peregrine looked at his companion with some interest. "What was she like when you knew her?"

Lord Sandersford's eyes looked somewhat mocking. "When she was a girl and a young woman?" he said. "Wild, graceful, beautiful. Her hair loose down her back as often as not. Confident, her chin always high, her eyes always flashing. It is hard to imagine, seeing her now, is it not?"

Peregrine considered. "No," he said. "I can see how all those qualities would translate into Grace as she is now."

Lord Sandersford's eyes rested keenly on the other. "You were a friend of Paul's?" he asked. "Not often does friendship call upon one to enter a marriage as you did. You are to be commended."

Peregrine looked startled. "Is that how my marriage appears?" he said. "Because I am so much younger than Grace, perhaps? I am afraid I tend to forget about that. It becomes quite unimportant when one grows familiar with another person, you know. Our marriage seems a very normal one to me, I do assure you. You must not think I did something even remotely heroic. Heavens, no!"

The viscount smiled. "You disappoint me," he said. "I have thought, you see, that I might look around me for a bride among all the hopeful little girls who are beginning to crowd the fashionable drawing rooms and ballrooms. I would hate to think that after a year or so of marriage I would no longer be aware of her youth and vigor. How very dull a picture you present."

"Then I must be very poor at conveying meaning through the medium of words," Peregrine said with a grin. "I wish you luck. And joy, of course."

Sandersford inclined his head.

"It is," a tall sandy-haired gentleman with large side whiskers and mustache said, stopping beside their table and bending slightly to look into the viscount's face. "Heaven bless us! Haven't clapped eyes on you for five years or more."

"Six," Lord Sandersford said, pushing back his chair and rising to his feet in order to shake hands with the new arrival. "I sold out six years ago, Maurice. And how have the Guards managed to survive without me?"

"Oh, tolerably well, you know," the other said with a bellowing laugh. "And they have had to do without me for the last three as well. Invalided out. My leg, you know. The knee never did heal properly. Should have had it sawn off, I daresay. Keeps giving out on me at the most awkward moments. I was kneeling at the altar for my own wedding— no one you would know, Gareth—and couldn't get up again." He guffawed with laughter once more.

"It must have been a priceless moment," Lord Sandersford said. "Would you care to join us, Maurice?"

He turned to Peregrine and introduced the two men. But his former army friend was in a rush. He excused himself after making plans to meet Sandersford the next day.

"Pleased to make your acquaintance, Lampman," he said. "And I look forward to hearing what you have been up to for the last six years, Gareth. No good, at a guess. Unless you have reformed. Female hearts and female virtue still strewn around in tatters at your feet, I suppose?" He left them, laughing.

Lord Sandersford resumed his seat. "That is what the Guards can do for you, Lampman," he said. "Some of us find afterward that we never can talk in anything lower than a quiet bellow. One wonders if he is capable of lowering his voice in his wife's boudoir, does one not?"

Peregrine excused himself a few minutes later.

The spacious houses and mansions of London's fashionable Mayfair filled up with the coming of April, and soon their wealthy and prominent residents were being offered a dizzying array of entertainments with which to amuse themselves for every moment of their days until summer should draw them home again or to one of the spas.

Ethel and Martin Howard decided that a ball given by Ethel's second cousin in honor of his own daughter's come-out would be a suitable occasion for Priscilla's first official appearance in society. Grace and Peregrine were invited, but then so was almost everyone who was someone in the social world. It was early in the Season. Many a hostess wished to establish the reputation of having attracted the biggest squeeze to her particular assembly.

Grace was looking forward to the occasion, her first grand ball at the age of thirty-six! She had not planned to dance until Peregrine laughed at her and asked if the rheumatics pained her enough that he should stop taking her walking during the daytime. And she had not planned to dress in just such a way. But Perry had gone with her to the modiste he himself had recommended and firmly forbidden all her early choices of both designs and fabrics for her evening gowns.

Was she afraid that a fashionable gown falling in elegant folds from a high waist might occasionally reveal the outline of her legs? he asked. Shocking! And—with a roguish grin for the dressmaker, who was spreading out a new set of plates for them to consider—was she afraid to reveal a little more of her bosom than a high neckline would allow? And, no, he would absolutely not hear of a turban to hide her lovely hair. Not until she was seventy years old at the very least. And if they were fortunate, perhaps those particular horrors would have gone out of fashion by then. Plumes, yes, if she really wanted, but a turban, no.

And he laughed at her again when she tried to pick out sober colors for her gowns. "Has all the black you have been wearing made you color-blind, Grace?" he asked. "Choose a different color from that gray. I insist. You cannot really want that, can you? What would you really like to wear if you did not have to consider at all what you think you ought to wear?"

She looked around at all the bolts of cloth spread around

them. "That red," she said daringly and half-jokingly, expecting another storm of protest.

"Then we are finally agreed," Peregrine said. "The red it will be for your first ball gown, Grace. And for the design, this, I think. Do you like it?"

She looked at the plate to which he pointed. "Oh, Perry," she said, "it is gorgeous. But I do not know if I dare."

"This one," he said, looking up to the dressmaker, his eyes twinkling. "And now for all the others. And you have my strict orders, madam wife, to think and see as a woman for the next hour or so, not as the sober dowager you are pretending to be."

So, almost two weeks later, she was wearing the red gown and staring at her image in the pier glass in her dressing room, wondering if she had stepped back in time. She had not expected to see herself so ever again, looking vivid and alive and, yes, feminine. Surely when Perry saw her, he would be startled at just how much bosom was showing and at just how much the fine silk did reveal of the outline of her body and legs. Only the heavy flounces at the hem kept it from clinging, she was sure.

And Effie had done wonders with her hair and the silver and red plumes that nodded above it. There was color in her cheeks, though none of it was artificial, and there was a brightness in her eyes that was unfamiliar to her gaze. She felt almost like Grace Howard again, the young Grace, the Grace before Jeremy.

She turned as the door opened behind her and Peregrine stepped into the room. She was suddenly self-conscious, convinced that she was making a foolish spectacle of herself, masquerading as a girl.

He closed the door behind his back and stood against it. And his eyes traveled down her body from the plumes to the toes of her silver dancing slippers and back up to her face again. "I am going to have to keep you at home, you know, Grace," he said. "This ball is supposed to be in honor of some poor young girl, and yet, if I take you there, no one will have eyes for anyone else but you."

"Perry," she said, pleased. "What a silly joke. But do I look all right? The color is not too vivid?"

"Blinding," he said.

"Is the bodice not cut too low?"

"Decidedly," he said. "I am not at all sure that it will please me to have other men see what a magnificent bosom you have, Grace. In fact, I am sorry now that I did not encourage the gray silk and the high neckline and the turban. I might have hidden you in a dark corner, then, and not have had above three-quarters of the men present realize that you were heavily disguised."

"How silly you are tonight," she said. "Oh, and Perkins has perfected another waterfall with your neckcloth, Perry. You do look splendid."

"Well," he said, "I cannot be quite outclassed by my wife, now, can I?"

Grace felt more lighthearted than she had felt in a long while as they drove the distance to Fitzroy Square, where the ball was to take place, and joined a line of carriages waiting to deposit their passengers before the double doors of the house. She was looking and feeling her best, she was on her way to the first grand ball she had ever attended, her niece was about to make her first appearance in society, and she had Perry at her side. She was going to enjoy herself and forget anything that might cloud her joy.

She was going to forget that Gareth was in town and had called on them two days before and stayed for almost a whole hour, making himself charming to Perry, looking at her frequently with those eyes that established ownership and that she knew from long experience meant mischief.

And she was going to forget that Perry was already going away from her. Oh, he still spent most of each day in her company and all of every evening and night. And she was not so unrealistic as to expect him to be with her for every moment. She had expected him to want to spend some time at his clubs and with former acquaintances.

She had no complaint whatsoever against him. But he was going away from her for all that. He had been unnaturally quiet for the last week, unnaturally serious. Not unkind, not in a bad mood, not silent, not even humorless. It was hard to explain in words. Perhaps she would not have even known that he was going from her if she had not lived long enough with him to know him very well indeed. But she did know him well, and so she did know that she was losing him.

It was inevitable, of course. It must have started at the opera, when that very lovely Lady Leila Walsh had reminded him that there were young people whose company and activities were waiting to be enjoyed. Yet he was married to a lady quite indisputably beyond the age of thirty. And it would have continued when Priscilla left them and took the sparkle and frenzied restlessness of her youth with her. And all their walks and rides together, all his outings alone, would have brought to his notice the young and the beautiful and the exuberant who seemed to have a monopoly on the springtime and the Season.

And Perry, because he was good and kind and honorable, was still spending most of his time with her and still treating her with deference, still entertaining her and buying her gifts by day and loving her by night. Perhaps he did not even know himself yet that their marriage was dying. Or perhaps he did know and was fighting the inevitable. Poor Perry!

But she did know and accepted the reality, though with a dull and hopeless pain inside. She had always known it would come to this and had protected herself from unbearable agony by refusing to allow herself to come fully alive under Perry's affection. But it had not happened yet. It was happening, but it was not finished. There was some time left yet. There was this evening and this ball. And she had Perry beside her, in the sort of teasing mood that she had not seen in the past week. She was going to enjoy herself.

Lady Madeline Raine had just rapped Peregrine on the knuckles with her fan and told him not to be impertinent. Her green eyes were dancing with merriment.

"If you are suggesting by talking so pointedly about this being my fourth Season that I have been unable to find a husband in all that time," she said, "then I shall direct Dominic to call you out. He is considerably taller than you,

sir. The very idea! Have you considered that perhaps I have
not wanted to find a husband?''

Peregrine grinned. ''If you will recall my exact words,
Madeline,'' he said, ''you will be forced to admit that I
neither said nor hinted at anything so unmannerly. I would
have to say that you protest rather too much. I suspect that
you have been touched on the raw.''

''Ah, sir,'' she said, ''you are unkind. Now that you are
respectably married, you think you may look in scorn at
everyone over the age of twenty who is not. I shall best you
yet, you know, by marrying a duke.''

They were dancing, and the flow of their conversation was
considerably hampered by the steps of the dance, which
frequently separated them. Grace, Peregrine saw, was still
standing at the side of the ballroom, talking to Lady
Amberley. But he did not worry about her. It was the first
of four sets that she had not danced.

He still could not keep his eyes away from her for more
than a couple of minutes at a time. He knew her to be
beautiful, of course. And that gown could reveal nothing of
her body that he did not know already. He knew her with
far more than his eyes only: he knew her with his own body
and with a long and intimate familiarity. But he still could
not stop himself from looking at her in wonder. There was
a beauty in her tonight that he had not seen before, a certain
glow from within that had forced itself past the calm of her
eyes and gave her vibrancy. He was not sure that he had
been entirely teasing when he had said that he did not want
other men to see her in all her beauty.

And yet he was proud of her and delighted at every male
head that turned for a second look at her. The room was
filled, of course, with young girls in their delicate whites
and pastels, and it was undoubtedly on them that most of
the male attention and admiration was focused. But there was
a mature beauty and attractiveness about Grace that drew
the eye almost like a magnet. Even Lady Sally Jersey,
surrounded by her usual court, did not outshine her.

''Even Edmund is here tonight,'' Lady Madeline was
saying. ''I would dare swear that he will not attend half a

dozen more balls in the whole Season. He would prefer to attend a salon and spend an evening in conversation on literary or political topics. Can you imagine?''

"It is very poor-spirited of him to be so dull,'' Peregrine said. "A whole earldom going to waste! It is enough to make the most sanguine of young ladies cross beyond bearing.''

"Oh,'' she said, "I might have known I would have no sense out of you, Perry. I forget that you are rather like Edmund when you are not tormenting the ladies.''

"Tormenting the ladies?'' he said. "When I have been rehearsing my charms for the whole of the past week?''

Peregrine had caught Grace's eye across the room. Lord Sandersford had joined her and Lady Amberley.

Gareth.

And all the joy went out of Peregrine's evening as it had been doing out of his life for the past week, whenever he could not keep that name at bay.

He had not wanted to believe it at first. And he still did not know for sure. He had not asked anyone. But the coincidence would have been just too great. It could not but be true. Sandersford must be of an age with Grace. He had been a soldier. He had grown up with Grace, knew a great deal about her, lived at no great distance from her father. And his name was Gareth.

He had been Grace's lover. And fathered her child. And abandoned her. She had loved him. And perhaps still did. And now, having seen her again, he had followed her to London.

And Grace's unhappiness over the last weeks, that something that was troubling her, was finally explained. She had met again the man she had loved. The man she still loved? And he wanted her again. Yet she was trapped in a marriage she had made for comfort and convenience. Marriage with a younger man, who could not hope to compete with the very handsome and charismatic figure of Gareth, Viscount Sandersford.

He did not know what to do, had not known what to do for a week. His first instinct had been to go home and confront Grace. She had lied to him before their marriage, when he had admired her for being so open with him and frank about her past. And she had deceived him during their visit to her home. He had felt a hurt anger against her, an anger that had bewildered him because it was an unaccustomed emotion for him, especially directed against his wife. Their relationship had been a remarkably tranquil one over more than a year of marriage.

But he had not confronted her. He knew, without having to think very deeply on the matter, that Grace had never lied to him or withheld any truth maliciously. And he knew that she must be troubled as much by the deception she had perpetrated against him as by the renewal of her acquaintance with Sandersford. Would he solve anything by telling her that he knew? Or would he make matters many times worse?

He did not know, and he did not know what to do. He did not know if he should try to prevent meetings between his wife and her former lover—should he take her home to Reardon Park perhaps?—or whether he should allow her to work out the problem in her own way. And he did not know if he should confront the viscount with his knowledge or stand back and let Grace make her own decisions.

He knew what he would do if he were a man, according to all the codes of manhood with which the people of his generation had been indoctrinated. He would probably challenge Sandersford to a duel and beat his wife and take her into the country. Or else he would turn her off, having discovered that her lover was still alive and still a part of her life, and send her back into the arms of the man who had taken her honor.

But he had always considered such codes silly and immature. Why should he think only of his own image, his own reputation, when there was another human being to be considered? He would prefer to think of what was best for Grace—and himself too—rather than of some inanimate code of behavior. He trusted her, when all was said and done, to do what was right. And if he must lose her, if that was what she would decide was right, then so be it. To hell with what the world might say.

Only one thing he did not consider, because he knew it

was not in Grace's nature to put him in such a dilemma. He did not ask himself what he would do if she should decide to take Sandersford as her lover again while continuing with her marriage. That question he did not ask himself. He knew that he would never have to provide himself with an answer.

He smiled at Lady Madeline as the music ended, and led her back to her mother.

"Sandersford?" he said pleasantly. "Ah, Edmund, where have you been hiding? Your sister tells me that you have been in town for four days already."

"And occupied by business ever since," his friend said, extending a hand to him. "But intent on enjoying myself tonight. Now let me see. The Courtneys and the Carringtons and the Cartwrights—the three C's, in fact—and the Misses Stanhope all send their regards to you and Lady Lampman, as do the Mortons and the rector and his wife. Have I forgotten anyone, Mama?"

"I think it would be safer just to say 'everyone,' dear," his mother said.

Lord Amberley smiled. "Now, why did I not think of that?"

"My dance, I believe," Lord Sandersford said, extending a hand for Grace's. "With your permission, Lampman."

Peregrine bowed.

"They make a handsome picture," Lord Amberley said, looking after them. "Lady Lampman is in good looks, Perry. You must be treating her well." He grinned.

"I must be on my way to claim Lady Leila Walsh's hand for the next dance," Peregrine said, "before someone else steps in and takes my place. She does not lose any popularity over the years, does she?"

His eyes were twinkling as he approached the lady in question and stood politely to one side while she explained to a disappointed youth that she had no space left on her card where she might write his name. He must enjoy the evening, Peregrine told himself, or appear to do so anyway. He must not appear to mope over Grace.

"Perry, there you are," Lady Leila said, turning her slanting hazel eyes on him. "I do not know why I did not grant that dance to poor Mr. Daniels, you know. I am still quite out of sorts with you for marrying without giving me a sporting chance of taking you away from her. And I will never forgive you for the trick you played at the theater. Can you imagine my mortification at letting my eyes stray past your wife and dismissing her as far too old for you, and greeting effusively a girl who was not even out at that time? Really, Perry, your jokes get worse and worse.''

"If you are going to scold," he said, "I will find the card room, Leila, and see if I cannot separate a few duchesses from their fortunes. You have that hair to live up to, I know, but you need not turn into a shrew.''

He grinned at her indignant rejoinder.

Strange, he was thinking. Since his marriage, he really had grown unaware of the difference in age between himself and Grace. She was just Grace to him, a person who had become very dear to him. He could not look at her even now and see a woman of thirty-six in comparison with his twenty-six. He could see only Grace, his friend and his lover. Did she look older than he? He supposed she must. Common sense said that she must. And London society appeared to be saying that she did.

His eyes strayed to where Grace was dancing with Sandersford, his handsome face smiling down into her upturned one.

Damnation. Oh, damnation!

8

Gareth had turned on the full force of his charm. Grace recognized all the signs. There was his smile, of course, which had always been more attractive than almost any other man's smile because of the whiteness of his teeth. And there was the very intense and appreciative look in his dark eyes and the way he had of crinkling his eyes at the corners when he laughed. And those eyes, though very direct, knew how to flutter down to one's mouth for the merest moment, or up to one's hair.

They had laughed about that deliberate charm when they were much younger. He had never used it on her then because she would immediately have accused him of being false. But he had used it on other girls, entirely for his own amusement and hers.

He was using it on her now, Grace saw as she danced with him. Except that now it was not a boy's charm any longer, but a man's seductive power. And he was a man now who knew the irresistibility of his attractiveness even more than the young Gareth had done.

"Well, Grace," he said, "I came to town to look about me for a young wife. I came here tonight for that purpose. And it could be a successful evening. We are surrounded by young ladies, a dozen or more of them pretty, I would imagine. Yet I find I have eyes for no one but you."

"Nonsense, Gareth," she said. "You forget that I know this approach of yours from long ago. Are you trying to make a conquest of me? Did you think it would be easy? And would it amuse you to know that it was still possible?"

They were dancing close to the edge of the dancing floor, close to the windows. He drew her away from the other dancers and stood with her in the relative shelter of the long velvet curtains.

"You are right," he said. "I was being less than sincere in my manner. And I have been lying, both to you and to others I have spoken to since arriving in town. I am not here to look over this new crop of beauties, Grace. What interest would I have in young girls who know nothing about satisfying a man's needs and appetites? I came here because of you. You know that, do you not? You must have expected me to come. But if I am to be honest, then so must you. Don't talk of my conquering you. There is no conquest to be made. Is there?"

He was Gareth, she told herself, looking up at him. He was that boy she had loved dearly for years as she grew to womanhood, the young man with whom she had been intimate for the span of a few days. He was Jeremy's father. He had started her son in her. She had always expected that he would be her husband. She had always expected that there would be several children. And now he was powerfully handsome. He frightened her, suffocated her.

"No, there is not, Gareth," she said, answering only his last question. "It is an impossibility. I am married to Perry."

He made a dismissive gesture with his hand. "A mere boy," he said. "A pleasant-enough boy, I will admit. And it was decent enough of him to rescue you from an awkward situation after Paul died. But a boy nonetheless. And one who favors young ladies, as is perfectly understandable, Grace. Look at him now laughing with his partner. Do you believe he does not fancy her?"

Grace looked obediently. Perry's fair head was bent to Lady Leila's flaming red one, and they were clearly teasing each other or flirting. There was nothing unusual about the scene. But Lady Leila was indeed very youthful and dashing. And extremely pretty.

"You do not need to cling to him and be constantly humiliated by his roving eye, Grace," Lord Sandersford said fiercely. "You have more beauty and more passion in your little finger than that young lovely will ever have in her whole person. But you need a man to appreciate both and bring them alive in you. Not a boy."

"You speak as if you think me undecided, wavering," Grace said, turning determinedly from the charming picture made by Perry and Lady Leila. "I am not, Gareth. My relationship with Perry, as I told you before, is entirely a private matter between him and me. And as for you, you are a part of my distant past. There is no question of resurrecting what there once was between us."

"Oh, liar, Grace," he said, his dark eyes gazing down intently into hers. "Are you trying to convince yourself? Ours was not a love that could easily die. I put the child in you, whom you claim to have loved so dearly because he was mine, Grace. That is a bond that cannot be shrugged off even in a lifetime."

"And yet," she said, "it was of so little importance to you that you married a wealthier woman even while that child was still inside me. Don't talk to me of lifelong bonds."

"I was a boy," he said. "A headstrong, conceited boy. Let us not judge each other now from this distance of time, Grace. You were not blameless yourself. You knew the risks and the moral implications when you decided to give me a husband's privilege."

"I was foolish," she said. "Foolish and irresponsible."

He took one of her wrists in his hand. "Let us not quarrel," he said. "We have both made mistakes, Grace —me in dishonoring you, you in allowing yourself to be taken, me in marrying Martha, you in marrying Lampman. Are we going to let those mistakes ruin what is left of our lives?"

"You have been widowed for many years, Gareth," she said. "I have been married for one. What happened to the years between? If you had made such a mistake, if you wanted so badly to be reunited with me, where were you during those years?''

"I did not know where you were," he said. He shrugged. "And I did not see you. It was seeing you again a few weeks ago that brought everything back to me and made me realize what a fool I have been.''

"I am sorry, Gareth," she said. "You are too late. Fifteen years too late.''

"No," he said, his hand gripping her wrist almost painfully, shaking it even. "No, I will not believe that, Grace. You are bitter. I can understand that. I did a dastardly thing to leave you alone with the child and the scandal. And it was remiss of me not to come for you after Martha died. But must you punish yourself as well as me? If you turn from me now, we will waste not only those years, but the rest of a lifetime.''

"Those years have not been wasted for me," Grace said. "I spent four of them with Jeremy. I have spent one of them with Perry. It is too late for us, I tell you, Gareth. Our love has long been dead. It is a thing of the past.''

"You lie, Grace," he said. She knew from old experiences that his temper was rising. His jaw was set and his eyes even more intense that they had been. "Are you convinced by your own words? Are you content to go through life with the beautiful boy, watching him flirt with every pretty young girl he sees, knowing that he will be amusing himself in private with more than a few of them? Can you tell me that you love him, Grace? That you think him worth fighting for? Humiliating yourself for? Tell me that you love him, that he is everything in the world to you as I once was. And still am, I firmly believe. Tell me and I will leave you alone.''

"No." Grace was glaring back into his eyes. He was as overbearing as he had ever been. They had had not a few fights in their younger days, sometimes very physical fights. "I will tell you no such thing merely because you demand it of me. And I will tell you nothing that concerns Perry. Nothing. My feelings for him and his for me are none of your concern. None, do you understand me?''

"You cannot say it, can you?" he taunted. His eyes strayed

to her lips. "You cannot tell me that you love him. Because it is not true, Grace. And cannot be true. He is a boy and you are a woman."

"Sh! Oh, please hush. People are beginning to notice." Grace, angry and dazed, was aware suddenly that Ethel was standing directly in front of them, a look of deep mortification on her face. "Please," she said again, opening her fan, waving it slowly before her face, and attempting to smile, "you must not quarrel here."

Lord Sandersford released Grace's wrist and smiled with practiced charm. "Ah, a timely reminder, ma'am," he said, inclining his head. "Grace and I were merely having a friendly difference of opinion. Just like old times."

Grace noticed for the first time that the dancing had stopped. All the occupants of the room were not looking at them, she found, glancing about her in some trepidation. But Perry was making his way toward them, his face rather pale. He was smiling.

"This dancing is warm work," he said. "Would you care to come with me in search of some lemonade, Grace?"

"Yes, I would," she said, reaching for his arm, for a haven of kindliness and safety. Reaching for home. "It is hot in here. Are you enjoying yourself, Perry?"

"My feet might be worn down to stumps by the end of it," he said, his eyes twinkling down at her, "but it is all in the cause of enjoyment, so I will not complain."

"We will go riding in the carriage tomorrow, then, instead of walking, and you may have a soft pillow beneath your feet," she said, patting his hand and letting her fingers linger there, absorbing his warmth.

Peregrine followed Grace into her dressing room later that night and stood leaning against the door, watching her remove first the plumes and then the pins from her hair. She had refused to have her maid sent for at such a late hour—or such an early hour, she had amended. He strolled across to the dressing table and picked up her brush as she shook out her hair.

"I think Priscilla did remarkably well for her first

appearance," she said. "Ethel succeeded in finding her a
partner for every set. And it was kind of Lady Madeline to
take such an interest in her, was it not, Perry?"

"Her friendship can do nothing but good for our little
niece," he agreed. "Madeline has been a very popular young
lady since she first came here. She could have married—
and well too—twenty times over in the last three years, I
daresay. Sit down, Grace. I'll brush your hair for you."

She sat obediently and closed her eyes as he drew the brush
through her tousled hair and continued with the conversation
about the ball and the fortunes of their various friends. And
he watched her face in the mirror. It was flushed with
tiredness.

He did not want to remember it as it had looked earlier
that evening when he had finished dancing with Leila and
glanced over to where she was standing against the windows
with Sandersford. He did not at all want to remember how
animated and wildly beautiful she had looked and how very
handsome her companion. They had been very deep in
passionate conversation, clearly oblivious to everything
around them.

He did not want to remember, or how distressed Ethel had
looked when he had met her eyes. Or how she had hurried
across to them and said something that had perhaps saved
them just in time from drawing public attention. Or how
Grace had looked at him as he came up to them, her
expression bewildered and remorseful. Or how she had
gripped his arm afterward and touched his hand and chattered
on about trivialities for all of ten minutes, quite unlike the
Grace he knew.

He did not want to remember. He gazed at her reflection
and tried to see her as a woman ten years his senior, a woman
too old for him. A woman more suited to a man of her own
age. Like Sandersford. But he could not see that older
woman. He could see only Grace, his wife, looking tired
and rather lovely with her red gown and her dark hair silky
and straight down over her shoulders.

He set the brush down quietly, and she opened her eyes

and smiled in the glass. She looked at him questioningly. The obvious next step at such a late hour was to undress and go to bed. But he had never been in her dressing room before when she was disrobing. He had never seen her without either her clothes or her nightgown.

"You will need help with all those buttons," he said. "Let me undo them for you, Grace."

She stood up a little uncertainly and turned her back to him. She bent her head, shaking her hair forward over her shoulders.

"I think someone must have thought up the idea of so many buttons down a lady's back to ensure high employment among female servants," he said. "You could not possibly manage without a lady's maid, could you?"

"And what about gentlemen and their tight coats and elaborate neckcloths?" she said.

"*Touché*," he said with a laugh, opening the lowest button.

The silk gown was lined so that there was no need of a shift worn beneath it. Peregrine put his hands lightly against her shoulder blades and moved them up to her shoulders. He slid them down to her waist and up under her arms to cup her full and naked breasts. He bent his head to kiss her shoulder.

Grace brought her head back to rest against his shoulder. She held her gown with both hands beneath her breasts. He continued to kiss her one shoulder, to fondle her breasts, to tease her nipples with his fingers until he knew her aroused, though she made no sign.

He wanted her as he had wanted her increasingly since their marriage. He could never have enough of her, of her shapely body, the special fragrance of her, that special something beyond each individual attraction or even the sum of those attractions that made her Grace. And he needed her, as he had come to do more and more each day since he had first taken her as his bride to his home and she had become its quiet mistress and his companion and lover. The thought of life without her was terrifying. Those two nights at inns on the journey to London had been bleak experiences indeed, even though he had known that he would have her again at the end of them.

And now was he to lose her altogether? Was she going to leave him for Sandersford? Was she going to overcome that temptation and stay with him and die a little and be gone from him anyway? Peregrine quelled his panic, felt the desire in his wife's breasts, and turned her in his arms.

And he kissed her hungrily: her eyes, her temples, her ears, her throat, her mouth. He reached out to her with his tongue, something he did not normally do. His lovemaking usually concentrated on making what he did pleasing to her. But he was losing her, and he was protesting his loss, and he was too agonized to be gentle.

"Let's go to bed," he said against her mouth, and stooped down to lift her into his arms, the gown still clutched to her waist. But when he set her down beside the bed, he stripped it from her and sent the rest of her flimsy undergarments to join it on the floor. She closed her eyes as he laid her down. Her color was high. He had never unclothed her before, even between the bedsheets. He had touched every part of her with his hands and his own body, but he had never removed her nightgown entirely.

Grace lay on the bed, her eyes closed, resisting the urge to reach out for the blankets to pull over her. She waited for Perry to undress himself and come to her. Her desire for him was more of a pain than a pleasure. There was an ache and a throbbing in her throat that could easily have her wailing and clinging to him if he did not come soon.

The evening had been an agony: Gareth and all the turmoil of her encounter with him, all the anger and the uncertainty. Her outrage that he should suggest a renewal of their love. Her conviction that he was in her past and that her feelings for him could never be rekindled. Her fear that perhaps after all he would exert his power over her, that perhaps a man one had once loved, a man one had given oneself to, a man whose child one had borne, could not after all be shrugged off. Her guilt at not having told Perry the truth and the nightmare of seeing that lie grow greater in magnitude with every passing day. Her fear that somehow Gareth would have his own way, as he always had, and force her into loving him again and not loving Perry any longer.

And her terrible fear of losing Perry, of seeing an end to the most peaceful and the loveliest year of her life. If her love for him did not fade, then surely his for her would. There was her memory of watching him at the ball, gay and smiling, dancing and talking with ladies of his own age and younger, teasing them, enjoying himself. And Gareth's words about him, blocked from her memory, large and loud in her memory.

She wanted to be at home. She wanted to be at Reardon Park with Perry in the dull routine of the quiet days that had given her more happiness than she had known in her life. She wanted to be there now and forever. And she probably never would be there again. Even if they went there physically at the end of the Season, it would probably never be home again. They would never be happy there again.

She was glad of the unaccustomed fierceness of Perry's lovemaking. She was glad that when he joined her on the bed he did not spend many minutes caressing her gently with his hands and his mouth, as he usually did. She was glad that he came down directly on top of her, that he came between her thighs and thrust up into her without any prelude. And she was glad that he lay heavy on her, not easing his weight onto his arms as he often did, moving deeply and ungently in her.

She relaxed and lay still for him, as she always did, and kept her eyes closed, and waited for that ache to be quieted. He would take it away for her, she knew. Perry had never failed her. The pain would go away, the throbbing, and her fears would be put at bay again—for a while, anyway.

And he came to her deeply, as he always did, and she held her intense satisfaction private to herself, as she always did, and turned in his arms as he lifted himself to lie beside her and pulled the blankets warmly around her naked body. And she raised her mouth for his drowsy kiss and moved her head to a position of comfort on his arm and closed her eyes.

   And she discovered that the ache she had been feeling was
not after all a physical thing and had not therefore been eased
at all by the beauty of what he had done to her body. The
magic was going away faster than she could learn to cope
with. Perry could no longer blot out the pain for her.
   And why was there pain? When had she allowed herself
to come back to life again?

   Desperation could not restore anything, Peregrine was
thinking, holding his wife to his side, his head resting on
the pillow, his eyes closed. His taking of her tonight had
been an utterly selfish thing. He had not made love to her.
He had used her for pleasure, for reassurance, for forget-
fulness. He had wanted her naked beneath him, and he had
wanted to bury himself deep in her to assure himself—and
her perhaps—that he owned her, that she was his, that no
other man could possibly have any claim on her. Sandersford had possessed her for a few days in the distant past.
He had had her for more than a year, and he had married her.
   But it was no good. There was no reassurance to be gained
from taking his wife as if she were no better than his whore.
And there would be no holding her by closing the grip of
his possession on her. The point was that she was not a
valuable property to be hoarded and hidden away. She was
a person whose strength of character he had come to respect
even before he had married her. And he could not keep her
merely because he owned her according to the law and the
church.
   Peregrine lay, silent and unhappy and apparently asleep
beside his equally quiet and wakeful wife until long after
dawn had rendered the candles on the mantlepiece pale and
redundant.

   Grace went walking in St. James's Park after luncheon the
next day with Ethel and an exuberant Priscilla. Peregrine
had gone to Tattersall's with the Earl of Amberley to look
over some horses that the latter was thinking of buying.

"I cannot tell you what a wonderful time I had at the ball last night, Aunt Grace," the girl said, and proceeded to do just that.

Grace and Ethel smiled indulgently and seemed quite satisfied to listen to a monologue that needed no participation on their part except an occasional murmur of assent or appreciation. There was something of an awkwardness between them that the girl's presence helped to mask.

"I danced every set," Priscilla said, "and with some very handsome and amiable gentlemen. Did you see me dance with Lord Eden, Aunt Grace? He is your neighbor, is he not? He is very handsome and very tall. I think I liked Mr. Johnson best, though. He promised that he would call at Cavendish Square and take me walking in the park one afternoon. And did you know that Miss Darnford whispered to me that Uncle Perry was very charming? She looked quite mortified when I told her that he was married to my aunt." She laughed gaily.

"I was gratified to find that Priscilla made friends with several young ladies," Ethel said. "One's first appearance in society is such an important and anxious occasion."

"I do admire Lady Madeline Raine," Priscilla said. "Her manners are so easy, and all the men like her. She was obliging enough to offer to pick me up later this afternoon when she goes driving with Lord Harris. She says that her brother will come too. Lord Eden, that is, not Lord Amberley. I was not presented to him, though he is very handsome too. And very grand. He is a friend of Uncle Perry's, is he not?"

They strolled on, admiring the freshness of the leaves on the trees and the grass around them, gazing in admiration at the flowers.

"Lucinda Stebbins is supposed to arrive today or tomorrow," Priscilla said. "I can scarcely wait. And so many entertainments already engaged for, Aunt Grace. Three balls already in the next month and two soirees, one concert, and one breakfast." She counted them off on her fingers. "And your dinner party. And the invitations have not finished coming in yet. Papa says that we may expect more now that

I have been seen in public and after I am presented next week.''

"I am even hoping that before the Season is out we will procure vouchers for Almack's," Ethel said. "Though I have cautioned Priscilla not to set her heart on it. If Martin had the title already, of course, things might be different. Though I am not sorry he does not.''

"And Lord Sandersford is to invite everyone out to his home outside London some time," Priscilla said. "It is less than a two-hour drive, he says, and the property very lovely. But I do hope he invites some other young people, or it might prove very dull."

"I did not know he owned property in this part of the country," Grace said.

"It belonged to his late wife, I believe," Ethel said hesitantly.

"I have so much to tell Lucinda," Priscilla said, twirling her parasol and performing a few skipping steps that drew an appreciative smile from a passing gentleman and a frown of disapproval from her mother.

And they would be invited, of course, Grace thought. And should she allow Perry to accept? Or should she beg him to make some excuse? Did she wish to avoid all future risk of private conversation with Gareth? Or did she acknowledge the need to face up to her past and settle once and for all her present and her future?

She did not want any change in her life. She wanted everything to remain as it had been for the more than a year since she married Perry. She had been happy in that year, or at least more contented than she had been at any other time in her life. And she loved her cheerful, smiling, gentle husband, with his private depths of learning and intelligence and insight. It was a cautious love, one that she had not expected to last. It was not the consuming passion that she had known with Gareth. But it had brought her undreamed-of contentment. She did not want it to change.

Yet she had the feeling that she must face up to Gareth, that she must find out what had happened to that passion, which had died such a sudden and bitter death. Was it dead forever? Or would it never die? as Gareth himself said. She did not want to find out. She did not want to love Gareth again. She did not want all the turmoil of that kind of passion, and she did not want any emotion that might destroy her love for Perry. But she had the feeling that she must take the risk.

It was useless, anyway, to try to cling to things as they were. Things as they had been, rather. Her relationship with Perry was already changing. She had felt it when they were at Pangam Manor. She had felt it since they had been in London. And she had known it the evening before, when they had been almost like strangers, watching each other cautiously, neither of them quite sure what was happening. But something was happening to them. It was not her imagination.

There was the way he had made love to her the night before. She had loved it at the time. It had suited her mood and her needs exactly. But since waking and finding Perry already gone from her side, she had felt upset to remember the fierceness of his passion. There had seemed to be none of the awareness of her as a person that had always characterized his lovemaking. In retrospect, he had reminded her somewhat of Gareth, though she had never entered into Gareth's passion quite as she had into Perry's the night before.

Grace shuddered.

"Lady Leila Walsh said last night that she has heard a rumor that the Prince Regent will be at the Duchess of Newcastle's ball next week," Priscilla said. "Do you think it could possibly be true, Mama? Aunt Grace? I should positively die of excitement if it is."

9

The next few weeks were surprisingly tranquil ones. They were filled with activities, ones that were largely shared by Peregrine and Grace. They had both sensed that the honeymoon period of their marriage was over and that a more difficult period, even possibly a disastrous one, was ahead for them. And both resisted the change and clung desperately to the quiet and affectionate closeness they had shared for more than a year.

They attended the opera together and heard the famous Madame Catalani in *Atalida*. They attended the Hanover Square Rooms one evening and listened to the concert there in company with a large gathering that included four of the royal dukes and Princess Alexandra, mother of the Princess of Wales. They watched a splendid and colorful military review in the park one afternoon and attended St. Paul's together for the Easter services. They visited an exhibition of paintings at Somerset House and another of paintings of famous cities at the Panorama. They visited the Tower again and spent a full afternoon in the armory there.

They attended some of the quieter evening entertainments as well as the balls and routs that attracted large squeezes. They spent a few evenings at Mrs. Eunice Borden's salon, meeting and conversing with the writers and poets and political figures with whom she liked to surround herself. She was a small, rather heavyset, curly-haired widow, somewhat younger than Grace, a particular friend of the Earl of Amberley. Indeed, Grace began to wonder with some curiosity if perhaps she was his mistress. His lordship was always there when they were, and he never left before them, however late they lingered.

Somehow, although they attended several of the more glittering entertainments of the *ton*, they avoided any more uncomfortable evenings like that of the first ball. And yet they both knew that they were living through an interval that could not last. And they both knew that they could not prolong it indefinitely. Although they never spoke to each other of their deepest desires, each wanted to go home, away from London, away from all those forces that seemed to be conspiring against their happiness. And yet each silently consented to stay.

And even in the midst of the tranquillity, there were still signs of strain. They met Lord Sandersford on more than one occasion, though Grace contrived never to be alone with him. At the opera one evening she declined his offer to take her into the corridor for some fresh air between acts, although he had looked to Peregrine for permission and had received a nod in return. And she sat next to Perry for the rest of the performance, their arms not quite touching, conversation between them dead, both of them taut with stress, while Martin and Ethel, Priscilla and Mr. Johnson laughed and exchanged comments on either side of them.

And there was the morning when they called at Cavendish Square to find Priscilla in mingled elation and despair. Four young ladies and three young gentlemen had arranged an expedition to Kew Gardens for the afternoon.

"But Lucinda declares that she will not go as she has no particular beau," Priscilla said, "though I have assured her that Mr. Johnson will be quite delighted to offer his free arm to her. It really does not signify that the numbers are not quite even."

"And yet," her mother said, "you must imagine how you would feel, Priscilla, if it were you without an escort."

"I would die," Priscilla assured the room at large.

Peregrine laughed. "If you think that Miss Stebbins would not die an equally horrid death to be escorted by an old married uncle of yours, Priscilla," he said, "perhaps I could make up the numbers. Would you mind, Grace? We have no other plans for this afternoon, have we?"

Grace encouraged the outing. It was just like Perry to step in with such cheerful kindness to save a poor girl from embarrassment. She did not even mind when he arrived home late in the afternoon and came directly to her sitting room to throw himself rather inelegantly into a comfortable chair so that he might tell her all about the expedition. It seemed that he had undoubtedly made a mortal enemy of Mr. Francis Hartwell, who had been forced to escort Miss Stebbins during the whole afternoon because Lady Leila Walsh had laid claim to Peregrine's arm. He was laughing by the time he finished.

"Do you think I might get called out onto a frosty heath at dawn, Grace?" he asked. "It sounds a deuced uncomfortable prospect to me."

"I don't think there are any frosty heaths left at this time of year, Perry," she answered, "even at dawn. I would say you are safe."

"Thank heaven for a wife's common sense," he said, laughing again. "Ah, you have finished embroidering that sprig of flowers, Grace, and I looked forward to watching you do it. What a shame. Kew had nothing to compare with it in beauty, you know."

"Silly," she said, holding the cloth up nevertheless so that he might see better the work she had done during the afternoon.

And there was that uneasiness in her again. It was not jealousy. She was not jealous of the young and vital Lady Leila, not suspicious of her husband, not accusing in any way. Only left with a feeling that there was perhaps more rightness in Perry's being with her and with those other young people than there was in his being with his own wife. And did he realize it too? Or would he come to do so soon?

Their own dinner and evening party were set for a day one week ahead of Lord Sandersford's two-day house party in the country. They had invited him—how could they not without admitting to each other an awareness of a potentially explosive situation they had never referred to? And they had invited all their acquaintances from both their homes as well as Peregrine's mother and aunt and cousin, who had arrived from Scotland a couple of days before, and a few other young people to make the gathering merrier.

Grace had been apprehensive about meeting her mother-in-law, but when they called upon her in Charles Street the day before their party, they received a gracious welcome. Peregrine's mother offered a cheek for his kiss and then hugged him. She stretched out both hands to Grace, looked her up and down, declared that she was in good looks, and then hugged her too. Perry winked at her over his mother's head.

Mrs. Campbell, too, Peregrine's aunt, greeted her with affectionate courtesy and proceeded to tell her that of course she had still not forgiven young Perry for imitating her late husband's Scottish accent so mercilessly during their last visit into England that a footman had burst into laughter and slopped a soup tureen over the tablecloth and almost got himself dismissed.

"I protest, Aunt," Peregrine said, laughing. "I could not have been above fourteen at the time. Ah cuid nae be sae ill-mannered noo, ye ken." He dodged her flying hand and caught her around the waist in order to plant a smacking kiss on her cheek.

"Grace, my dear," Mrs. Campbell said, "how do you endure it? You must be a saint, for sure."

They all laughed, and Grace felt accepted as one of the family.

And throughout the five-course dinner at which she presided the next evening, she continued to hug to herself that warm feeling of belonging. She looked down the length of the table to where Peregrine sat, entertaining his mother on his right and Ethel on his left, and felt again how wonderful it was to be a married lady with a definite place in society. And she marveled anew at how she could have lived for so many years at the rectory in a type of suspended animation. Then she caught the rather mocking eye of Gareth, seated halfway down the table.

And she knew she would not be able to avoid him for the

whole evening. A chill of something like fear set her to refusing her favorite dessert and stumbling in her conversation with Mr. Stebbins beside her.

They had thought that perhaps the younger people would wish to dance. But no one suggested it. They seemed content for a while to entertain themselves at one end of the long drawing room by playing the pianoforte and singing. And then they formed two teams for charades and played with a great deal of shrieking and laughter. Some of the older people wandered over to watch while others stayed closer to the fire and talked.

Peregrine had been drawn into the game in order to make up even numbers and was having so much success that he was being loudly accused of cheating by the opposing team. Grace sat behind the teapot, talking to Lady Amberley and her mother-in-law until both ladies smiled at an unusually merry burst of laughter from the opposite end of the room and strolled across to see what was happening. Grace was not at all surprised when Lord Sandersford took their place almost immediately.

"There is something quite strange about this situation, Grace," he said. "The bulk of your guests amusing themselves with great energy at the other end of the room while you sit here behind the teapot in demure domesticity. The Grace I knew would have been in the very center of that activity."

"The Grace you knew was considerably younger, Gareth," she said. "Would it not look extremely peculiar for a matron of my age to be romping with the very young?"

"And yet your husband does," he said quietly.

Grace said nothing. She stacked the cups more neatly on the tray beside her.

"I could do violence, Grace," he said. "I want to shake you out of your torpor."

"You are quite unrealistic," she said. "You expect me to be as I was fifteen years ago. I was only a little past twenty then. I am close to forty now. I cannot stay a girl forever."

"Nonsense," he said. "Age has nothing to do with the question. You were alive then. You are half-dead now. You have been avoiding me, Grace. Are you afraid of me?''

"Of course I am not,'' she said, her eyes dropping from his momentarily. "But you cannot expect me to seek you out either, Gareth. I am married to Perry.''

His lips tigthened. "I might end up doing murder, you know,'' he said. "Look at him, Grace. Look at the man to whom you insist on remaining loyal. He is a boy. A thoughtless, laughing, undoubtedly empty-headed boy. Though I will grant you, a tolerably pretty one. And you call him husband? I will not accept it. I give you due warning that my patience is running out. You cannot tell me that you feel any attachment to him beyond some gratitude perhaps. He did rescue you, I grant, after Paul died, though you might have come to me if only you had known that I was widowed and back home.''

Grace's silence was stony.

"He was at Kew with Lady Leila Walsh last week,'' he said. "Did you know? Did he remember to tell you? Oh, with a few other young people as well to add some respectability. But very much with her, nonetheless. Do you not know that she means to have him, Grace, and that he has every intention of being had? If it is not already an accomplished fact, that is. Are you blind, or do you refuse to see?''

"And do you mean to have me, Gareth?'' she said in some anger. "And do you believe that I have every intention of being had?''

"No,'' he said, "to the second half of what you said. You are a coward, Grace. You are afraid to examine the state of your own heart and act on what you find there. Are you afraid of the scandal? Are you afraid your Peregrine will divorce you? It is very unlikely, I do assure you. He will be happy to let you go your way while he goes his. And I do not care that much''—he snapped his fingers—"whether we can be legally wed or not when you come to me. We belong together. We will be married in all ways that matter.''

"Yes,'' she said, "I know that you do not set much store by marriage, Gareth.''

He laughed and tried to take her hand, but she moved it

away in order to adjust the angle of the teapot. She was finding his presence suffocating again. She was very aware of him, as she always had been—of his broad shoulders and his long-fingered hands, his dark hair and handsome face. She was aware and she was frightened. She could feel the pull of his power over her, but did not know the nature of that power. Did she still love him? Or did she hate him? Was she afraid of him? Or was it herself she feared?

"Sometimes," he said, "and with great relief, I see flashes of the old Grace. There was pure spite in those last words, my dear. You are still angry over my desertion, are you not?"

"My son lived the whole of his life without a father," she said.

"Well," he said, "I was not responsible for his early death, Grace."

"And the whole of his life as a bastard."

"I am sure your family was far too well-bred ever to use that word in his hearing," he said.

"But it was used in my hearing," she said. "And it was used by a few to comfort me after he died. I must be relieved, it seemed, to know that my son would not grow up to know himself a bastard."

"Come on," he said, his voice grim at last, "tell me more. This has to all come out before we can get anywhere, you and I. I think we may even come to blows before it is all over. But, yes, Grace, I mean to have you. And you will have me. Because at the bottom of your anger is your love for me. So come on. Keep talking."

"They put the label on the wrong person," Grace said. "It was his father who was the bastard. And who *is* a bastard. You are trying to destroy my life all over again, Gareth. I have been happy for more than a year. Happy! But you must kill that happiness. I hate you now as I have hated you for years."

He smiled. But his eyes were burning down into hers. "This is better," he said. "Now we are approaching the truth. We are not there yet, but we are on the way. Keep talking."

"No!" Grace picked up the teapot with hands that were not quite steady and poured some into her empty cup. "Not again, Gareth. I am not going to forget my surroundings again as I did in that ballroom. No." She drew a few steadying breaths. "Do tell me about your late wife's property, the one you have invited us to next week. Is it large?"

"It is large enough," he said, "for us to find some privacy, Grace. We will continue this, ah, discussion there, perhaps even conclude it. We will have everything out in the open that has been festering in you for years. You will have the chance to strike at me with your fists or your fingernails if you wish. But the moment cannot be avoided. I promise you that. Now, Lady Lampman, was there anything else you wished to know about my property?"

"No, I thank you, my lord," she said. "You have been most specific."

She met Peregrine's eyes across the room and did not even try to quell the ache inside her. She knew now that it would not go away and that she could no longer expect Perry to take it away for her.

Lord Sandersford's house at Hammersmith overlooked the river and was so beautiful, Ethel declared, that it was amazing that his lordship had not made it his principal seat. But the viscount merely smiled and explained that home is something one feels in one's blood and heart and has nothing necessarily to do with obvious beauty.

His town guests had been invited to stay overnight. Ethel, Martin, and Priscilla were among this number, as were the Stebbinses and two male cousins of his late wife's. And, of course, Grace and Peregrine.

Peregrine knew as well as Grace did why they were there, that these two days in the country somehow represented a crisis in their marriage. He had known it from the moment their invitation had arrived, and even before that probably. And he had seen it very clearly at his own home the week before. He had expected Sandersford to contrive to have a private word with his wife there. And he had expected that same look of intensity in their faces he had seen at the ball.

He had expected too that Grace would not be happy afterward, that she would be feeling guilt and uncertainty. The crisis was coming, something far more powerful than had yet happened, and something that could not be averted. Oh, yes, it probably could be prevented, Peregrine granted. If he chose to assert his masculinity, his rights as a husband, there were probably several courses he could take to protect what was his own. He could take his wife home and keep her there. A very simple solution. Or he could confront her with his knowledge, forbid her to speak alone with Sandersford ever again. And he had no doubt that Grace would obey him. Perhaps she would even be relieved to have all the stress of the situation lifted from her own shoulders.

But he could not take either of those courses. He could only take the apparently unmanly course of staying quiet, of leaving his wife free to find out and to live her own destiny. Perhaps it was only in that week of his intense unhappiness that Peregrine realized fully what his feelings for his wife really were. And it was only in the same time period that he realized fully the nature of love. The terrifying nature. For love cannot take anything for itself. It can only give and leave itself wide open and defenseless against emptiness and pain and rejection.

And so Peregrine took his wife to Hammersmith with no comment upon the white, set face that had been hers for all of the previous week or on her eyes, which held desperately to their calmness during the carriage ride, in which they were accompanied by Priscilla and Lucinda Stebbins.

And in Hammersmith he allowed Grace to stay close to him without in any way following her around. He let her take his arm and hold to it throughout the tour of the house given by their host, knowing that that same host was far too skilled a man to allow her to stay there at his side for the whole of the rest of the day and the morning of the next.

They stopped in the gallery that overlooked the river and became so absorbed in examining the rare collection of Chinese porcelain there that they were scarcely aware of the glorious view from the window that had the other guests exclaiming in delight. And in the music room they admired all the various musical instruments collected by Lord Sandersford's mother-in-law.

"It is as well that we do not own these things, Perry," Grace said, "or I would spend half your fortune on music lessons so that I could play them all."

"And I would spend the other half so that I could play them too," he said. "Then, with no fortune left, Grace, we could wander the countryside, like the minstrels of old, earning our daily bread with our music."

"That sounds good," she said. "I will carry the flute, Perry, and you can load the pianoforte on your back."

They both laughed. "Perhaps it is as well we do not own them," he said.

And they walked in the gardens and down by the river and agreed with the other guests that they were fortunate indeed to have been granted such a gloriously warm and sunny day for their visit after more than a week of indifferent weather. They stood and watched as two of the cousins rowed Priscilla and Miss Stebbins out on the water, and agreed that they were quite content to keep their feet on firm—and dry—ground.

They sat side by side on the terrace to take tea and listened as Lord Sandersford, at his most charming, entertained his guests with amusing anecdotes of military life. And Peregrine felt Grace's arm brush his during a gust of laughter over one of the stories, and smiled down at her. Soon after, all the guests retired to their rooms to rest for a while and to get ready for dinner and the evening party, to which several of the neighboring families had been invited.

It would be that evening, Peregrine thought as he stood in his dressing room that opened off one side of the bed-chamber he was to share with Grace. He buttoned up his shirt slowly and smoothed out the lace at the cuffs so that it covered his hands to the knuckles. There was to be dancing in the lower drawing room, Sandersford had announced, to accommodate the young people who had been invited. And doubtless the doors onto the terrace would be kept open on such a warm evening.

It would be that evening. He was powerless to prevent it, or rather, he had chosen to be powerless. He must only watch to see that the confrontation when it came was not entirely against Grace's will. He knew that she did not want it, that she resisted the moment. He knew also that she did want it, that she recognized its inevitability. But even so, the moment must not be forced on her against her will. Against that at least he could and would protect her.

Lucinda Stebbins had not taken well during the first weeks of the Season. A little overplump for most tastes and with hair that tended to be more yellow than blond and that she wore in an unbecoming style with masses of tight ringlets, she could not lay claim to any great prettiness. And her tendency to become tongue-tied or giggly in company and to blush in uneven patches of red did not add to her attractions.

Yet she was an innocent and sweet-natured girl, Grace knew, and one whom Perry had very kindly taken under his wing. He sat next to the girl at dinner and had her giggling with amusement rather than embarrassment before the end of the first course. And he danced the first country dance with her in Gareth's large lower drawing room.

Grace was happy to see that one of the cousins led her into the second dance and lingered to converse with her afterward. He was a particularly small and thin young man. It was rather unfortunate perhaps that he tried to overcome these deficiencies by padding out the shoulders of his coat and the calves of his legs and by wearing a lavender and yellow striped waistcoat and extremely high shirt points, and by putting a quizzing glass to frequent and absurdly languid use. Grace had sat next to him at dinner and had found him to be a perfectly sensible young man once she had penetrated beyond the bored superficiality of his opening remarks.

Priscilla, of course, was preening herself before the obvious admiration of the other cousin and two tolerably handsome and eligible neighbors. She had taken well with the *ton* and was clearly enjoying every moment of her triumph.

"Of course," Ethel was saying to Grace and Mrs. Stebbins, "Priscilla will not even be eighteen for another five weeks. We have no great wish for her to fix her choice this year. She is far too young to marry. We merely wish for her to gain experience."

"Lucinda will doubtless be considering some of her offers this year," Mrs. Stebbins said, "since it is doubtful that Mr. Stebbins will consent to bringing us here for another Season. He is so hopelessly rustic, Lady Lampman. Of course, we wish to choose an eligible husband for her. We do not have to accept the first offer she receives."

It was strange, Grace thought, that she had never been brought to London for a Season. She could not now remember if there had even been any question of her coming. She certainly could not recall craving any such thing. If she had, doubtless she would have had her way. In those days her father had been quite unable to deny her anything she had set her heart on.

But she had been in love with Gareth by the time she reached the age to make her come-out. And planning to marry him and live happily ever after with him, They were to travel together, visit all the fashionable cities of Europe together. There had been no need of a come-out Season.

She had thought herself very strong-willed and independent, Grace thought now, watching the dancers perform a quadrille and smiling at her husband, who was with a flushed little girl who could not be a day older than sixteen. And yet she must have been extraordinarily like a puppet on a string. Gareth's puppet. She had been twenty-one years old when he went away. They had been talking of marriage for four years. Had he ever really intended to marry her? The idea that perhaps he had not was a novel one. But not by any means an impossible one.

Gareth had always had his way. They had quarreled and fought, sometimes quite physically, but she could not now recall any important matter on which she had won. Most notably, he had refused to marry her before going away, after giving her any number of very good reasons for not doing so. At the same time he had overcome her objections to their lying together before he went. And she had lain with him with a stubborn and foolish disregard of the consequences and conceived his child.

Far from being the strong and determined girl that she had always thought herself, she had in fact been a weakling. And very, very foolish.

"It was at just such a party that I first met Martin," Ethel was saying. "I did not like him at first because he rarely smiled. I thought him haughty. But it is amazing how different a person can seem once one makes the effort to get to know him well. Martin is really a man of great sensibility, and he is frequently unsure of himself."

Mrs. Stebbins tittered. "Papa chose Mr. Stebbins for me," she said, "because he had a modest fortune and we had an ancient name to uphold. Papa's great-grandfather was Baron March, Lady Lampman. Unfortunately, his grandfather was a seventh son. I do think it important for fortune and good family to mingle. Provided that the fortune has not been made in vulgar trade, of course."

Her father should have brought her to town, Grace thought. He should have insisted that she make her come-out, be presented at court, mingle with the *ton*, meet other young ladies of her own age and other eligible young gentlemen. Perhaps she would have grown up, acquired a degree of common sense long before she had. Perhaps she would have seen Gareth more clearly if she could have compared him to others. Perhaps she would have understood his selfishness sooner.

But would it have made any difference? she wondered. She had been a headstrong girl. Doubtless she would have fought her father every step of the way and closed her eyes and her mind to any experiences that might have saved her from her own future. She had been in love and hopelessly blind. Jeremy, or his older brother or sister, might well have been born a few years earlier if her father had tried to separate her from Gareth.

But had she ever completely shaken off the power Gareth had over her even though her eyes were now opened? Would she ever do so? She watched him conclude a conversation with a small group of men at the other side of the drawing room and begin to make his way toward her. She knew that it was toward her he came. She knew that this whole party had been planned with her in mind, and especially this evening's entertainment. Gareth was bound on getting her alone, and he would do so. Partly because Gareth always got what he wanted. And partly because she would not be able to resist finding out what the end of their association was to be. If it was the end that was now coming and not a new beginning. One never knew when it was Gareth with whom one dealt.

Ethel leaned toward her suddenly and whispered for Grace's ears only. "It is a warm night, Grace," she said, "and will doubtless be very pleasant outside. You may say that you and I have just agreed to stroll on the terrace if you wish."

Grace looked at her, startled. But she had not misunderstood. Ethel was flushed and embarrassed, not quite meeting her sister-in-law's eyes.

"Only if you wish," Ethel said. "I do not know how you feel. I never did know. But I have liked you this time. And Perry. I like Perry." She turned back to reply to a remark made by Mrs. Stebbins.

"Not dancing, Lady Lampman?" Lord Sandersford said, bowing in front of her chair and including the other two ladies in his smile. "I grant you that my drawing room is nothing in comparison with the ballrooms you have danced in during the last weeks, but you are used to country living."

"I have danced once with Perry," Grace said.

"And you must dance the next with me," he said, stretching out a hand for hers. "As your host, ma'am, I must insist on it." His dark eyes looked mockingly down into hers.

"Such a distinguished company, my lord," Mrs. Stebbins said.

He bowed his acknowledgment of the compliment while Grace could feel Ethel looking at her. She put her hand in Lord Sandersford's and rose to her feet.

"Thank you, my lord," she said.

"And now, Grace," he said, having maneuvered her with

consummate skill across the room to the opened French doors, stopping on the way to smile and exchange a few words with several of his other guests, "it is time for you and me to disappear for a while. Is it not?"

"Yes, Gareth," she said, looking steadily at him, "I think it is."

He looked at her appreciatively. "You always had the courage to meet a challenge face to face," he said. "I am glad you do not feel it necessary to simper and protest." He offered her his arm. "Shall we take a turn on the terrace, ma'am? It is, as you just remarked, a warm evening."

Grace took his arm and walked with him into the darkness of the night.

Peregrine, withdrawing his eyes from the doors, informed Miss Keating with a grin that if she expected him to stop stumbling in his steps, she must find somewhere else to fix her very blue eyes than on his face.

Miss Keating giggled, blushed, asked if Sir Peregrine really thought her eyes blue, not merely a nondescript gray, and proceeded to gaze at him with even wider eyes.

10

"I do not wish to go off the terrace," Grace said as Lord
Sandersford led her across it, ignoring the two older gentlemen who were in conversation farther along. "It would not
be right."

"We will walk down by the river," he said. "We have
a great deal to say to each other, Grace, and if your mood
of last week prevails, we may well wish to raise our voices
and even our fists. The terrace is altogether too public."

Grace said no more but allowed herself to be led in silence
down over the darkened lawn, past shrubberies and flower
beds, to the water's edge. Yet again he was having his way,
she reflected bitterly. But there was sense in what he said.

"Now," he said finally, releasing her arm and turning to
face her, "we are alone, Grace. No one is watching or
listening. Neither of us has any need of a mask. Let us speak
plainly, then. I want you. And I do not speak of a clandestine
affair behind the esteemed Peregrine's back, though I have
no doubt it would be an easy matter to cuckold him. I want
you to leave him, provoke a divorce if you will so that we
may marry. But if we cannot do so, then to hell with
marriage. We will live openly as man and wife and dare the
world to censure us."

"You have not changed at all, Gareth," she said. "You
are as selfish now as you were as a boy. You want! That
is all that matters, is it not? You do not know or care what
I want."

"Tell me, then," he said. "But you must be honest, Grace. You will not get away with saying what you think you ought. The truth! What is it you want?"

"I want things to remain as they are," she said. "As they were before I met you again, Gareth. I don't want change. I was happy."

"Things cannot remain as they were," he said. " 'Were' is past tense, Grace. You have met me again. And you 'were' happy. You are not now. Are you?"

"No," she said.

"Then something has to change," he said. "But you cannot go back, Grace. We can never go back. Only forward. You are unhappy because you know yourself married to the wrong man. You are unhappy because you have come alive again after fifteen years. And you know that you still love me. And always will. Tell the truth now."

"How can I love you?" she said. "How can I love you, Gareth? I stopped loving you a lifetime ago. I hate you. No, not that. I am indifferent to you."

His face was angry, she saw in the moonlight. "Liar!" he said. "We will have the truth spoken, Grace. The truth at last. You hate me, perhaps. I will accept that. You are not indifferent to me."

"How could you do it," she cried suddenly, her eyes kindling. "How could you do it, Gareth? You knew you were my whole world. You knew you had ruined me, that I could hope for no other husband. And you knew I was with child. You knew. And you had said that you loved me. Many times. And you expect me now not to hate you?"

"No," he said. His eyes were burning into hers. "No, I expect your hatred, Grace. Tell me more."

"I carried him alone," she said. "I bore him alone. I had a hard time giving birth to him, and there was no one at the end of it all to rejoice with me. You were not there, Gareth, when my son was born. You were married to your heiress."

"Yes," he said.

"He was a bastard," she said. "Jeremy was a bastard. My father never looked at him, yours never acknowledged

him. He was a nonperson. A beautiful, innocent child. He
was your son, Gareth. Your son! You never cared about his
existence. Or his death. Or about me. I hate you. I hate you!"
She raised both fists and pummeled at his chest.

He did not defend himself. She was surprised to see him
looking exultant when she glanced up, distraught, into his
face.

"Now we are getting somewhere," he said when she
finally stopped punching, the sides of her fists resting against
his chest. And he took her by the upper arms and lowered
his head and kissed her.

She could have pulled back. It was several moments before
he moved his hands from her arms and encircled her with
his own. But she did not pull back. He was so very unmis-
takably Gareth, though she had not been in his embrace for
fifteen years, though he had been little more than a boy then
and was now a powerful man. His embrace was all confident
demand, his mouth pressed to hers with a fierce urgency,
his hands boldly exploring her body. There was the familiar
taste of him, and smell of him, that could only be Gareth.

She felt her knees weaken as she sagged against him. She
felt fear at the evidence of his arousal, dread at the seeming
inevitability of her own response. She fought to think of
something else. Someone else. Perry.

"Grace," he whispered against her mouth, "my sweet
love, I want you. God, how I want you! Lie with me here.
Now. Follow your heart. Give me your answer here with
your body. You will never be sorry. I swear it."

She pushed against him and felt as if her heart would pound
through her ribs and burst from her body. "Gareth," she
said, "I do not love you. I do not want you. I hate you."

"Yes," he said fiercely, "I did a dastardly thing to you,
Grace. I have no defense. I knowingly deserted you for
wealth. And our child. And I was too ashamed to seek you
out afterward. But I never stopped loving you. I cannot go
back and amend the past. I wish I could, but I cannot. I can
offer you only the future and my devotion for the rest of our
lives."

"And yet," she said, "you would destroy me again. You know that I am married. You know that I have been happy. And you know that I want none of you. And yet you persist in forcing yourself on me."

"That is unfair," he said quietly. "You know why you were invited out to Hammersmith, Grace. Yet you did not refuse the invitation. You know why you were brought out here tonight. Yet you came freely. And you did not fight my kiss a moment ago. You are afraid to admit the truth."

"No," she said. "The truth is that you are evil, Gareth, that you cannot resist the urge to try to seduce me again. I want none of you. I want you to leave me alone."

He laughed softly. "Grace," he said, "you are such a coward. You used not to be. Is your marriage worth fighting for?"

"Yes, it is!" she cried.

"Why?" he asked. "What is good about it?"

"We are friends," she said. "We do things together. We are content together."

"Friends! Content," he said mockingly. "What a yawn, Grace. Is he good in bed?"

"What!" Her eyes snapped to his, shocked.

"Is he good?" he asked. "Does he satisfy you? Does he have you often? Ever? Or is this just a very maternal sort of relationship for you, Grace?" His eyes were mocking. "I cannot imagine the laughing boy being particularly skilled in sexual passion. And you need passion, Grace. I know. I have had you, remember?"

"You know nothing of my marriage," she said. "Nothing. It is the most valuable thing in my life. Yes, it is worth fighting for."

"And yet," he said, "you are out here arguing the matter with me. Happily married ladies are not tempted by former lovers, Grace. Why did you come?"

"I don't know," she said after a pause. She swallowed. "I don't know."

"I do," he said. "You love me, Grace. You don't love the boy. You merely feel sorry for him. You need not, you know. He will be quite happy to be released to the company of the sweet young creatures he favors.''

"I love Perry!" she protested.

"So!" He laughed gently. "Perhaps I should kill him, Grace. Would you like me to play jealous lover? I notice that he does not do so. And I would be very surprised to have a glove slapped in my face by Sir Peregrine Lampman. I doubt that his knees would keep from knocking together as he did so.''

"I hate you, Gareth," she said. "I hate you. I only wish I could be indifferent. You were right to say that I am not. I find that old wounds have not healed, after all. They are raw and festering again. But there is no love in me for you. None! We have talked. It is what you wished and what I felt necessary. Well, it has been done. And it is finished now. I want you to leave me alone.''

"Never," he said. "Not until you can tell me that you have no feelings for me whatsoever. And I know that day will never come, Grace. I love you, and I mean to have you.''

"No," she said, "you do not love me, Gareth. If you loved me, you would wish for my happiness. You would leave me alone with Perry.''

"Ah," he said, "but you said you are content with him, Grace. Or *were*, rather. Contentment is not happiness, or the past tense the present. You will be happy with me one day. I promise you that.''

"So," she said unhappily, "nothing has been settled. I have wasted my time coming out here with you. I am still not free of you, am I?''

"Grace," he said, passing a hand beneath her chin, "you never will be, my love. The sooner you realize that, the sooner your past contentment can give place to present and future happiness. No, nothing has been settled. You will be seeing more of me.''

She gazed at him in despair. "I thought my punishment was at an end," she said. "Now I see that even in this life I cannot escape it for long.''

He laughed. "A strange punishment," he said, "to give

in to your own love and to come to the arms of the man who
loves you.''

Grace turned without another word and began to stride
back toward the house.

Lord Sandersford followed silently some distance behind.

Peregrine became aware that Lord Sandersford had
returned to the house as he stood drinking lemonade with
Priscilla and a small group of the younger people. But several
minutes of anxious watching and much smiling and teasing
did not bring Grace into his view. At last, when the dancing
had resumed after a break, he left the drawing room as
unobtrusively as he could and went upstairs to their room.

At first he thought she was not there. The candles that were
burning on the mantelpiece showed him an empty bedchamber and a darkened dressing room at either side. But
he looked into Grace's dressing room anyway. She was
sitting in the darkness, facing away from him.

''Grace?'' he said softly, and moved across the room to
stand behind her and lay a gentle hand against the back of
her neck.

Apart from dropping her head forward, she made no
response.

''Do you need to be alone?'' he asked. ''Shall I go away?''

''Perry,'' she said. Her voice had the weariness of years
in it. ''Lord Sandersford is Gareth. Jeremy's father. He did
not die, and I knew it all the time. I lied to you.''

''Yes,'' he said.

''You knew?'' Her hands were twisting in her lap, he could
see. ''And you have not confronted me? You have not thrown
me out?''

''Thrown you out?'' he said. ''You are my wife, Grace.''

''My former lover is still alive,'' she said. ''You would
not have married me if you had known that, would you?''

''What difference would it have made?'' he asked.

She put up her hands to cover her face. ''I have been
outside with him tonight,'' she said. ''You must have seen
us go. He did not force me to go, Perry. I went freely right

down beside the river with him. I think we must have been gone for half an hour. He wants me to go away with him.''

He lifted his hand away from her neck. "Yes,'' he said. "And are you going, Grace?''

She shuddered. "Perhaps you will wish me to,'' she said. "I have dishonored you, Perry. I have not been unfaithful to you, but I have done what I have just said. And I listened to him.''

"Grace.'' He moved around to stand in front of her and squatted down on his haunches. "I can understand that seeing him again after all these years has put a severe strain on your emotions. I can understand that perhaps your feelings for him have been revived. I know that perhaps now you feel trapped in a marriage that was made largely for convenience. But I know you better than you seem to think. I know that you have not been unfaithful to me without your telling me so. And I know that if you leave me, you will not do so lightly and you will tell me quite openly what you must do. You have not dishonored me. I will not have you feeling the burden of that guilt.''

She was rocking back and forth, her hands still spread over her face.

"Do you love him still?'' he asked, his voice tense despite his efforts to remain calm. "Do you wish to go with him, Grace?''

"I want to stay with you,'' she said, her voice so full of misery that his sense of relief was short-lived. "I want to stay married to you, Perry.''

"Then you shall do so,'' he said, reaching out a hand to cover one of hers.

But she drew back from him. "Perry,'' she cried, "he kissed me. He held me and he kissed me, and I did not fight him off, though I would not lie with him as he wished me to do. I let him kiss me.''

Peregrine swallowed awkwardly. "Are you quite sure you wish to stay with me?'' he asked.

"Yes!'' Her voice was fierce, though she still did not take her hands from her face. "I want to stay. But you surely cannot wish me to, Perry.''

"You are my wife, Grace," he said. "You will stay with me if you wish to do so."

"Perry." She dropped her hands and looked up at him finally, though their faces were mere shadows in the darkness. "I hate him. I did not think I would after so long. I would have expected to feel nothing at all. But I hate him as if it all happened yesterday."

He nodded sadly and got to his feet. He held out a hand for hers. "Come on," he said, "let's go out of this darkness."

But she shrank from his hand. "No," she said, "don't touch me, Perry. Not yet."

Because she was feeling guilty and soiled. Soiled by Gareth's touch. Soiled more by her own moral weakness in going down to the river with him quite freely and in allowing him to plead with her to go away with him, and in allowing herself to remember and to feel a fearful sort of attraction to him again, and in allowing him to kiss her and hold her intimately and explore her with his hands as if he were still her lover. Because she had not washed herself and scrubbed herself and made herself clean for Perry. And because she knew again, seeing him stand there before her, that he was the very best thing that had ever happened in her life past or present, excepting only Jeremy. And she had nothing good to offer him in return. Not youth or beauty or vivacity. Not honor. And not even total fidelity since their marriage.

She could not put her hand in his. Not yet.

His hand closed on itself and dropped to his side. He stood before her for several moments as if he would say something. Then he strode from the dressing room and from the bedchamber.

"You forgot that Sandersford was to show us the stables this morning?" Martin asked Peregrine when he joined him in the morning room next day.

"No." Peregrine looked over the top of the morning paper and smiled. "No, I did not forget."

"Well," Martin said, lowering himself into the chair next

to Peregrine's, "you did not miss much. The stables themselves are impressive, but not many horses are kept here since
it is not Sandersford's principal seat."

Peregrine closed the paper and set it down on the table
at his elbow.

"Grace is well?" Martin asked. "I have not seen her this
morning."

"Yes, she is well," Peregrine said. "Just tired after a busy
day, I imagine."

Martin looked at his brother-in-law, looked away,
coughed, and picked up the discarded paper. He looked
uneasily to the door to see if anyone else was about to enter.
"I can't understand why you will allow it," he said at last.
"It's none of my business, of course."

"No," Peregrine said, not deeming it necessary to ask his
brother-in-law to clarify what he was talking about, "but you
are her brother. I understand your concern."

"You know who he is, of course?" Martin said. He did
not wait for an answer. "He was aways a scoundrel, with
too many good looks and too much charm for his own good.
One of the takers of this world. And Grace could never see
it. She was besotted."

"She is not an impressionable girl any longer," Peregrine
said.

"Well," Martin said, "you will be fortunate if he doesn't
take her from you as he took her from her family when she
was a girl. I would look to it if I were you. Not that it is
my business how you choose to deal with your own wife,
of course. This is deuced awkward. I should have kept my
mouth shut."

"No," Peregrine said, "I am not offended. You love
Grace, I see, and I can only honor you for that. Perhaps I
do not handle matters as other men would. Perhaps my
methods are entirely wrong. But I will tell you this, Martin:
I love Grace, too, and if you will pardon my saying so, I
will add that I love her many times more than any brother
possibly could. She is my wife, you see. And together she
and I will work out this situation."

Martin coughed again. "Sorry to have mentioned it," he said. "I thought it just possible that you did not know who he is or that you hadn't noticed what has been going on."

Peregrine smiled. "You must be pleased with Priscilla's success," he said. "And what about your son? Because I have never met him, I sometimes forget that I even have a nephew as well as a niece."

"Young fool," Martin said fondly. "He is just like we all were at his age, I suppose. Pursuing pleasure and getting into scrapes are of far more importance than studying and making an educated man of himself."

Ethel had linked her arm through Grace's and drawn her out from the breakfast room onto the terrace. "The sky is awfully heavy," she said. "I do hope it is not going to rain again. Yesterday it seemed that the weather was going to change for the better."

"Yes," Grace said. "But I always console myself for bad weather with the thought that we would not have such very green grass and such lovely flowers if we did not also have so much rain."

"Well," Ethel said, "I hope at least that it will hold off until we have returned to town this afternoon."

"Yes," Grace agreed.

"Grace," Ethel said on a rush, "I am very concerned about you. It is none of my business, of course."

"That is what you used to say," Grace said with the shadow of a smile, "and I used to agree with you whole-heartedly. I was a horrid girl, was I not? I can scarce believe that that person I remember was me."

"He was a very attractive man," Ethel said. "I used to think secretly that it was quite understandable that you would not listen to reason. And now, of course, he is even more attractive. But, oh, Grace, he has not changed."

"No," Grace said, "he has not. But I have, Ethel. And you need not worry about me. Or about Perry. You like Perry, don't you?"

"I was shocked when I first saw him, I must confess,"

Ethel said. "He looked so very young and was so very youthful in his manner. But I think you have made a fortunate match, Grace. Both Martin and I are very fond of him. And Priscilla, of course. And Papa." She laughed suddenly. "Papa said, 'That young puppy is more than my Grace deserves.' I think those were his exact words."

"Did he say 'my Grace?' " Grace asked, looking at her sister-in-law with some interest. "That is how he always used to refer to me."

"Yes," Ethel said, "he definitely said that."

"Well," Grace said, "you are not to worry about me. I am not about to run off with Gareth. I hope never to see him again once we have left London."

"I am glad," Ethel said. "And Martin will be too."

"Tell me what plans you have for Priscilla in the coming weeks," Grace said with a smile. "You must be very pleased with her."

"I am," Ethel said. "And very glad that she has not settled her affections on any one particular beau. I was rather afraid that she might. We really do not want her to do that this year when she is so young. I don't think I could face losing my girl for another year or two yet."

11

It was fortunate, both Grace and Peregrine thought, that
Priscilla and Lucinda Stebbins were so talkative on the way
back to London that their own silence seemed quite
unremarkable. Priscilla, of course, was always in high spirits.
This occasion was no exception. She had two days' worth
of new people and new experiences to exclaim upon, and
weeks more of the Season in town to look forward to and
speculate upon.

But even Miss Stebbins was unusually voluble. Did
Priscilla and Lady Grace not think Mr. Paisley handsome?
Not precisely handsome, perhaps, but in his own way really
quite well-looking? Gentlemen did not have to be tall in order
to be handsome, did they? Besides, character was far more
important than looks. And amiability. Amiability was
important, did not Sir Peregrine agree? Mr. Paisley did not
go into London very often, but he was planning to attend
Lord Sandersford's theater party next week. And she was
going to ask Papa if they might attend too, since she was
ever so eager to see Mr. Kean act. She had heard so much
about him.

Peregrine recalled that Mr. Paisley was the thin, padded
cousin of Sandersford's late wife. He smiled indulgently at
the eager, flushed face of Lucinda Stebbins, remarked that
her presence at the theater might distract Mr. Paisley's mind
from Kean's performance and that therefore she might be

142

doing him a marked disservice by attending herself, and he winked at her.

Lucinda giggled and blushed and was content for her friend to dominate the conversation for the rest of the journey home.

Peregrine himself was very aware of his wife seated beside him, her arm brushing against his occasionally when the carriage swayed unexpectedly before she had the chance to grab the strap with which to steady herself and keep away from him. And try as he would, he could think of nothing to say to her. And he could not bring himself to look at her because there would be nothing natural in his expression and he would be acutely uncomfortable.

They had not spoken, beyond the merest commonplace, awkwardly delivered and with no direct eye contact, since he had left her dressing room the night before. And they had not touched beyond the accidental contact of their arms in the carriage. He had slept in his dressing room. Or at least he had spent the latter portion of the night in his dressing room, slumped in a chair that was definitely not designed to be slept in, trying to empty his teeming and racing mind, trying to remind himself that it was good news he had heard in her dressing room. He had dozed fitfully, his head cradled uncomfortably on his arms, which he had spread on the high marble top of the washstand.

It had been good news. She had been alone with Sandersford for half an hour. She had talked with him, even allowed him to kiss her. And she had decided that she wanted to stay with *him*, that she wanted to continue with their marriage. It was what he wanted, what he had scarcely allowed himself to hope for in the past week.

And yet she had not wanted him to touch her. She had shrunk from his touch. She had decided to stay with him but would not let him touch her. And so there was no triumph at all, no joy in her decision. She had not been able to break her marriage vows, but her heart was with the man she had rejected that night.

And what could he do about it? He could not encourage her to leave him, to walk away from her marriage and plunge herself into the middle of a scandal. He could not do that.

He must respect her decision as he had sworn to himself that he would do, no matter what that decision was. And so he must keep her with him as his wife, knowing her unhappy, knowing that she must force herself to remain close to him, to remain his wife in every way.

He loved her. He had been prepared to let her go if she found that Sandersford was essential to her happiness. He had been prepared to keep her if she decided otherwise. But he had not even considered that matters might be this way. He was not at all sure that he was prepared to have her person only, knowing that her heart was elsewhere. She had never been wholly his, of course. He had always known that a large part of her was in the grave with her dead son and her dead lover. Or at least, that was what he had always believed. He had not known until recently that that lover was still alive. But he had always believed that at least he could bring her comfort, perhaps contentment.

And what was he to do now? Was he to live with her in silence for the rest of their lives? Without touching her? He could not do so. He loved her and wished more than anything for her happiness. But he was no saint. He was very human. If she had left him, he would have taught himself somehow to cope with her absence. But she had not left him. And so she must remain his wife. He must somehow carry on with his life as if these two days had not happened. Unless she cringed from him openly as she had done the night before. He would not be able to bear that. He would not be able to touch her if that happened again.

Peregrine reached out as Priscilla chattered on and touched the back of Grace's hand with his fingertips. She looked down at his hand and then rather jerkily across to look somewhat below the level of his eyes. She said nothing and looked away again almost immediately. But she did not remove her hand.

She had been sleeping, or pretending to sleep, when he had gone into their bedchamber the night before. It had been very late. He had wandered outside long after all the other guests had either taken their leave or gone to bed. And he had gone into the library on his return indoors, knowing by the sliver of light beneath the door that his host was there.

Sandersford had not looked surprised when Peregrine had walked in without knocking. And he had not risen. He had been sitting slouched down in a leather chair beside the fireplace, an empty glass dangling from the hand that was draped over the arm. He had not been foxed exactly, but Peregrine had guessed that he had had more than the one drink. He had regarded his guest with mocking eyes.

"Ah, the outraged husband," he had said. "Where is your glove, Lampman? You need a glove to slap in my face if the thing is to be done properly, you know."

Peregrine had walked right into the room and taken the chair opposite Sandersford's. "I have no wish to fight you," he had said. "I only want to ask that you leave Grace in peace now that she has made her decision."

Sandersford had laughed. "You find you can be generous in your triumph, do you?" he had said. "You fool! Do you think that Grace has chosen you? Do you think that she does not love me? Do you think that I could not take her away from you? Do you believe that I will not do it one day? You are a mere boy, Lampman, trying to understand the emotions of a woman."

"She is my wife," Peregrine had said. "Both duty and inclination dictate that I protect her from harm and from harassment. I have stepped back to allow her to make her own decision about you because I know that in the past she loved you and bore your child. Now she has decided, I hope the matter is final in your mind too."

"Do I detect a threat?" Lord Sandersford had asked.

"No," Peregrine had said, "only a plea for decency. Did you once love her, Sandersford? Do you love her now? Leave her in peace then. You brought ruin and pain enough into her life once. Make some atonement now."

Lord Sandersford had leapt to his feet, his hands in white fists at his side. "By God," he had said, "if it were not shameful to whip a puppy, Lampman, I would whip you now. What do you know of Grace and me and what was between us? By what right do you judge me and lecture me, you sanctimonious fool? She was mine once. I had her body and soul, do you understand? And you think that she is yours now because she accepted your legal protection after the death of her brother? Do you think you have ever possessed her? Do you think she is yours? She is mine. She always has been and always will be.''

Peregrine had kept his seat. But his face had paled. ''I will not engage in such an argument,'' he had said. ''As if Grace were a possession to be wrangled over. Did you ever see her as a person, Sandersford? Did you ever consider her feelings? Did you ever wonder when you left her with child what she felt, what she suffered? Do you have any idea now of the torment you are putting her through? Leave her alone now. Do something decent in your life.''

Lord Sandersford had brought himself under control. He had refilled his glass with brandy, not offering any drink to his guest, and resumed his seat. ''You are the torment in Grace's life, not me,'' he had said. ''Do you not realize that she sees you as a boy, that you have become the child she lost? She will not harm your good name by leaving you. She will not risk hurting you. She has chosen rather to renounce the great passion of her life. But it will not be forever, Lampman. She will see soon enough that you are are indeed like her child, a growing man who has to be given up to a younger woman. Do you think I have not seen your preference? And Grace will see it too. You have not seen the last of me. I will come for her when the time is right.''

''I had hoped,'' Peregrine had said, ''that you were not quite the scoundrel you seemed, Sandersford. I had hoped that perhaps there was some explanation for your treatment of Grace in the past, or at least that you would have outgrown your total selfishness. I had hoped that if she rejected you tonight, you would accept her decision and decide to put your love for her before your own selfish desires. But I see it is not so. I am sorry. Good night.'' He had got to his feet and made for the door.

''What?'' Lord Sandersford had said, sneering. ''No threats to kill me if I ever come near your wife again, Lampman?''

''No.'' Peregrine had turned back to him. ''No threats,

Sandersford. I can see no good coming from violence. And
I feel no compulsion to prove my masculinity to you or
anyone else. Only if you harass her, if you force yourself
on her against her wishes, will I be forced to take action
against you. Not otherwise. Good night.''

"You are a coward,'' Lord Sandersford had said with a
laugh. "A lily-livered boy beneath my contempt, as I
suspected when I first set eyes on you.''

"Strangely,'' Peregrine had said before letting himself
quietly out of the library, "I find myself incapable of being
wounded by your opinion of me, Sandersford.''

Grace's hand had turned beneath his, Peregrine noticed
as he smiled ruefully at Priscilla and admitted that he could
not answer her question because his mind had wandered
shockingly over trying to list mentally all the young
gentlemen who had been slain by her and Miss Stebbins in
the past few weeks.

"A long list,'' he said. "Twenty-four already when your
question jolted me back to reality. And I cannot now
remember if I had included Mr. Paisley on that list. I think
not. Twenty-five, then.''

Both girls laughed.

Grace's hand was lying palm-up beneath his fingertips.

It was not easy, they both found, to pick up a marriage
after such an emotional crisis, to piece it together again, and
to continue with it. The events of the past weeks inevitably
left their scars. And their uncertainties. Neither was quite
sure how the other felt. Each wondered if the other was
reluctant to continue with the marriage at all. But those same
events had left a shyness, an awkwardness, that made it
difficult, if not impossible, for them to talk openly about their
feelings.

But the marriage did continue. After an almost silent
journey from Hammersmith, they endured a dinner at home
during which they made labored conversation, and an evening
at Mrs. Borden's, when Peregrine turned in relief to his

friend the Earl of Amberley for conversation and Grace almost forgot her woes in her fascination at a conversation with a portrait painter. And later that night Grace, lying cold and rigid with tension in the bed she had shared with her husband since their arrival in London, discovered that they were still to share it.

She knew that he had misconstrued her shrinking from him the night before. She knew that he had been deeply hurt. But she had been unable all day to explain to him that it was from herself she had shrunk, not from him. How could she explain when doing so would mean referring again to all those matters that she wished to put behind her? And how could she simply tell him that she loved him? Perhaps he would not wish to hear it.

They had married for convenience, he had said the night before. The words had stung. She had not been able to shake them from her mind all day. And they were true, of course. Simply true. They had not been spoken out of any desire to hurt or to set her down. They were true. She had known all along. She had not loved Perry any more than he loved her when she had agreed to marry him. It was only since— and so gradually that she could not say when it had happened exactly—that he had come to mean all the world to her.

There was no reason whatsoever to expect that the same thing had been happening to Perry. And she had no complaints. He had always treated her with the utmost gentleness and affection. He had shown understanding and respect for her feelings and her personhood in the events of the past few weeks. There was nothing to complain of. But, oh, it hurt to hear him say the bald truth with no conception whatsoever that their marriage had become for her far more than a thing of convenience.

She did not believe Gareth. She did not believe that Perry craved younger women and that sooner or later it was inevitable that he take a mistress. She did not believe that. She knew Perry a great deal better than Gareth did, and she knew that he was faithful to her, and would remain so. But was there some unhappiness in him, some longing to be able to look at a younger woman with desire perhaps? Was he bound by a marriage that could never bring him real happiness even though he would never be unfaithful to it?

She could not ask him. There was no way of knowing the answer. But she was terrified that her behavior of the night before would drive a wedge between them so that their marriage would never bring them anything else but misery and entrapment.

It was with some relief, then, that she watched him come from his dressing room into their bedchamber on their first night back in town. She watched him with large and wary eyes as he crossed the room, sat on the edge of the bed, and touched her cheek with his fingertips. His face was more serious than she had ever seen it.

"You said that you wish to remain married to me, Grace," he said. "It is what I wish too. But I cannot contemplate half a marriage. If my touch is abhorrent to you, you must tell me now and I will have to make some arrangement whereby we can live separately. I will not touch you against your will."

"Your touch is not abhorrent, Perry," she said, and she reached up to take his hand and bring the palm against her cheek. "And I do not want half a marriage either."

He searched her eyes before rising to put out the candles.

But Grace was not sure half an hour later, as she lay awake beside her husband, not quite touching him, that their lovemaking had brought them any closer together. She had been unable to relax, unable for a long time to respond to his hands and his lips, which had slowly and patiently tried to gentle her. Memories of Gareth's demanding, searching hands and mouth the night before kept intruding and making her feel unclean again. She had had to keep herself tense in order not to shudder.

And Perry had come to her eventually before she was ready and had hurt her, though she had shown her pain only by tensing yet again. It was only toward the end, when he had buried his face against her hair and she had known that he knew, that she had felt herself come finally to meet him, so that she had held him to her and leaned her head against his and swallowed a lump in her throat. He had moved away from her after a few minutes and not put an arm beneath her head as he usually did.

She did not think he was sleeping. He was too still to be asleep.

"Perry," she whispered. She touched him lightly on the arm.

He turned his face toward her.

"Perry," she said, "do you really want to stay here any longer? Are you enjoying the Season?"

"You want to go home?" he asked.

"Yes." She could not read his tone. "But only if you do. We have accepted several invitations for the next few weeks."

"Then we will spend tomorrow morning penning our regrets," he said. "Will the day after tomorrow be soon enough, Grace?"

"Yes," she said. "Oh, Perry, it seems so very long since we were at home."

"Too long," he said. He leaned forward to kiss her on the lips and then turned over to face away from her.

And so their marriage had resumed, Grace thought as she lay awake and knew only much later by his deep breathing that Perry slept. It was better than she deserved, better than she could have hoped for the night before. But there was an emptiness that was remarkably like pain lodged somewhere in the region of her stomach. And even the fact that they were together and had just made love and that they were planning to return home together in two days' time had not taken away that emptiness.

She was frightened.

"Oh, Perry, do look. Oh, the flowers!" Grace sat forward on the carriage seat, her face close to the window as it had been for the last two miles, though there had been no possible way that she could see Reardon Park for all of that distance. But she had seen it now: the square, classical house, the trees, and the late-spring flowers that he and she had planted together the year before, all in full and glorious bloom.

Peregrine moved closer to her and looked over her shoulder. "Home," he said. "One glimpse of it is worth more than a thousand days spent anywhere else in the world. I am afraid I will never be an adventurer, Grace."

"Me neither," she said. "Oh, Perry, I could cry."

"That would be remarkably foolish," he said. "You would not then be able to see the orchard, which is about to come into view. And the servants would take one look at your face and think you were sorry to be back. The flowers do look splendid, Grace. There are so many of them that I am afraid we did not leave any to grow downward to bloom in China."

"Well," she said, "I say, let the Chinese plant their own flowers if they want them."

It was as if they had stepped out of one world that morning when they had left the inn at which they had spent the night and been transported in a matter of five hours into another world. Peregrine vaulted out of the carriage when it drew to a halt before his front doors, and turned to lift his wife down. He totally ignored the steps that the footman had lowered for their convenience. They were home and they were together and they had smiled at each other in genuine delight before the carriage had stopped completely.

Almost, he thought as he held to her waist for a few moments after her feet touched the ground, and he smiled down at her again as if all the awkwardness and stiffness and unhappiness and all the efforts to pretend that everything was normal between them had vanished during the final stage of their journey. Almost as if they could revert immediately to the quiet contentment they had enjoyed here together during the first year of their marriage.

"Happy?" he asked before releasing her.

She nodded, though her lips were trembling. He might have folded her to him and kissed her and told her that he loved her and would keep her safe and at peace for the rest of her life if the coachman and the footman had not been bustling about with two of the servants from the house and his valet and Grace's maid, all intent on emptying the baggage coach, and if their housekeeper had not been standing in the doorway, bobbing curtsies, her face wreathed in a smile of welcome.

"That surprised we were, my lady, to hear just this morning that you were on your way home already," she said when Grace moved forward to greet her. "And that glad. You go upstairs and wash yourself now. I have had hot water sent up already. And there will be warm scones and good strong tea in the parlor before you know it."

"Thank you," Grace said. "It is so very good to be home."

And it was good, Peregrine agreed. He had never been a great lover of London and the fashionable world. Now the very thought of both was enough to make him shudder. He did not believe that he would ever want to go back there again or ever leave Reardon Park again.

It was good to settle once more into the routine of their quiet life. It was good to wander in the garden and in the orchard and to see the beauty and the color with which his wife's skill and imagination had surrounded them. And to see the promise of roses in the arbor. It was good to be back among his own books and to be able to relax in his own worn chair in the library and read to his heart's content and watch again his wife quietly embroidering in the chair opposite his. Good to read to her again and to discover again that if he shared his thoughts and ideas with her, she would show interest and be perfectly capable of matching her intelligence to his.

And it was good to be back among their friends again. News of their return spread quickly, and not an afternoon passed for several days without bringing with it at least one visitor. The rector apologized for his good wife's absence, but he was delighted to announce that the latest addition to their family had arrived but three weeks before. Mrs. Cartwright lamented the fact that with both them and the earl's family gone, life had been very dull but that perhaps now there would be a little more company again. Mr. Watson came to return a book of poetry he had borrowed before Christmas.

Mr. and Mrs. Carrington were so much their usual selves that Peregrine could have laughed aloud at them, and did after they were gone and he was alone with Grace again.

"Such a fine new gown, to be sure," Mr. Carrington said with a shake of the head as he looked at Grace's muslin dress. "I daresay you will not be talking to such rustics as us any longer, Lady Lampman, and we will be as dull as we have been since you all went away, you and Amberley and the rest of them."

"William," his wife scolded. "The very idea! Lady Lampman will be thinking you are serious. Take no notice of him, my dear. William does like to tease."

"Well, I have a new coat," Peregrine said, smoothing his hands down the lapels, "made by Weston, no less. And I have been seriously wondering whether everyone in this part of the world is not now beneath my notice. Of course, if I turn my back on all my neighbors, there will be no one to admire my superior appearance, will there?"

"Exactly," Mr. Carrington said. "So you need us, after all, you see, Lampman. And we need not be dull, you will be relieved to know, Viola."

"Well, really," Mrs. Carrington said indignantly. "Your husband is every bit as bad as mine, Lady Lampman. You have my sympathy. But then he always was a dreadful tease."

"Viola gets awfully violent when she once loses her temper," Mr. Carrington said. "We had better take our leave, my dear."

"Since we have been here an hour already, I agree we should," Mrs. Carrington said. "But what he says is quite untrue, Lady Lampman. Me violent? The very idea!"

Grace joined Peregrine in his laughter after they had left.

The Misses Stanhope too were quite their usual selves. Miss Stanhope described for Grace exactly how they had decorated the altar at church for Easter, using the lace cloth she had made the year before expressly for that purpose, and how they had missed Lady Lampman when it came time to arrange the flowers. And Miss Letitia tittered at Peregrine's compliments and declared that if she had a new cap every

time dear Sir Perry thought she did, she would have a whole
dresser stuffed full of them.

Yes, it was good to be home again. Almost as if they had
never been away. Almost. But not quite.

There was something between them. It was hard to explain
it, impossible to put it into words, hard even to grasp it in
coherent thought. They spoke frequently and freely on all
topics. And yet there was a constraint in their conversation,
something that they avoided with such care that they could
not even name that something to themselves. They could sit
in comfortable silence with each other. And yet sometimes
that silence became loud with that unspoken something. They
went about together and enjoyed the friendship of their
neighbors. And yet they watched each other, not out of
jealousy or suspicion, but out of some emotion or fear they
could not name.

They lived together as man and wife, and yet their lovemaking was somewhat less frequent than it had been before.
And though they were both satisfied by each encounter and
knew the other at least not repelled, they both wondered
sometimes, entirely against their will. Grace wondered if he
did not dream sometimes of a younger woman. Peregrine
wondered if she pined for the man she had loved since she
was a girl.

And both remembered that they had made a marriage of
convenience and that for the other it was still so. Each
believed that love had grown on one side only.

12

As the second year of their marriage drew to its close, both Grace and Peregrine could reflect that it had been restored to the relative contentment they had known at the end of the first. Perhaps the only real difference was that now each of them knew what both had felt but not acknowledged the year before. And so there was a somewhat lesser contentment. It was not easy, each found, to love deeply when one believes that that love is not reciprocated. And yet each was thankful for the companionship, the loyalty, and the affection of the other.

They invited Grace's family to visit them for Christmas. The invitation was refused—the weather and therefore the roads were likely to be bad, and Oswald would be coming home from school for a few weeks. But they did promise to come later, perhaps in February if the winter turned out to be not too long and hard. Even Lord Pawley said he would come. He wished to see the grave of his younger son, Ethel added in a postscript to the letter she wrote Grace.

Grace was pleased. The reconciliation with her father that had begun the spring before had not been completed, she felt. They had been very close at one time. The gap between them after their estrangement had been correspondingly wide. She looked forward to entertaining him in her own home, and she certainly could not visit him at Pangam Manor so soon after her last visit. There was still a bewilderment, a fear about her feelings for Gareth. Not fear of him and what he might do to her, but fear of herself and a return of that weakness that had blinded her to his faults when she was younger and drawn her into a passion that had deprived her of all reason and morality.

In the meantime there was Christmas to look forward to again. Decorating the church with the Nativity scene; caroling with the Mortons and the Carringtons outside all the village homes and some of the outlying cottages too; taking baskets of food to the sick and the poor; helping the Countess of Amberley organize a party for the children at Amberley Court; buying and making gifts for servants and friends and for each other; conferring with the housekeeper and the cook on the foods to be prepared; bringing inside armfuls of holly to decorate doors and mantels; commiserating with each other over scratched hand and pricked fingers. There seemed to be a hundred and one tasks to be done, all equally delightful.

There was the usual party at Amberley Court on Christmas Day, beginning late in the afternoon so that each family would have plenty of time in which to enjoy its own company and open gifts and eat the Christmas goose before bundling up warmly for the carriage ride to Amberley.

But they were not to enjoy the warmth of the blazing log fire in the Amberley drawing room for long, it seemed. Lord Eden and Lady Madeline, who had not had a chilly journey to endure a half-hour before, were all impatience to persuade the younger guests that a brisk walk to the beach, two miles away along the valley in which the house was situated, was just the thing to settle their Christmas dinners and make room for all the good things still to come at tea and dinner.

Young people are ever resilient, Peregrine thought, settling more comfortably into his chair and feeling with some complacence that the heat of the flames was almost too hot on his feet. Walter Carrington and his younger sister, Anna, immediately leapt to their feet, eager to be on the way. And the four Courtney boys were no more reluctant. Miss Morton and her younger sister agreed to join the party when they saw how many young gentlemen there would be to escort them. And the rector's two older children, bouncing before their mother as if they thought that such motion might mesmerize her brain and induce her consent, begged to be allowed to go along too.

The Earl of Amberley grinned. "Sometimes," he said, "being a host has distinct advantages. Especially when it is a chilly Christmas and a crowd of mad youngsters suggests a walk of a mere four miles. I must stay to entertain my wiser guests, of course. But don't let me hinder you, Perry, my lad. Perhaps these young people will need the steadying influence of an older man."

"Oh, very steady," Lord Eden said with a shout of laughter. "I am only five years younger than you, Perry, and I can remember some of the scrapes you and Edmund used to get into. You were quite my idol at one time."

"At one time?" Peregrine said, delighting the Misses Stanhope and Mrs. Cartwright with his look of mock horror. "You mean I have lost my reputation for daring and recklessness? This will never do. My coat and my hat immediately, if you please."

"Oh, splendid," Lady Madeline said. "I was terrified that Dom and I were going to be the seniors of this expedition." She smiled impudently at Peregrine.

"May I come too, Perry?" Grace asked. "I like the thought of the exercise. I certainly feel the need for it."

"You mean you will do this quite voluntarily?" he asked. "Without being tricked into it, as I have been? You are quite heroic, Grace."

"Dear Lady Lampman," Mrs. Morton remarked to Miss Letitia. "She does keep herself young for Sir Perry, does she not? I would not welcome such an expedition even if I could be taken in a carriage with a hot brick for my feet."

"It would keep a lady young to be married so late in life to such a handsome, cheerful gentleman as Sir Perry, though," Miss Letitia replied with a sigh that might well have been one of envy. Peregrine had not failed to remark on the handsomeness of her new cap—and it really was new this time, a Christmas gift from her sister.

The young people, together with Grace and Peregrine, were soon on their way, striding energetically and noisily along the valley through which a stream flowed to the sea. Anna Carrington, who had decided five years before, at the age of ten, that she was going to marry her first cousin, Dominic, when she grew up, linked her arm through his and tripped along at his side, and reminded him of the birthday she had celebrated less than two weeks before and of the fact that in another year she would be finished with the horrid schoolroom for good and would be almost grown up.

"And will dazzle not a few gentlemen when you are finally let loose on society, Anna," he said good-naturedly.

"Oh, do you think so, Dominic?" she said eagerly. And she added ingenuously, "And you too?"

"You are already dazzling me," he said, "with those rosy cheeks. No, don't frown and look offended, you goose. They look very becoming."

Madeline walked with Howard Courtney and chattered determindly about any topic that came to mind. Howard had had a painful *tendre* for her for years, and though she had told him almost four years before that she could never look on him as more than a friend, he seemed unable to meet her without flushing and becoming tongue-tied. If only he were not such a thoroughly nice person, she thought with an inward sigh, she could perhaps despise him and feel no sympathy for him at all.

Walter Carrington took Miss Hetty Morton on his arm, reflecting glumly on the fact that she was not even quite as old as his sister and no foil whatsoever for his advanced eighteen years. It was a great shame that Miss Susan Courtney had been away at her aunt's since the summer. She was growing up fast, and she was such a very pretty and timid little thing.

The older Miss Morton was proud to have the others see that she walked with two gentlemen, both her arms occupied. It was true that they were only two of the younger Courtney boys. And it was true that she had been privately annoyed to see that child Anna monopolize the attention of Lord Eden again. But even so, it was gratifying to know that there were two gentlemen eager to accompany her. It was something to tell Mama later.

Peregrine held Grace's arm snug against his side. They both wore woolen scarves wrapped twice about their necks. "You are a marvel," he said. "There are not many married ladies who would prefer a brisk walk in the December air to a cozy chat by the fire."

"The sea and the beach are at their loveliest in the winter," she said. "And you know I love the outdoors, Perry. I just hope these very young persons will not feel inhibited by my very elderly presence."

He grinned. "I would wager you could outwalk and outwork all of them put together, Grace," he said. "Your nose distinctly resembles a cherry, by the way."

"No, no," she said. "This is the Christmas season, Perry. A holly berry would be a more appropriate comparison, surely. Not that I can see my own nose to judge, of course. But I can see yours."

"*Touché,*" he said with a laugh. "Ah, look, there is the sea already. The tide must be almost full. What a pity. I like to see the wide beach when it is out."

"But this sky looks splendid reflected in the water," she said. "Look, Perry. Lots of heavy gray clouds scudding across the sky with the sunshine behind them. And the sea looks like silver. Molten silver."

Peregrine laughed. "Most people would say it is a nasty dull day and cold into the bargain," he said. "You have a lovely creative mind, Grace. A poet's mind."

The valley opened out onto a flat golden beach with steep cliffs either side. But now, almost at full tide, not a great deal of the sand could be seen. They all walked out until they were almost at the edge of the incoming water. Anna squealed as Lord Eden threatened to pick her up and hurl her into the closest breaker.

"Shall we stroll along at the edge for a while?" Peregrine asked. "I don't think we are likely to be trapped against the cliffs yet. And if we were, we would merely have to climb up."

"Gracious," Grace said. "Is it possible?" She gazed up

the almost sheer height of the cliff. "I suppose it is something you did during your boyhood, Perry. And something that was strictly forbidden, I presume."

"Right on both counts," he said meekly. "It looks as if we were both rather reckless and disobedient young people, Grace. We deserve each other, don't you think? And we dare to stroll sedately along the beach here, avoiding all those noisy, frolicking youngsters, for all the world as if we never dreamed of behaving in such a riotous manner when we were their age. We are frauds, my dear. Should we turn back, do you suppose, and confess to them?"

"Oh, Perry," she said, "you speak as if you are an old man already. Do you not long to join in with their high spirits."

"Join in?" he said. "Good Lord, no, Grace. I am no boy, my dear. I have been a sober married gentleman for almost two years."

"Is that what I have done to you?" she said.

He looked down at her, eyebrows raised. "Made a married gentleman out of me?" he said. "Yes, certainly."

"I meant the sober part," she said.

"Not at all," he said. "I distinctly remember laughing at least three times only today. But not frolicking, Grace. That would be somewhat undignified at my age, would it not?"

"I am sometimes afraid that perhaps you crave young company," she said.

"And you do not think of yourself as young, I presume," he said. "Do you think that way, Grace? Because I like to tease young girls, perhaps? But I like to tease the older ladies too, dear. Miss Letitia Stanhope would be severely disappointed if I did not pretend each time I see her that I think her cap to be new and most charming. I like women. It is so easy to please them, to make them happy. In a quite superficial manner, of course. But I like to make people happy. You do not think I flirt, do you?"

"No!" she said. "No, I was not being in any way critical, Perry. I was not, believe me."

He took her gloved hand in his and squeezed it. "I am not sorry I married you, Grace," he said. "If that is what you meant." There was a small silence. "Are you ever sorry you married me?"

"No," she said.

He waited for her to say more. She seemed about to do so. But she did not.

"That is good," he said. "I suppose all married people sometimes wonder. But it is difficult to ask, is it not?"

"Yes," she said. "I am not sorry, Perry. Truly I am not."

He squeezed her hand. "We should turn around and walk back," he said. "But it is relatively comfortable walking with the wind almost behind us, is it not? I am not sure I have the courage to turn around."

"I think the only alternative is to go up over the cliff, then," she said. "The tide is coming in fast."

"And so it is," he said. "I am sure you would have the energy to climb up, Grace, but you might find it a little too much to haul me up with you. Let's turn back, then. Ugh! I knew it."

"Oh," Grace said. "I feel as if my breath is being blown back down my throat."

"I almost wish we had chosen to spend Christmas Day alone," Peregrine said. "I always feel most contented strolling with you. However, I suppose we must be thankful for so many congenial neighbors and friends."

"Very much so," Grace said. "And you cannot pretend that you are not going to enjoy the evening, Perry. Music in the drawing room and games and probably dancing. And plenty of conversation and food."

He grinned. "Trust my wife to know me rather well," he said. "Grace, you have holly berries for nose and cheeks. And brightly shining ones too."

"I know," she said. "I assumed that the wind was having the same effect on my face as it is having on yours."

As the evening progressed at the house, it seemed that Grace was perfectly right. Peregrine turned pages of music for Miss Hetty Morton and Anna Carrington, whose extreme

youth caused the other young gentlemen to ignore them much
of the time. He played a hand of cards with the rector's wife,
Miss Stanhope, and Mr. Courtney and a game of spillikins
with the rector's young children. He danced with his wife
and any other lady who happened not to have a partner when
the music began. And in a robust game of blindman's buff,
he was roundly accused of cheating when twice in a row he
caught a tittering Miss Letitia despite his blindfold.

Grace was standing to one side of the pianoforte late in
the evening when there was a general lull in the festivities
following supper, browsing through some music. Peregrine
was at the opposite end of the room laughing with a group
of others at Mr. Courtney's protestations that he would not
be able to squeeze one more morsel of food inside himself
until at least New Year's Day.

"At least you know that you will not waste quite away,"
Mr. Carrington said. "You could lose two stone without
anyone noticing."

"William!" his wife said. "Oh, take no notice of him,
Mr. Courtney."

"Perhaps I should hire myself out to Arabs for desert
crossings," Mr. Courtney said good-naturedly. "Is there a
shortage of camels, do you think?"

"Oh, do look," Mrs. Cartwright said with a titter. "Look
where Lady Lampman is standing."

"The pianoforte must have been moved," Lord Amberley
said with a laugh. "The mistletoe was meant to be directly
above the stool. No one seems to have noticed it just where
it is."

"I would wager Lady Lampman does not know it is there,
the poor dear," Mrs. Carrington said.

"Well, Perry," Lord Amberley said, "what are you going
to do about it?"

Peregrine got to his feet while most of the ladies smirked,
Miss Stanhope blushed, and Miss Letitia clasped her hands
to her bosom.

"Grace," Peregrine said a moment later, "do you realize
the great danger you are in?"

She looked at him, startled out of her concentration on the music. "I beg your pardon?" she said.

"Do you not see what is threatening right above you?" he asked.

She looked up in some alarm only to have the ceiling blocked from her view by his face.

"You are standing directly below the mistletoe," he said. "You cannot expect me to resist such invitation, can you?"

And then he kissed her on the lips, quite lingeringly enough to satisfy their audience at the other end of the room. Peregrine heard a smattering of applause, a few giggles, and a "Bravo!" as he lifted his head and grinned down at his wife.

"Perry," she said. "Everyone will have seen."

"I'm afraid so," he said. "And you had better move from there, or I will be forced to kiss you again."

Grace moved with some haste, and yet there was a warmth of feeling in her as he laid her hand on his arm and took her across the room to join their laughing neighbors. It was a warmth that had begun with their morning of gift opening and entertaining of the servants and had continued with the evening spent with congenial friends. If it could only be like this always, Grace thought, seating herself beside her husband and not removing her arm from his sleeve.

The carriage ride back home was a cold one, though they had a hot brick at their feet and a heavy blanket to wrap around their knees. Peregrine put an arm around Grace's shoulders as soon as they were on the way, and she snuggled her head against him.

"Tired?" he asked.

"Mm." She closed her eyes. "I wish every day could be Christmas. There is something so very special about it, isn't there, Perry?"

"Yes," he said. And he moved one hand up beneath her chin to raise it, and kissed her.

It was rather absurd, Grace thought somewhere behind the fog of contentment and rising desire she felt over the next half-hour, to be sitting in the chill interior of a carriage with one's husband of almost two years, both dressed in heavy winter garments, kissing for almost every moment of the journey, softly and slowly exploring each other's mouth with lips and tongues, touching each other's face with gloved fingers, murmuring to each other in words that had no meaning to the ear, but only to the heart.

Equally absurd, and enchanting too, to be taken directly to her bedchamber when she arrived home and to have her husband dismiss her maid and his valet for the night and proceed to undress her himself as he had done on one other occasion and to have him kiss her all the while and worship her with his hands and take her to the bed to make love to her over and over again until finally they clung together damply and drifted toward sleep from pure exhaustion.

And absurd perhaps to imagine that he loved her, loved her with all his being and for all time and not just because it was Christmas and everyone feels love and good will at that season.

"Perry," she murmured against his warm and naked chest.

"Mm," he said, kissing the top of her head.

And they both slept.

Perhaps Christmas would have stayed with them even beyond the New Year if Grace had not received a letter from Ethel. Certainly the magic of that day and night did not fade in the days following Christmas but bound them together in the warmth of a deeper affection than they had known before. But the letter did arrive, and it came to drive a wedge between them again.

Not that there was anything upsetting about Ethel's letter. It was filled with news of the family, in which both Grace and Peregrine were interested, and hopes that the planned visit could be made in February or March at the latest, even though they were all suffering from colds at the moment of writing.

What was upsetting were the two enclosures. One was a separate note from Ethel, for Grace alone. The other was a sealed letter also addressed to her. It was from Viscount

Sandersford, Ethel explained. She had not wanted to take it from him or send it in such clandestine manner to Grace. She was sure that Martin would blame her for doing so if he ever found out the truth. But Lord Sandersford had been very insistent. He had told her that Grace would want the letter. He had told her that if she did not send it secretly, he must do so openly and doubtless upset Grace's husband. Ethel did not know at all if she did the right thing.

Grace felt sick. She sat in her sitting room, Gareth's unopened letter clasped in one hand. She did not want to open it. She wanted to pretend to herself that Gareth was dead. She did not love him. She wondered how she could ever have done so. She wanted to forget about him. But of course he was not dead and she could not forget. Whether she liked it or not, he was a very real part of her life. She had loved him; she had shared the intimacy, even if not the reality, of marriage with him; he was Jeremy's father.

She sat for a long time with the letter in her hand. Then she got to her feet, strode from the room, and almost ran down the stairs. She opened the door to Peregrine's study in a rush, not waiting to knock first, and drew to a sharp halt when she saw that he was with his estate manager.

"I am sorry," she said. "Excuse me, please."

Both men jumped to their feet.

Peregrine came toward her, his eyes steady on her face. "What is it?" he asked. "Do you need me?"

"It can wait," she said. "Please excuse me."

But he held up a staying hand and turned to the manager. "Will you excuse us?" he said. "I shall come and see you later."

The man bowed and left the room.

"What is it, Grace?" Peregrine turned back to her, concern in his face. "Something has happened to upset you. Was there bad news in Ethel's letter? Your father?"

She did not answer but put Gareth's letter in his hand almost as if it were to scald her.

He looked down at it and turned it over in his hand. "It is sealed," he said, "and addressed to you, Grace."

"It is from Gareth," she said. "Lord Sandersford."

"I see." He stared down at the letter for a long and silent moment before handing it back. "It is for you, Grace. Not for me."

She swallowed and took it into her own hands again. "Yes," she said. And she knew that whether she opened it or not, he was there again. Gareth. Her past. The things that would always come between her and Perry. And she knew that Perry would never make her life easier by telling her what to do. And it was that very fact that made her love him so dearly. Perry respected her as a person. He would never dominate her as her husband, even to make her life easier and their marriage more enduring.

She turned, left the room without a word, and climbed the stairs to her sitting room again. And opened the letter.

He could not live without her, Gareth wrote. A lifetime punishment for a youthful thoughtlessness was too much to bear. She must come to him. Or he would come to her. He had struck up enough of an acquaintance with the Earl of Amberley the previous spring to impose on his hospitality for a few weeks. He loved her and he would not believe that she did not love him, though he understood she was trying hard to remain loyal to her husband. He had visited Jeremy's grave almost daily since his return from London and wept there for the son he had never known and the love he had so carelessly thrown away.

The words blurred before Grace's eyes. Could he not have spared her that? And was it true? Had he finally recognized that they had had a son together and that Jeremy had been a real person, quite distinct from either of them? But she did not want to know if it was true. And she doubted that it was. Had he written that only because he knew that that of all details would weaken her? Gareth crying at Jeremy's grave! At their son's grave. She shuddered.

And what was she to do? Write to tell him that she would not come and did not wish to see him again? He would ignore her denials, she was sure. Gareth would just not believe that her love for him was dead. Gareth had always got what he wanted.

And the dread grew in her that somehow, totally against her will, he would get his way again. He would exert his power over her once more, a power she had welcomed as a girl and willingly acquiesced in. She could never make a willing surrender to him again. She hated him. But hate is very akin to love. And he knew that. He had been quite undismayed by her hatred. She was terrified that her very hatred would draw her to him.

And away from Perry. She loved Perry. His gentleness and his laughter and his quiet affection represented all the goodness and peace that had been missing from her life until she was already in her mid-thirties. And she had begun to think that perhaps she could enjoy those things for the rest of her life. But always thoughts of Gareth aroused memories of her guilt and doubts of her own worth.

She did not deserve goodness and peace. She did not deserve Perry.

She was going to lose him. And in the worst possible way. He was not going to cast her off. She knew he would never do that even if perhaps he did sometimes regret being married to a woman ten years his senior. And Gareth would not force her to go. Even Gareth would not resort to abduction. No, she would end up going quite freely to her own destruction. And she would do so in order to punish herself for a past she could never quite forgive herself for. It was inevitable. The prospect terrified her.

She was going to fight it. She was too strong a person to do anything as weak as destroy herself.

But she was very much afraid.

13

Peregrine was doodling on a sheet of paper with a quill pen that badly needed mending. It scratched over the surface, setting his teeth on edge, and sent out occasional little sprays of ink to dot the page.

To be a man and a gentleman had always seemed to be an easy thing to accomplish. To have the courage to face life and live it according to one's own moral principles. To stay within the bounds of law and religion. To treat other people with dignity and respect. To protect the weak and the innocent. It all sounded easy. He had never thought himself lacking in courage or principle.

But courage was not the question with him now. The question was what was right and what was wrong. What exactly was involved in treating another person with respect? In what way exactly was one to protect the weak? It was so easy to be a gentleman in the abstract, so easy to act the gentleman with the masses of people one met in the course of months and years. But it was not easy at all to know the right course of action to take with his own wife, with the person who mattered more to him than anyone else.

It had all started up again, this business with Sandersford. Just at a time when he had been hoping that perhaps she had finally put the past behind her. Just at a time when everything seemed to be going so marvelously right with their marriage. Since Christmas Day and its wonderful, magical ending he had dared to hope that perhaps she loved him now with an undivided love, notwithstanding all the emotions and passions of her past. And it was so difficult to persuade himself to settle for less than love. Respect, loyalty, affection even, just did not seem enough to satisfy him any longer.

But his hopes had been dashed again. That damned letter! Peregrine set down his pen and leaned back in his chair, one hand over his eyes.

Had he acted in the right way? He had found himself quite unable to break the seal of that letter. It was addressed to his wife. It was from the man who had once been her husband in all but name. The man she had loved. And still had powerful feelings for, even though he did not know the true nature of those feelings. He had not been able to open that letter and read it, even though she had brought it to him herself.

And so he had given it back to her. Was he mad? Was he a man? His wife's former lover had sent her a letter in secret, undoubtedly a love letter, and he had permitted her to read it, encouraged her almost. He had refused to interfere. Should he not have torn it to shreds and gone after Sandersford to ensure that he was never again inclined to interfere in the sanctity of his marriage?

But he could not. He could not play the high-handed husband. He could not keep a wife with him by force. He could not present a veneer of respectability to the world and have a festering sore of a marriage in private. He would rather lose her than keep her against her will.

But she had brought the letter to him, unopened. Why? Was she pleading for his help? Did she want him to take the burden of the problem on his own shoulders? Had he let her down? Was he forcing her into a course of action she did not want to take?

Why could they not talk about it? A huge silence seemed to surround the topic of Sandersford and everything he had been to her, and was. Why could they not speak of it, know each other's mind and heart? There are some things too deep and too painful for words, he concluded. He could face the prospect of losing Grace if she should ever decide that she must return to the lover of her past. But he could not face bringing on the moment, hearing the brutal truth from her lips in response to a question of his. He was a coward, then?

Peregrine reached the door of his office just as it opened and Grace came in. She held out a written sheet of paper to him.

"I have read the letter," she said. Her voice was quite toneless. "And I have written a reply." She held his eyes with her own.

He took the letter from her hand and folded it into the creases she had already made. He did not look down at all while he did so. "Then you must send it," he said. "Grace, why did you bring me his letter? And your reply? Do you need my help?" He bit his lip when tears sprang to her eyes.

"I did not want to do anything behind your back, Perry," she said.

He lifted one hand, changed his mind about laying it against her cheek, and set it on her shoulder. "May I help, Grace?" he asked.

She shook her head. "I wanted you to read the letter or tear it to shreds and forbid me ever to be in communication with Gareth again," she said. "That was foolish. You would never do anything like that, would you, Perry? For it would not solve anything but would certainly ruin our respect for each other."

"I want to stop your pain," he said. "I want to take it on myself. But I can't. That is one thing we can never take away from another person."

"He wants me to go to him," she said. "Or he will come here for me. I have written back to say that I will not go and that I will not see him if he comes here." She had her eyes tightly closed.

Peregrine's hand squeezed her shoulder unconsciously. "Do you love him, Grace?" he asked. Every blood vessel in his body seemed to be throbbing.

"No," she said. ."No, I don't love him. I hate him." There was a pause. "But there is something. I think perhaps I belong with him. I think perhaps I don't belong with you, Perry. I have wanted to do so, but I am afraid that I don't."

He could feel the pain of her first sob tearing at her as

she put her hands over her face. He could feel it because he shared it. He gripped both her shoulders bruisingly, not even realizing that he did so, and bent his head forward. He could not even pull her against him to comfort her and himself. She did not belong in his arms any longer.

It had happened then, his mind told him quite dispassionately. It had happened at last. It was too late now to unask the question. He had asked it, and she had replied. It had happened.

He whirled around suddenly, grasped a porcelain figurine that happened to be within his reach, and hurled it toward the fireplace. It smashed satisfyingly against the mantel, and the pieces tinkled noisily into the hearth.

"Damn it!" he said between his teeth. "Damn Sandersford. And damn you, Grace."

He stood facing away from her, his hands in fists at his sides, appalled by the echo of his own words. There was perfect silence behind him. She had stopped sobbing.

He was surprised by the calmness of his own voice a few minutes later as he moved forward to nudge together the pieces of porcelain in the hearth with the toe of his boot. "You will be wishing to leave, then?" he asked, and turned to her.

She looked at him with reddened, frightened eyes. "Leave?" she said. "Leave here? You are asking me to, Perry? Oh, God, has it come to this, then? But I don't want to go. I don't want to be with Gareth again. I want to be here with you. I want to be safe with you. But I have told you that I do not belong with you any longer. And you hate me now. How could you not? Oh, God, what is happening?"

"Perhaps we are both being hysterical," he said, turning and walking back to the desk, rearranging the objects lying on its surface, putting some distance between them. "I don't want you to leave, Grace. And you do not want to go. Not yet, anyway. You seem unsure of your feelings. Stay then until you are."

"That is unfair to you," she said.

He laughed rather grimly as he crumpled the sheet of paper on which he had been doodling earlier. "What, then?" he said. "I don't want you leaving me, Grace, when you are not even sure that you wish to do so and when I do not wish you to go. And I suppose I must be thankful that you have been honest with me. You might have hidden that letter." He turned to look at her. "Stay with me. Stay at least until you know you can no longer do so. I know you will tell me when the time comes." Was his voice as cold and abrupt as it sounded to his own ears? he wondered.

"When?" she whispered. "Are you so sure then of my final decision? Is it inevitable, Perry? And could you bear to have me stay permanently after all this?"

He smiled suddenly, unexpectedly, and just a little grimly. "Let us not be morbid," he said. "I think my head is going to explode into a thousand pieces if I don't get it into the outdoors immediately. Come for a walk with me, Grace. Look, it is trying to snow out there."

"I can't, Perry," she said.

"Yes, you can." His smile had taken a firmer hold of his face. "We will take a brisk walk along the lane. I must have you with me to make beauty and poetry out of those heavy gray clouds and all the bare branches. No, you are not to cry again. I forbid it. Absolutely. Shall I send someone up for your outdoor things, or will you go yourself?"

"I'll go," she said.

So, Peregrine thought, completing the unnecessary task of tidying his desk after Grace had left, life continued on, did it? Tears dried, wounds were bound up, and life continued. Only in grand tragedy did a catastrophe happen in one sweep. In real life it came in a series of small agonies. And perhaps in the end it never came at all. Or perhaps it did. But regardless of the outcome, life continued. Life had to continue.

He glanced uneasily at the porcelain pieces on the hearth and pulled the bell rope to summon a servant.

The news that Grace's father and brother were coming to stay at Reardon Park with the latter's wife and daughter created a stir of pleased anticipation in the village of Abbotsford and the surrounding areas. These people had discovered the year before, of course, that Lady Lampman was not as alone in the world as they had once thought but that she did have family members whom she had visited with her husband. But to know that those people were coming was a great salve to their curiosity and a boost to their social expectations, which tended to lag during the winter, once Christmas was over.

The added news that Lord Amberley was to entertain Viscount Sandersford at about the same time added an extra buzz of excitement. Was he an eligible gentleman? Mrs. Morton asked Mrs. Carrington. Mrs. Courtney, present when the question was asked, privately lamented the fact that her Susan was still away at her Aunt Henshaw's and not like to be home again until April.

The Earl of Amberley himself was surprised by the news of the imminent arrival of an uninvited guest. His acquaintance with Lord Sandersford was of short duration and was not by any means an intimate one. But his sister reminded him that the viscount was a neighbor of Lady Lampman's brother and had known Lady Lampman herself all his life.

"To be sure," he said. "I had forgotten. And he had them all out to Hammersmith for a few days, did he not, just before Perry and Lady Grace came home? I daresay he wants to be a part of this gathering at Reardon Park."

"He is very handsome," Madeline said. "Should I fall in love with him, do you suppose, Edmund? Or is he a little old for me?"

"Heaven help us," her brother said. "You fall in love often enough when we are in London, Madeline. Can you not wait until we return there before doing so again?"

"Oh, I suppose, so," she said with a laugh. "Besides, I don't believe I could bring myself to fall in love with a gentleman beyond the age of thirty. And Lord Sandersford must be closer to forty. What a strange man he must be, though, to invite himself to the home of a virtual stranger."

"I am quite sure he knows of my friendship with Perry," Lord Amberley said. "And I am very pleased to be able to oblige Perry."

The Countess of Amberley began to organize a dinner party

in honor of her son's guest and Sir Peregrine's, and Mrs.
Morton had to pay a call on both Mrs. Cartwright and Mrs.
Carrington before she could decide whether to give a card
party or a charades party. She finally decided on a combin-
ation of both.

Everyone agreed that the end of February was the very
best time to be expecting visitors in the neighborhood. The
winter had made everyone dreary, and spring had only just
begun to show a few tantalizing signs that it was on the way.
Lady Lampman and Sir Peregrine had told them after church
that there were a few brave snowdrops blooming already at
Reardon Park. But then everyone knew that the Lady
Lampman had only to look at a patch of bare soil to persuade
a flower to grow there. It hardly seemed fair, Mrs. Courtney
commented cheerfully to her spouse during the carriage ride
home.

It was strange, Grace thought, how life went on. No matter
how bad things became, provided one survived at all, one
somehow picked up the pieces of the disaster and went on
living. She had proved it in the past. Gareth's leaving. The
scandal of her pregnancy. Gareth's letter announcing his
marriage. Her son's death. The dreadful quarrel between
Paul and their father. Her leaving with him. Life had
continued. She had felt dead for nine years, had even
welcomed the land of the half-dead. But she had lived on,
and she had eventually come back to full life.

And now she was surviving again. Barely surviving, she
sometimes felt, but living on nonetheless. She was still with
Perry. Somehow she was still with him. And not just living
in the same house with him. They talked to each other, read
together, walked together, watched together for signs of
spring. They treated each other with a wary sort of courtesy.
No, perhaps with more than just courtesy.

It was true that they no longer lived as man and wife. She
had waited in their bedchamber the night after Gareth's letter
came, the night after Perry's terrible outburst, shivering, to
tell him that she could no longer share the room with him,

not at least until she could offer him her undivided loyalty. But she had waited all night. He had not come then or any night since.

She missed him dreadfully. And she wanted him. But she could make no move toward him until she was quite sure of herself beyond any doubt at all. She was quite sure that she loved him and always would. But then, she had known that for a long time. It was herself she was unsure of. She was not quite sure that she belonged with him, that she deserved him, that she had anything of value to offer their marriage. She was almost sure, but not quite.

And was their reconciliation entirely up to her anyway? Would Perry take her back even if she asked? She had been terribly disloyal to their marriage. And he had been furiously angry during that one short outburst when he had thrown the figurine. Could she expect that he would willingly forgive her to the extent of returning to their bed again?

She was glad that her family was coming. Their presence would be a distraction for both Perry and herself. And she had a feeling too that if ever she was going to straighten out her life finally, it was not only Perry with whom she had to deal but them too. And she missed her father. Having seen him again the year before, she realized how much of both their lives they had wasted apart from each other.

She felt sick on the afternoon when Lord Amberley paid a call on them and announced with a smile that Lord Sandersford was to be his guest for a few days at the end of the month. She did not dare look at Perry.

"Sandersford is your father's neighbor, Lady Lampman?" the earl asked politely.

"Yes," she said. "We grew up together."

"You will be happy to have both your family and a neighbor close to you again, then," he said.

"Yes." She called on the calmness of manner that had seen her through nine years with Paul.

"I thought you were on your way back to London soon, Edmund," Peregrine said. His voice sounded quite normal.

"Yes," Lord Amberley said. "Mama and Madeline are

eager to be on the way. Dominic left two weeks ago. But we can wait until our guest leaves. I will be quite happy to have him, I do assure you.''

Grace felt sick. And yet almost relieved at the same time. There had been a sense of waiting for the past two months. Nothing was over. Nothing had been settled. Now something would happen once and for all. And the confidence was growing in her that this time she was going to free herself from the power Gareth had exerted over her in one form or another for much of her life. This time she was going to take the initiative. And this time she would win.

Her only hope was to fight now, years and years too late. But, no, it was not too late. She was thirty-seven years old, but she was not dead yet or anywhere close to death, she hoped. She had a great deal of living yet to do and a great deal to live for. Oh, a very great deal.

On the whole, she was glad that Gareth was coming to Amberley Court. Even though Perry looked white and tense in the days between Lord Amberley's visit and the arrival of her family. Even though he looked at her with haunted eyes. Yes, she was glad. Soon she would be able to offer him her undivided loyalty, if he was willing to accept it. Her love too, if he wanted it. The look on his face made her hope. But she would not think of that yet.

Not until she was quite, quite sure of herself.

All the expected visitors arrived before the end of February. Grace's family, who came first, were all in the best of health. Lord Pawley was even walking without his cane and seemed quite content to sit most of the time in a room with his famly rather than keep to his own room. Priscilla was her usual exuberant self and had almost eight months' worth of news to divulge to her uncle and aunt.

It was several days later before word reached Reardon Park that Lord Sandersford had arrived at Amberley Court. But Ethel clearly knew that he was coming. She took the first opportunity of their being alone together to raise the matter with Grace.

"I should not have accepted that letter to send to you," she said. "It was quite against my better judgment to do so, and I have never been able to summon the courage to confess to Martin. I sent it eventually only in the hope of saving you from just such an encounter as this, Grace. Or maybe you have invited him. Maybe you welcome his coming. I don't know. I just wish I had not got involved."

"You must not blame yourself," Grace said. "And you must not be afraid for me or for Perry."

Ethel looked both dubious and troubled, but Grace would say no more. She followed Peregrine to his dressing room after the rector brought them the news that Lord Amberley's visitor had arrived. She stood inside the door while he looked at her in some surprise and dismissed his valet.

"Perry," she said as soon as they were alone, "I wish you to invite Lord Sandersford to tea one afternoon. Preferably tomorrow. Will you?"

He looked at her cold, set face and did not smile. "Yes, if you wish, Grace," he said. "I shall invite Edmund and the countess too. I will suggest tomorrow."

"Thank you," she said.

They looked at each other for a few moments longer, and then she turned to leave because there really was nothing more to say.

And they did not see each other alone again until late the following afternoon. In the morning Grace went into Abbotsford with Ethel while Peregrine took Martin and Priscilla to call on the Mortons.

The arrival in the afternoon of Lord Amberley, his mother, and their guest, and the added presence of Mr. Courtney and his daughter, Susan, who had returned early from her aunt's, made the whole situation somewhat more comfortable, Grace found after curtsying to Gareth and motioning him to a chair close to her own. She could better ignore the tense look on her husband's face, a look that she knew was mirrored on her own, the disapproving frowns of her father and Martin, and the anxious, guilt-ridden glances of Ethel.

She waited until Susan and Priscilla were in the midst of

an excited exchange of views on fashion and everyone else seemed to be fully engaged in conversation before rising to her feet.

"May I show you our garden, Lord Sandersford?" she asked politely. "I am afraid there is not a great deal of color yet, but the daffodils are in bud."

He rose to his feet, a smile on his handsome face.

Grace was fully aware of his great height, the breadth of his shoulders, the aura of masculinity that had always surrounded Gareth from as far back as she could remember.

"I would be delighted, ma'am," he said.

She did not look at Peregrine. She held her shawl tightly about her as they went outside and walked past the flower beds and down into the orchard.

"I thought you might make it difficult for me," he said. "I thought you might refuse to see me at first."

"No," she said. "I have been looking forward to your coming, Gareth." She looked up into his handsome, smiling face. "I have a number of things that I wish to say to you."

"There is only one that I wish to hear," he said. "When will you come away with me, Grace? Immediately? There is no point in further delay, you know."

"I will not be going with you," she said, "ever. And for one simple reason, Gareth. I have no wish to do so. No, perhaps there is another reason even more important. I have no need to go away with you. You see, I have finally forgiven myself for the past and I have no further need to punish myself with you."

He laughed. "What is this?" he said. "You have been feeling guilty, Grace? You have been punishing yourself with me? Whatever do you mean?"

"I sinned against all the moral laws of our society and church when I gave myself to you," she said. "My father's faith in me was broken when he knew I was with child. I brought great shame and embarrassment to him and Martin. I caused a dreadful rift between Papa and Paul. And Paul died without any reconciliation between them. I gave birth to an illegitimate child and he died at a time when I was not taking care of him. I was sleeping that afternoon, having persuaded myself that I had a headache as a result of a fancied insult from Ethel. And after Paul's death I took an easy route to securing my future by marrying a man ten years my junior, who offered out of the kindness of his heart. That is a great deal of guilt for one human being to carry around, Gareth."

"Nonsense," he said. "We were in love; what we did was not wrong. And everyone else on your list made a free decision, Grace. You are not responsible for other people's actions."

"We were not in love," she said quietly. "You used the wrong pronoun, Gareth. *I* was in love. *You* have never loved. You do not know the meaning of the word. I fed your self-love when we were young by worshipping you and allowing you to dominate me. I satisfied your appetite for the last few weeks you were at home until you could get away and meet more desirable females. And wealthier ladies. You did not love me. And you never had the least intention of marrying me."

"That is not true," he said. "You know it is not true, Grace. Ours is the love of a lifetime. It is still more powerful than any other emotion in our lives. You are afraid to admit the truth."

"No," she said. "At last I am not afraid to admit it, Gareth. It has always been easier to believe that we shared a great love. But I was a fool and a dupe, and I can only feel enormous relief that you were not just a little more honorable than you were. I would have married you and now I would either be living a life of great misery or be so thoroughly convinced that your selfish, amoral attitude to life was right that I would have lost all sense of right and wrong."

"I will prove to you that you still love me," he said, grasping her arm in a painful grip.

"I have done a great deal of wrong in my life," Grace said, "but I have atoned and will atone. It is hardest to forgive oneself for the dead, but I have done it. I took Papa to see Paul's grave yesterday, and he told me that he admired Paul more after their quarrel than ever before in his life. So maybe there was some small good in their quarrel, after all. And

I have forgiven myself—finally—for Jeremy. I was wrong
to lie with you, Gareth, but Jeremy was not wrong. And I
have looked back and seen that what Perry once told me was
right: it is never wrong to give life. I devoted myself to my
son utterly while he lived. And I was not neglecting him at
the end. It was perfectly acceptable to send him off with a
governess. Ethel had done so with Oswald and Priscilla. I
was not to blame. He lived as happy a life as I could give
him. I have forgiven myself.''

"The child was part of me," he said. "You can have me
to love instead, Grace. For the rest of our lives.''

"No," she said. "I do not quite understand why you
pursue me now, Gareth. You never did love me, and I am
no longer young. I think it must be the challenge. Had I
returned home destitute and broken after Paul's death, I think
you would not have afforded me a second glance. But I was
married when you met me again, and happily married, to
a man whose youth must have challenged your masculinity.
I think that must be it. But I do not really care. Whatever
your motive, you have failed. I have no feelings for you at
all, not even hatred.''

"You are not happily married," he said fiercely. "To that
boy, Grace? Nonsense! You feel a mother's concern for him.
You are afraid he will be hurt by your leaving. He will
survive, never fear.''

"One wrong which I have been longest in forgiving myself
for," she said, "was marrying Perry. Guilt over that has
haunted me for almost two years. And I allowed you to fan
it. Only recently have I realized that in fact I did no wrong
and that there need be no guilt. I love Perry with all of my
being, and though I have made him suffer because my guilt
drove me back into your power for a long time, I will spend
the rest of my life trying to make him happy. Perry married
me freely and has not failed in his affection for me and his
kindness toward me even during this past difficult year.
Perhaps he should be married to a younger woman. But the
fact is that he is married to me and has shown no sign of
being sorry it is so. You cannot destroy my marriage, Gareth,

or even spoil it any longer. You have no more power over me."

"Liar, Grace," he said. "Oh, liar."

"Yes," she said, "you will have to convince yourself that I am being untruthful. I am not sure that you are able to cope with failure, Gareth. But then I have not really known you for sixteen years. Perhaps I do you an injustice. Perhaps you have a stronger character than I think."

"I love you," he said. "That is the strongest fact of my life, Grace."

"Then you must prove it by leaving me to my happiness," she said.

He still held to her arm. His eyes smoldered into hers. "I could win you if I wanted," he said. "I could make you admit that you love me, Grace. And I will do so one day, I do assure you."

She shook her head. "Tea will be ready," she said. "We must go inside. I am not going to ask you to cut short your visit to Lord Amberley, Gareth, or to stay away from me in future. I know I would waste my breath to do so. But I will tell you this: it will not matter to me in the future how often you put yourself in my way. It simply will not matter."

He looked searchingly into her eyes for a few moments before releasing her arm. "Do you know, Grace?" he said. "If you had been like this at the age of one-and-twenty, I think I might have married you, after all, and be hanged to all the money that Martha brought me."

They walked side by side and in silence back to the house.

14

Peregrine went outside to see the Courtneys on their way. They were taking Priscilla with them, on the request of Susan, who appeared perfectly delighted to have a fashionable young lady to befriend. Mr. Courtney assured Ethel and Martin that Miss Howard would be returned to them safe and sound before bedtime.

Lord Amberley and his mother did not stay much longer. They rose to leave as soon as their guest came back indoors with Grace.

"You have a lovely garden," Lord Sandersford said.

"I can bear to look at it now," Lady Amberley said with a smile for Grace. "But don't expect me to come anywhere near here when all the daffodils are in bloom. Or later, during the summer. I shall be just too envious. Lady Lampman will have at least twice as many flowers as anyone else within five miles, I do assure you, Lord Sandersford."

Lord Amberley shook hands with Peregrine and bowed to Grace. "We may expect you all to dinner, then, the day after tomorrow?" he asked.

"Yes." Grace smiled. "That will be very pleasant, my lord."

She went outside with her husband again to wave the Amberley carriage on its way. But there was no chance to talk. Martin had come out behind them.

"You are fortunate to have such pleasant neighbors," he said. "Do you feel like a game of billiards, Perry?"

* * *

It was good to have visitors, Peregrine thought hours later. One was forced to live and function, to carry on talking and eating and doing. Even when one felt like curling up in a corner somewhere and ceasing to live, or like lashing out with one's tongue and one's fists at everyone who had the misfortune to cross one's path.

She had asked him to invite Sandersford to his own home, and he had meekly complied. And she had asked Sandersford to step out into the garden alone with her, and they had been out there for almost half an hour. While her own husband sat inside conversing pleasantly with their other visitors. Was he an utter fool? Was she making a fool of him?

But, no, he would not believe that. *Could* not believe that. She would tell him. When the time came for her to leave, she would come and tell him first. He stood at the window of the bedchamber that had been his for the past two months and leaned his forehead against the windowpane. And he gave himself up to a rare moment of self-pity. And loneliness. He saw her every day, lived with her, talked with her, and was probably more lonely than he would be if she had left him already. Then he would be able to allow the healing to begin. Now he waited in anticipation of a wound that would tear him apart.

He turned at the light tap on the door and tied the belt of his dressing gown around him. "Come in," he called without moving.

He watched Grace in silence as she stepped inside the room and closed the door behind her. She was not beautiful, was she? He could not remember ever thinking her quite so when she had lived at the rectory with Paul. Her face was too narrow, her eyes too large in comparison with the rest of her features. And she was not young. There was no youthful bloom in her face, only the character that seven-and-thirty years of living had carved there. Perhaps no one else in the world would look at her and call her beautiful. But everyone else would look at her with the eyes only. To him she was more beautiful than the loveliest rose in her garden.

She watched him from her large eyes. She wore a white silk robe over her nightgown. Her dark hair was loose down her back.

"Perry," she said, "are you willing to take me back?"

"Take you back?" He looked at her in incomprehension. "I have never sent you away, Grace."

"We have not been a married couple since Christmas," she said. "Will you have me back again? Will you forgive me?"

"Have you back?" He frowned. "I have not put you from me. You told me that you did not think you belonged with me. I would not force myself on you, Grace."

"I have broken his power over me," she said. "I do not love him, Perry. I have not done so since months before Jeremy was born. But I have been afraid of him."

"Afraid?" He took one step toward her. "Had he threatened you? Hurt you? Why did you not tell me, Grace?"

She shook her head. "I was afraid that he was my punishment," she said. "My destiny, I suppose. I had been happy for a year when I met him again, and then I thought that perhaps I did not deserve happiness. I had done a great deal of wrong in my life."

"We all have," he said.

"I know." She clasped her hands before her and looked earnestly at him. "I have come to realize that. And I cannot do anything to change the past. I can influence only the present and the future. And I do not wish Gareth to have a part in either. I have told him that. And I have told him that he may put himself in my way as much as he wishes in the future without in any way upsetting me. I have no feeling for him at all except indifference. I do not even hate him any longer."

"You want to continue with our marriage?" Peregrine realized suddenly that he was holding his breath.

"Yes." She moved her hands to clasp behind her. "If you wish it, Perry. I fully realize that perhaps you will not. I will return home with Papa and Martin if you would prefer it."

"Grace." He spoke her name softly, reproachfully. "You

are my wife. And will remain so while we both live. I would not have divorced you, you know. You would have been free to go, but you would have remained my wife."

She tried to smile. She grimaced instead.

"I have missed you," he said softly.

"Have you? And I you." But she held up her hands sharply in front of her as he moved toward her. "Perry," she said, "I am with child."

He stopped in his tracks and stared at her.

"It is true," she said. "I called on Doctor Hanson this morning when Ethel came into Abbotsford with me. I thought that for some reason I could not conceive, Perry, but it is not so. I am able to give you a child. I think it must have happened at Christmastime."

"Grace." Peregrine felt as if he were looking at her down a long tunnel. "Is it safe?"

"At my age?" she said. "Doctor Hanson says that I seem perfectly healthy and that I should not have any great problems. You are pleased, Perry?"

He moved toward her at last and took her hands in a firm grip. "I will not forgive myself if you . . . if anything happens to you," he said.

"Having a child is always a risk," she said. "But women older than I am are giving birth every day, Perry. And it is not my first." She flushed. "There is no need to be especially frightened for me. I am not afraid. This is something I want to do. I want to give you a child."

"Oh, Grace." He lifted one of her hands to lay against his cheek and turned his head to kiss the palm. "We men are selfish brutes. For the first few months of our marriage I confess I did worry a little. I thought perhaps you would not want all the burdens of motherhood again. But then I forgot the danger to you and concerned myself only with my own pleasure."

"You are not happy, are you?" she said. "I thought it might please you to have a son. Or a daughter."

"A son," he repeated, "or a daughter." He felt a buzzing in his head as though he were going to faint. "We are going to have a child, Grace. A baby." He laughed rather shakily.

"Of course I want a child. Oh, of course I am happy."

He caught her to him then and held her, his eyes tightly closed, terror for his wife's health and very life warring for control of his mind with elation at the knowledge that his child was growing in her.

"Perry?" She lifted her head for his kiss.

And, oh, it had been so long. His arms had been so empty without her, his bed so lonely. He had spent two months trying to condition himself to the probability that she would never occupy either again. But he had missed her. God, he had missed her. He wanted Christmas back again. He wanted it to be like that with her again. When they had started a new life in her.

He put her from him and swallowed. "You are with child," he said.

"It does not matter." She flushed. "Doctor Hanson talked about it. He said it does not matter until the last months."

He touched his fingers to her face. "In our bedchamber, then," he said. "Not here. I heartily dislike this room, Grace."

She smiled and turned back to the door.

Peregrine settled his wife's head on his arm almost an hour later and made sure that the blankets were close about her. She was warm and naked against him. And relaxed. It had been as good as at Christmastime. She had made love with him, and he had felt her come to him at the end. He rested his cheek against the top of her head. And she was his. She did not love Sandersford, had not loved him for years. She wanted to continue with their marriage. And she was with child by him. They would have a nursery in their home. A son or daughter. Their child, his and Grace's.

If the child survived. And if Grace survived. But he would not think such morbid thoughts. Childbirth was always dangerous, though it was also the most natural process in the world. He would not expect the worst. He would not feel guilt at having so carelessly impregnated a woman of close to forty years. As she had said, this child would not be her first, and women older than she were giving birth every day. Seven-and-thirty was not so very old. She was his wife. He had loved her. The child had sprung from his love.

And he would not allow the thought to poison his happiness that perhaps he had trapped her, after all, despite his wish to leave her free to decide her own future. She must have suspected the truth for the past month. She had found out beyond all doubt only that morning, a few hours before her confrontation with Sandersford. But she did not love him, she had said. She had been afraid of him, afraid that he was her destiny, and not wanting it to be so. She would not have wanted to go with him even if she were not with child.

It was so. She was his. Perhaps she even loved him, though she had never said those words and he had never asked her. He tightened his arm about her and pressed his cheek to her head. She lifted one hand to his chest and murmured something in her sleep.

Ethel had been shocked. "You are quite sure, Grace?" she had asked in the carriage on the way into Abbotsford.

"No," Grace had said. "I am going to Doctor Hanson so that I may be sure. But I cannot think what else it can be. I am far too young for the change of life. And I believe it is true. There is a certain feeling in the mornings—not a biliousness exactly, not a dizziness exactly—that I remember from when I was carrying Jeremy."

"Is it wise?" Ethel had asked. "I mean . . ."

"You mean that I am far too old to be giving birth," Grace said. She flushed. "But, yes, it is wise. Perry deserves children just like any other man. And I want to give him a child. Just this one. There probably will be no more. It has taken two years this time. I love him, you see. And I want his child for me too, for purely selfish reasons."

"I did not mean . . ." Ethel leaned forward and touched Grace's hand. "I did not mean to insult you, Grace, truly I did not. I just never thought of such a thing, which is very foolish because you have been married only a short while and you are still quite young, so it is only natural that you would both wish for a family. I am happy for you."

And during the carriage ride home, after they had paid

a call upon the Misses Stanhope and the call on the doctor, Ethel took Grace's hand in hers and squeezed it.

"I am so very happy for you, Grace," she said. "I have been thinking of it all morning, and I have been growing as excited for you as if it were myself. Everything is all right between you and Perry, then? I have been terribly afraid . . . And Gareth at Amberley Court."

Grace shook her head. "Gareth is my past," she said, "my foolish past. Perry is my present, and he and our child are my future."

"And yet Gareth has been invited for tea?" Ethel said uneasily.

"Yes." Grace smiled at her. "I suppose there must be a definite ending to something that has figured so large in my life. My love for Gareth was a very powerful force, Ethel. And without Gareth there would not have been Jeremy. And Jeremy is still as important to me as Perry and this new child are to me now. This afternoon will be the end with Gareth. Then I can start living my present and looking forward to my future."

"Oh, be careful." Ethel looked troubled. "Do be careful, Grace. That man frightens me."

Grace merely smiled.

"Grace." Ethel sat back in her seat and looked uncomfortable. "I have wanted to say this to you since last year. In my mind I have said it a dozen times, but it is so hard to do so when I am face to face with you."

Grace looked inquiringly at her.

"I feel such guilt," Ethel said. "I used to hate you, you know." Her face was blotched with uneven patches of color. "You were so beautiful and so self-assured. And even when you had Jeremy, you bore yourself so proudly that I was furious with you and quite determined to hate him too. I couldn't, of course. He was such a handsome child and so good-natured. But I was jealous. And I hated you for the time you devoted to him and Priscilla and Oswald too, when I was so frequently tired with those headaches I have always suffered from. And your papa always used to watch Jeremy so hungrily when he thought no one was looking."

"It is all best forgotten," Grace said, twisting the rings on her finger.

"Yes," Ethel said, "but it must be spoken of first. Because I like you now, Grace, and I think we can become friends if there is no barrier between us. I was so wretched with guilt after you left. I thought of you with Jeremy gone when I still had my children, and with Gareth gone and Papa and Martin estranged from you. And I never had the courage to write. I wanted to, but I never could. And when you wrote and I knew you were married, and after you had accepted my invitation to visit, I wanted nothing more than to write again and tell you not to come, after all. I was too embarrassed to face you."

"We do terrible things to our own lives and those of the people around us, don't we?" Grace said. "So many years wasted, Ethel. But we must put them behind us. If we are to make amends, we must do so. For I have been at least equally to blame for the coldness there has been between us. How I hated you for having the respectability of marriage when I had been deserted and left with an illegitimate child. And we might have been sisters all these years."

"Well," Ethel said, "we will have to make up for lost time. How is Perry going to react, Grace? I do wish I could see his face when you tell him. He will make a wonderful father, you know. And I know from experience that you will be a wonderful mother."

They smiled at each other, a little embarrassed, and both turned to observe the scenery passing the carriage windows. There would be an awkwardness for perhaps a day or two. But there would be a friendship after that. And they both felt a warmth in the knowledge, though they could not yet quite share their thoughts.

Somehow, no one quite knew how, everyone in the neighborhood knew of the impending event long before it became evident to the eye. No one doubted the integrity of Doctor Hanson. He would certainly not have violated a patient's trust. And Grace and Peregrine told no one apart from Grace's family and Peregrine's mother by letter.

Of course, Mrs. Hanson had been at home to entertain Ethel while Grace had consulted with the doctor. And she had been known on occasion to whisper confidences to her close friends, the Misses Stanhope, on the strict understanding that the secret stop with them. And the Misses Stanhope were known to have the greatest trust in the silence of their friend Mrs. Morton. And Mrs. Morton was known fondly to the rest of her neighbors as a bit of a gossip. It was never malicious gossip, of course, and could therefore be readily forgiven. There was nothing malicious about spreading the glad tidings that dear Lady Lampman was in a delicate condition.

She was a little old to be having her first child, to be sure, Mrs. Courtney confided to Mrs. Cartwright, but she herself had been somewhat past her thirtieth year when she had had Susan, and Susan's birth had been the easiest of the six she had been through, counting the stillborn one—her second. And there was certainly nothing wrong with Susan. She was quite as pretty as any other girl in the neighborhood, Miss Morton and Lady Madeline Raine included, for all they were in a class a little above Susan's.

Dear, dear Sir Perry, Miss Letitia said to her sister with a sigh and a sentimental tear, would be so pleased. Imagine him a father and it seemed but yesterday he was a rogue of a boy up to no end of tricks. How delightful it would be if the child turned out to be a son and they could have another little mischief to look forward to.

And to think that Lady Lampman had been married from their very own home, Miss Stanhope reminded every one of their neighbors, some of them on two separate occasions. Such a dear, dignified lady.

"Well, Viola," Mr. William Carrington said when his wife had hurried into his library with the news after the departure of Mrs. Morton, "so Perry and his good lady have been doing their duty to the human race, have they? And decidedly tardy they have been too. How long have they been married?"

"Two years," she said. "I just hope that it will be safe

at her age, William, considering that it is her first. Poor dear lady, I do hope so.''

''She cannot be very much younger than you, Viola,'' her husband said. ''And we completed our family fifteen years ago. They put us to shame, do they not? I feel a distinct gleam developing in my eye. Look closely now. Can you see it?''

His wife threw up her hands and shrieked. ''William,'' she said. ''What an idea. At our age? It makes me blush just to think of doing—you know. But to have another child!''

''Well, then,'' he said, ''you should know better than to regale me with such disturbing news, Viola. I am afraid I am just going to have to make you blush, my dear. I feel quite like doing—you know.''

''William,'' she said, blushing quite sufficiently to draw a roguish gleam to his eye. ''Not here. Someone might walk in at any moment. Oh, do pray remove your hand and behave yourself.''

''In our room, then,'' he said. ''You may precede me there, Viola, since you would clearly die of mortification to have me lead you there in full view of the servants.''

''William,'' she said. ''Sometimes I think you will never grow old gracefully.'' She withdrew from the room without further argument.

Her husband closed his book and replaced it on the shelf unhurriedly before going in pursuit.

The Earl of Amberley, his mother, and his sister were preparing to leave for London and the Season when Mr. Courtney broke the news to them during a visit with his daughter.

''I am so very glad for Perry,'' Lady Amberley said to her son when they were alone. ''He is a man who needs to be surrounded by children. I have been very much afraid that they were unable to have a family of their own.''

''I think the marriage has been quite successful,'' Lord Amberley said. ''They seem fond of each other, would you not say, Mama?''

She nodded. ''He seems so devoted to her that I wonder

sometimes if perhaps she is a domestic tyrant," she said, and frowned. "But that is unkind. I do hope I am wrong. And I am glad that she is to have a child. Every woman should have that experience."

It seemed that Mrs. Hanson was not privy to all her husband's secrets. Word certainly did not get past the doctor that Lady Grace Lampman's baby was in fact not her first. He had completely hidden his shock behind the cool professional manner that he presented to all his patients under all circumstances. But the fact might certainly make the birth a little easier for her, he had explained, though there was no knowing when the pregnancies were fifteen years apart. There were, however, dangers to both the mother and the child when the mother was well past her thirtieth year.

Lady Lampman was, of course, in good health and had looked after herself well and kept herself fit, he said. Her chances were good. But he would not lie to her and assure her that there was no danger.

Grace lied to Peregrine in that one detail only. She assured him on that first night and during the months to come that there was no danger at all beyond the ordinary. And she refused utterly to give in to fear. It was there, and sometimes she awoke in a cold sweat in the middle of the night. But she was not going to give in to it. She would curl into Peregrine's sleeping form for warmth and comfort and concentrate on her happiness.

And she was very, very happy. Happier than she had been at any time in her life. Happier than she had ever dreamed of being. If only she could live through this pregnancy. If only the child would live and be healthy. If only it could be a son. A son for her to give her husband.

But she would not think of the ifs. She was going to give Perry an heir. She was not going to give him a chance ever to regret marrying a woman so much older than he. She was going to make sure that never again would the laughter be in danger of dying out of his life. And the future was hers. Theirs. He had taken her back. He had wanted her, said that he had missed her, said that she would always have remained his wife even if she had gone off with Gareth.

And she had his child in her, making her tired, making her feel nauseated in the mornings, growing in her, very much there in her even though he did not show for several months or move in her enough for her to feel. She had all the bulk and weight and ungainliness of advanced pregnancy to look forward to and all the agony of childbirth. She was entirely, utterly, deliriously happy.

Lord Sandersford had left Amberley Court the day after the dinner given there in his honor. He sent his regrets to Mrs. Morton, with the explanation that urgent and unexpected business made his immediate return home imperative.

Everyone at Reardon Park had attended the dinner, though Priscilla had confided to Grace with a giggle that it was a great shame that Lord Eden was not still there. But Lady Madeline would be there, and Walter Carrington, who was very young, to be sure—only one year her senior—but of pleasing appearance and easy manners.

Lord Sandersford, dressed with London elegance, looked extremely handsome and had clearly set out to behave with the most engaging of manners. But Grace was not to be intimidated. She did nothing during the evening to seek him out and nothing to avoid him. When he suggested after dinner that she partner him for a hand of cards with Lady Amberley and Mr. Carrington, she complied with a smile for all three and a remark to Mr. Carrington that he would not find her so easy to defeat as he had at Christmas. And she briefly touched Peregrine's hand with her fingertips when he rested it on her shoulder as he came to stand behind her.

Lord Sandersford gave her an enigmatic smile when she took her leave of him later in the evening. "I will be leaving here in the morning, Grace," he said.

"Will you?" she said. "I will wish you a safe journey, then."

"No regrets?" he asked. "No last-minute panic? If you are to change your mind, it must be done now, Grace. I have decided that I will not be coming back."

"I am happy here, Gareth," she said. "Very happy."

"Damn him," he said, taking her hand and lifting it to his lips. "I never thought to lose a lady I fancied to a damned milksop. It is a humbling experience, my love."

"Good-bye, Gareth." Grace smiled.

"What a very strange man," Lady Amberley said to her son after luncheon the next day, their guest having taken his departure. "Why did he come, do you suppose, Edmund?"

"I don't know, Mama," he said. "But I was watching him last evening. I had the strangest feeling that perhaps he is sweet on Lady Grace Lampman."

"On Lady Lampman?" she said. "Oh, surely not. He is such a very handsome and charming man."

"Lady Lampman is not without beauty," he said. "I think she was probably extraordinarily handsome as a girl. I sometimes wonder about her past. There was never a mention of a family while her brother was alive, was there? Yet last spring she and Perry took themselves off to visit that family. And now a mysterious suitor from the past perhaps?" He grinned.

"Nonsense, Edmund," she said with a laugh. "You cannot possibly make a romantic figure out of Lady Lampman for all that I like and respect her."

"I think she probably jilted Sandersford at the altar twenty years ago," Lord Amberley said, "and ran away with her brother to hide from his wrath. And now he has found her again and is trying to convince her to run from Perry. Grand romance triumphant at last."

"Edmund!" She laughed merrily. "Now I know what you must do during all the hours you like to spend alone. You are writing novels. Your secret is out. My son the novelist."

"She in the meantime has grown passionately fond of Perry," Lord Amberley said. "And the lover has been sent on his way disconsolate. He will doubtless expire from a broken heart."

"I have not been better entertained in years," she said, getting to her feet. "I would love to stay to hear more, dear, but I have promised to go with Madeline to visit Viola. It is time to return to ordinary, mundane life. How sad!'' She bent to kiss her son's cheek as she left the room.

15

Spring always brought mixed blessings to those who lived most of their days in the countryside or in a small village remote from any large urban center. There was the splendor of new life all around—new leaves on the trees, new flowers to cover the earth with color and fill the air with fragrance, new calves and colts to frisk about on spindly legs, new lambs with fresh white coats to frolic among the more staid, dirtier numbers of their elders, new warmth from a kindlier sun. And there was greater freedom and comfort of travel. One could bear to sit in a carriage for half an hour without piled blankets and heated bricks. And there was relief from winter chilblains.

But spring also took away to London or other large centers whole families, whose presence was sorely missed. Always the Earl of Amberley and his family. Last year Sir Peregrine and Lady Grace Lampman. This year the Carringtons. And Lady Lampman's family, whom everyone agreed were most genteel and amiable, returned home at the end of March. All were missed. And it would be summer before everyone could be expected to return and the round of social events be well enough attended to make them worth organizing again.

It was already quite evident to the eye that the rumors concerning Lady Grace Lampman's delicate condition were quite correct when unexpected and very welcome news reached the village from Amberley. The earl was returning early from London with the countess and the twins and Sir Cedric Harvey, close friend of the former earl's and a regular summer visitor at the court. And if that were not enough to raise everyone's spirits, there was the added detail that Mrs. Oats, the housekeeper, had been instructed to prepare for the arrival of three or four other visitors a week later. And then, as a final touch of pleasure, the Carringtons too returned home.

In the event, the return of the Carringtons was by no means the least of the events. Mrs. Carrington visited Mrs. Morton the day after her return home and left that poor lady in a perfect dither, since by the time her visitor had left, there were not enough hours left in the afternoon in which to call upon all her acquaintances with the news. She decided upon the Misses Stanhope, since at least she would have the satisfaction of observing the effects of the startling announcement on two separate faces.

The expected guests at Amberley Court were the earl's new fianceé and her mother and brother, no less. And it seemed that the betrothal had been contracted in great haste and under somewhat scandalous circumstances, Miss Purnell —that was the lady's name—having been hopelessly compromised by one of Lord Eden's pranks, which had been intended for Lady Madeline.

"Then why is it that Lord Eden is not marrying the lady?" Miss Stanhope asked with great good sense.

"No one seems to know," Mrs. Morton said, nodding sagely as if to indicate that she knew very well but felt it indelicate to gossip about such matters. "But the earl gave a grand garden party for his betrothed in London. The Carringtons were there."

"I daresay his lordship considered dear Lord Eden just too young to take a bride," Miss Letitia suggested. "But is she pretty, Mrs. Morton?"

"Quite handsome, according to Mrs. Carrington," Mrs. Morton replied. "Very dark in coloring."

"And do you suppose the nuptials will take place here?"

Miss Stanhope asked. "It would be entirely fitting. And before the summer is out, do you think?"

The ladies had a comfortable coze about all the possibilities surrounding the news. And Mrs. Morton went home with the satisfaction of knowing that she had created a stir in one household and that she would be sure to call upon Lady Lampman and the rector's wife and Mrs. Courtney and Mrs. Cartwright the next morning before the Misses Stanhope, whose morning it was to decorate the church with flowers, were abroad.

Grace was glad of the diversion presented by the new arrivals. Her pregnancy had made her restless. Nine months seemed altogether too long to wait for an event whose outcome was so very uncertain. And once the increased tiredness of the first months was behind her, she found herself full of energy and compelled to be busy every moment of the day. Even her embroidery, always one of her favorite pastimes, seemed far too passive an activity. She wanted to be out digging in her garden, striding along lanes and roadways, cleaning the books in the library from ceiling to floor.

Dr. Hanson had told her that she must rest, that physical activity must be cut to the minimum, that she must remain indoors except when she had a carriage to take her somewhere. And even then she must be sure not to travel on the rougher roads—and that command excluded almost every road in their neighborhood. Unfortunately, he had given this professional advice in Peregrine's hearing, though he had not mentioned the dangers that he had told Grace of during her first consultation with him.

And Perry was being very protective, fetching pillows for her back and a stool for her feet whenever she sat down, forbidding all work in the garden, and allowing sedate walks that were all too slow and all too short only under the severest of protests. It was very irksome.

And quite gloriously delightful. She had been so very alone for years and years. And now she had a man fussing over her, worrying over her health, giving her commands, and being quite insistent that she obey most of them. She saw a new side to Peregrine during those months. He had never been a man to give orders. He commanded respect entirely through the kindliness and integrity of his character. But he had been very angry the morning he had caught her on her hands and knees at the edge of a flower bed, picking out some weeds with her fingers, and had taken her quite ungently by the arm and conveyed her to the privacy of the library.

There he had told her, without the merest glint of humor in his eyes, that if he caught her doing any such thing again until after her confinement, he would forbid her to leave the house without his escort. She had not asked how he would enforce such a rule. She had had no doubt as she had listened to him in silence that somehow he would. It was only the second time she had ever seen him angry.

Memory of that incident could make her smile secretly for weeks afterward. And she would sit, restless and impatient, quietly sewing, her feet resting on a stool, for many hours when Perry was with her, his nose inevitably buried behind a book, glancing down with satisfaction and hidden excitement at the swelling that was her child, feeling him move in her and kick at her, knowing that when she got to her feet again she would feel the extra weight of him. And she would think that it was quite impossible to be any happier in this life. And she would shift in her chair, often drawing Peregrine's eyes and the offer to bring her another cushion, and wonder if the nine months would ever, ever be at an end.

The arrival of Lord Amberley's betrothed and her family necessarily brought more activity and more excitement into their lives. The earl had always been Peregrine's close friend. And she liked him too. He was rather like Peregrine in some ways. He was gentle and kindly. But he was far more reserved than Perry. One felt that one liked the man but that one really did not know him at all. But both felt that he deserved a good wife, one who would know him and understand him and make him happy.

Peregrine would not be able to forbid her to attend all the

social activities that must follow upon such an event, Grace thought with satisfaction. She would be able to forget her restlessness for a while.

And she was right. The only matter on which he was quite inflexible was that they not host any grand entertainment themselves. Nothing more grand than an invitation to tea.

"They will take one look at you and understand perfectly, Grace," he said with a grin. "And it is quite obvious that you have not been merely overindulging in food, or you would be fat all over."

And so they went to the Courtneys' dance and card party, where they met Miss Purnell for the first time. Grace liked her. She was darkly beautiful and quiet, though she was not shy. There was a poise and a charm about the girl that was somewhat at variance with her age. She must be about the age Grace had been when she had had Jeremy. And Grace thought that there was a fondness between the girl and her betrothed, though they danced together only once during the evening.

Grace was forbidden to dance, but she had accepted the command with a smile. "Very well, Perry," she had said. "I will be good, as you will see. But on one condition: you must not feel obliged to hover over me all evening. You must enjoy yourself."

"And I cannot enjoy myself by staying with you?" he had asked.

"No," she had said. "You know what I mean, Perry. You must promise."

"I promise," he had said solemnly, holding his right hand in the air.

But it was a mixed blessing, she found, this renewed spate of social activity. It curbed her restlessness, filled her days and her thoughts with activities that helped a long nine months to their end. But it reminded her again of how old she was to be bearing what everyone around her believed to be her first child. Much as she delighted in her growing bulk when she was at home, much as she liked to look at herself privately in a mirror, standing in profile, her hands over the rounded shape of her womb, which held Perry's child, in public she sometimes felt ungainly and unattractive. And embarrassed.

And she found herself again, as she had used to do, watching Perry when they were in company together, watching his gaiety, his smile, and his dancing eyes, listening to his laughter, and feeling that she was too old for him, too serious, too unattractive. There was no jealousy in her, only an unwilling and an unreasonable sadness.

Unreasonable because Perry had shown her nothing but affection since their marriage. And because since she had sent Gareth away and since she had told her husband that she was with child, his every look and action had shown concern for her as well as affection. She was the most fortunate of women. She was the happiest of women, she told herself over and over again.

There was only one thing lacking in her happiness. Only one very small detail. Perry had never said that he loved her, that she was all the world to him. It was a very small detail. His looks said those things. His actions said those things. And even if he did not feel that ultimate commitment to her, he was the kindest and most considerate of husbands. And he had given her a child and filled the one remaining emptiness in her life.

It must be her pregnancy, she decided, that was making her temperamental: delirious with happiness one moment, stirred by doubts and fears the next.

Peregrine, for his part, felt a similar mixture of emotions. On the one hand he was happier than he had been at any time in his life. Finally he felt that he could relax in the knowledge that his marriage would continue. And continue not just because it was too difficult and too troublesome to end, but because they both wished it to do so.

Grace had sent Sandersford on his way and claimed to feel nothing but indifference for him any longer. And her behavior during that dinner at Amberley had seemed to bear out her claim. She had shown no preference for her former lover or even any shrinking from him and no sign of distress after their final leave-taking.

The only apparent sadness she had shown since had been

at the churchyard where he had taken her and her father the
day before the latter returned home. The two of them had
cried in each other's arms at Paul's graveside while he had
stood quietly by. And of course she had been quiet and
dejected for two days after the departure of her family. But
that mood had paradoxically delighted him, showing as it
did that her reconciliation with them was complete. Even
the stern Martin had hugged Grace as if he had wanted to
break every bone in her body before following Ethel and
Priscilla inside their carriage.

It was very good, Peregrine found, to be able to relax
again, to know that his wife was his. It was good to talk with
her again on any topic that interested him, read to her, watch
her about the tasks he was willing to allow. It was good to
be free to love her again. And it was very good indeed to
watch her growing larger with their child, growing more
beautiful to his eyes with every passing day.

And he was terrified. Afraid that the child would die, either
during the nine months or—worse—at birth. How would he
ever comfort Grace if she should lose this second child,
coming as it was so long after the first? After the beloved
son who had died? He could survive the pain. The only
person he really needed was Grace, though he did of course
ache with longing to hold this child of theirs. But Grace?
Would she be destroyed by the loss of her baby?

And he was terrified that Grace would die. Would he be
as fearful if she were ten years younger? he wondered. Was
it natural to fear for the life of the woman one had
impregnated? He would not want to go on living without
Grace. He would have done so, of course, had she decided
to go with Sandersford. He would do it doubtless if she died
in childbed or from any other cause. But he would not want
to. And if it was the bearing of his child that killed her, he
did not think he would ever be able to talk himself back to
life again. Unknown to Grace, he had had a private talk with
Doctor Hanson, and he knew full well that the dangers that
faced both her and the child were only enhanced by her age.

He was aware of her restlessness, though he did not understand its causes. He knew that it irked her to sit indoors and

allow him to coddle her, to watch the gardeners do every task in her beloved garden while all she could do was walk sedately through it, her fingers itching to get down among the flowers to perform their miracles. He knew that when they walked, she fretted at his slow pace and willed him to take just a few more steps before turning to go back home again. He knew that she longed to do more visiting and more entertaining.

And he gave in, against his better judgment, when Amberley's betrothed arrived and various social entertainments were planned in her honor. He took Grace to the Courtneys' informal dance, the Carringtons' picnic, Amberley's garden party, among other things.

But he ended up feeling uneasy. She could do nothing strenuous, of course. She could not dance or walk any great distance. And he found himself watching her almost constantly, though she had begged him not to feel obliged to keep her company at every moment of every entertainment. He was proud of her, proud that their friends and neighbors would see that she carried his child. And he ached with love for her, observing her converse with Miss Purnell and others with her usual quiet charm.

And he wondered if she was happy. There was no reason in the world why she should not be. She had freely chosen to stay with him—or had she? She had been pregnant before that infernal letter from Sandersford had arrived. And she had told him that bearing a son was what she wanted to do— she very rarely admitted the possibility that it might be a daughter. And she seemed perfectly contented with his company by day and his lovemaking by night. Indeed, it could no longer be said that he made love *to* her almost nightly. To his wonder, he had found since their reconciliation that he made love *with* her.

There was no reason to believe her unhappy. But he found himself, quite against his will, watching her with ladies of almost her age, ladies with grown children, and he wondered if she perhaps found it humiliating to have a younger husband who had forced her into beginning a new family.

And always, returning to haunt him against all reason, was

that knowledge that when she had made her decision regarding Sandersford, she had not after all been free to make a free choice. He had begotten his child in her perhaps a week before that letter came.

It was absurd. He had every reason to be happy. He *was* happy. But he watched his wife with unwilling unease. Did she love him? She had never said she did. And it did not matter if she did or not. Love was only a word. She showed him love, or respect and loyalty and affection anyway. They were enough. Quite enough.

But did she love him? Absurdly, totally absurdly, he was afraid to ask. And afraid to say the words himself for fear they would be unwelcome and embarrass or even distress her.

Grace attended the wedding of the Earl of Amberley and Miss Alexandra Purnell in the village church during September, and the wedding breakfast afterward at Amberley Court. There were only two weeks remaining until her expected confinement, and she was feeling quite huge, but she assured Peregrine that she was quite well and that riding in the carriage could not do her the harm that it might have done a few months before.

But she did not have to plead. He was quite as eager as she for her not to miss such a rare and glorious event as the marriage of the Earl of Amberley. And he reassured her when she mentioned her size that they were not in London, where perhaps the presence of a very pregnant lady in public might be frowned upon. In the country, people were far more tolerant and willing to accept life for what it was.

"The only thing you must absolutely promise me," he said with a grin, "is that you will not begin your pains in the middle of the church service or the wedding breakfast. Not only would you divert everyone's attention from the bride, but I might give in to the hysterics or a fit of the vapors."

"I promise," she said, and spread her hand over her swollen abdomen. "Oh, Perry, this son of yours is going to be a boxer, I swear. I sometimes wish he did not have to practice on me."

"Your daughter is going to be a dancer, is she?" he said, lifting her hand away and setting his own in its place.

Grace liked the earl's bride very well and had been pleased to find her a regular visitor during the past couple of months when she was confined more and more to her home. They would be friends, Grace liked to think until she remembered that there must be a fifteen- or sixteen-year gap in their ages. And yet their husbands had been childhood friends and the earl was, in fact, two years older than Perry. It was a little awkward, but it was an awkwardness that she was going to have to accustom herself to. And not before time. She had been married to Perry for two and a half years.

Were all marriages as hard to adjust to as hers was proving to be? she wondered. Even if husband and wife seemed suited in every way, were there still inevitable problems of adapting to each other once the nuptials were over?

She watched the earl and his bride as they stood and kneeled together at the front of the church. They were a beautiful couple and seemed very well-suited in character. Would they live happily ever after from this day on? If rumor was at all true, their association had certainly not had an auspicious beginning. But at this particular moment they were very deeply in love with each other. That seemed very obvious to Grace.

And gracious, she thought later as she watched the earl and his new countess move among their guests after the wedding breakfast, those two had known physical love already. And she flushed in shock at her own improper intuition and glanced self-consciously at Peregrine, half-expecting that he would have read her thoughts.

"Are you feeling quite the thing, Grace?" he asked, leaning forward and covering her hand briefly with his.

"Yes, thank you," she said, "I am quite well. Your son must be sleeping. Will they be happy, Perry? I do hope so. I like them both excessively."

"I could never quite picture Edmund married," he said. "He is a handsome devil, of course. I used to be envious of his good looks. But he is a very private person too. They seem fond of each other, though, don't they? I suppose if they want a happy marriage, they will have it. It all depends on how much they want it, doesn't it?''

They were interrupted at that moment by Lady Madeline and Lord Eden, the latter looking extremely dashing in the green uniform of an officer of a rifle regiment. Madeline was clinging to his arm. A few months before at the age of two-and-twenty, rather late in life, he had finally defied his family's reluctance and fulfilled a lifetime ambition to buy himself a commission in the army. He was off to Spain the following week to join the British troops there.

''It all depends on how much they want it.'' The words echoed in Grace's mind for the rest of the day and the days to come. Marriage was not quite so simple, though, was it? Both she and Perry doubtless wanted a happy marriage, and had from the start. And they had that now, did they not? But it had not come easily and it had not come merely from the wanting. They had both had to work hard and give a great deal to achieve the measure of harmony and contentment they now knew.

And she could still not say that they were perfectly happy. Happily-ever-after happy. There were always the niggling doubts. Perhaps such happiness was impossible to achieve in real life. Perhaps because a married couple must always be made up of two distinct people, perfect harmony, perfect togetherness was an impossible illusion, the stuff of dreams and romance. Perhaps she and Perry were as happy as a married pair could ever hope to be.

And perhaps people never reached a pinnacle of happiness, even an imperfect one. Perhaps one could never say that now one was as happy as could be, and that was the way things would always remain. She and Perry would always have to work on their marriage, fight to retain the contentment they had won. That was true of any marriage, she supposed. For theirs perhaps it was more so than usual. The age gap would always create awkwardnesses and doubts and feelings of inadequacy in both of them. But the problems would never be insurmountable unless they chose to make them so.

When she was eighty and he seventy, the age difference would be almost unnoticeable, she thought with a smile of amusement.

"Not allowed, Grace," Peregrine said, taking her by the elbow. "I absolutely forbid you to enjoy a joke that I cannot share. Out with it."

"I was thinking that when I am eighty and you seventy, no one will notice the age difference," she said.

He grinned before looking at her a little more seriously. "Do you think they notice now?" he asked. "Do I look so much younger than you, Grace? I do not see it when I look in the mirror and when I look at you. And I doubt that our friends do. We are just Perry and Lady Grace to them. I don't plan to still be crawling about among flower beds when I am seventy, by the way. Your eighty-year-old knees will have to take you alone then, I'm afraid. I will not be able to keep up with you."

She laughed.

"I think we might just be able to get close to Edmund and his bride now," he said.

The new Countess of Amberley held out both hands to Grace as they approached, and smiled warmly. "I am so honored that you came, Grace," she said. "Are you very uncomfortable? You should not be standing so much, should you?"

Grace took her hands. "You look very beautiful, Alexandra," she said. "And of course I cried at the church, just like every other lady present. Except you, that is. And I am quite well, thank you."

The countess looked up, bright-eyed, at her new husband, who was talking with Peregrine. "Perry has promised Edmund that he will send word as soon as your time comes," she said, "so that Edmund may go and pace the floor with him. I will not come. I don't believe that you will feel like making social conversation at that time." She laughed and squeezed Grace's hands. "But I will come and visit afterward as soon as I may and duly admire your child. You must be very excited. And frightened?"

Grace smiled. "Yes, both," she said. "I am glad the weather has been kind to you today. And I am glad that you decided after all that the wedding would be here. The Misses Stanhope were ready to hold a wake, I believe, if you had removed to London or Yorkshire."

"Papa favored St. George's in London," Lady Amberley said. "And I am not at all in the habit of defying Papa. But Edmund and I decided this together. This is where we belong, where we love to be even though I came here for the first time only a few months ago. It made sense that we also marry here. Oh, and today I am so glad. I have all my friends around me and I have never had friends before. You must know what I mean, Grace. Do you know?"

"Yes," Grace said. "This is a special part of the world. We are fortunate, you and I, that our husbands live here."

"Our husbands," the girl said with a breathless laugh. "How strange that sounds, and how very lovely." She looked wonderingly at the earl again, and he smiled and moved to her side.

"Lady Lampman," he said, "I must tell you how grateful I am that you have come to our wedding. It would not be quite right to be without my oldest friend on such a day, and one who got me into so many scrapes as a boy, I might add. Yet I am sure he would not have come and left you at home alone. If you will pardon me for noticing your, ah, condition, I must say that I think it heroic of you to have traveled all these miles."

"You don't know Grace," Peregrine said with a grin. "I have had to have new locks put on all the garden sheds so that she does not sally forth into the garden at the dead of night to create new flower beds. And I have to tie her arm to my side when we are out walking so that she does not break into a gallop. You are looking at a man who is almost worn out from the exertions of chasing after a, ah, pregnant wife, Edmund."

"Perry," Grace said, and all four of them laughed.

"We are pleased to have you here anyway, Lady Lampman," the earl said, extending a hand to her, "aren't we, Alex? And if you wish to take Perry to sit down before he collapses, ma'am, please feel free to do so.''

Peregrine took Grace's arm and smiled down at her as bride and groom turned away to greet another group of well-wishers. Her eyes were bright, her cheeks flushed with color, sure signs of fatigue. ''I am going to order the carriage to be brought around,'' he said. ''And you may not argue with me, Grace. You are tired and I am in the mood to play tyrant. Besides, that daughter of mine is going to wake soon and want her dancing lesson again. Or has she started already?''

''I think he is stirring,'' she said. ''And I am in the mood to play obedient wife, Perry. I am tired, I must confess. But do you mind leaving early? I am afraid I am spoiling your enjoyment.''

''I am expecting a child too within the next two weeks, you know,'' he said. ''Has no one told you? I feel excitement too, and emotional turmoil, and anxiety, and fatigue. And, no, you need not look at me with suspicion. I am not teasing you. I have never been more serious.''

16

It was awkward to hold Grace in the carriage on the way home, Peregrine found. He could not just cuddle her against him as he could remember doing during the same journey late on Christmas Day. But by sitting sideways himself, he did manage to cradle her head on his shoulder and take some of her weight against himself. She was very tired. She held both hands over the bulk of her pregnancy. Perhaps he should not have allowed her to attend the wedding, after all.

"I am glad we came, Perry," she said, as if she had read his thoughts. "Was it not all very splendid?"

"Very," he said. "Are you comfortable, Grace?"

"Mmm," she said. "I think they are going to be happy."

"Do you?" he said, and wriggled her head into the warm hollow between his neck and his shoulder. He held her while she relaxed more against him and while her breathing became deeper and more even.

He was thinking of his own wedding, in the same church more than two years before. He had been a married man for more than two years! It seemed impossible. And yet that wedding and the weeks that had preceded it could be something from another lifetime altogether. As he held his sleeping, very pregnant wife against him, it was hard to believe that she was the same woman as the quiet, dignified sister of his friend the rector, whom he had married to save from the humiliation of having to seek employment.

He had cared for her then. He had thought he cared. And

he had thought it such a simple thing, to marry her and to comfort her for the rest of his life. Even after she had told him her history, he had thought that it would be easy. And yet marriage had proved the most difficult undertaking of his life. It was impossible, he believed now, to be married and not become totally involved in the relationship. At least, it was impossible for him.

Grace was now more dear to him than anything or anyone else in his whole life. She was a person now, a complex, dearly beloved person, not just the figure of respect and, yes, pity that she had been at the start. But even love brought its own complications, its own doubts and fears and dissatisfactions.

Somehow, through two and a half difficult years, they had reached a plateau of harmony and contentment. Even love, perhaps. Certainly love on his part. But he could not be certain that this state of affairs would remain for the rest of their lives. Or even that he wished it to do so. Marriage was a living, dynamic relationship that must keep growing if it was to survive. They would have to want to be happy if they were to be so. That was what he had said to Grace earlier about Edmund and his bride. But the same applied to himself and Grace and to any married couple.

They must want to be happy. He did. He wanted it badly enough to be prepared to work at his marriage for the rest of his days. Did Grace? He could only have faith that she did. There were no certainties when one was married. Because, however close one became to another person, one never became that person. That person was always a different being. It was a risky and a troublesome business, marriage.

Would he do anything as rash as marrying Grace if he had it all to do again, knowing what he now knew? Would he choose to live if he could go back beyond his mother's womb and have the choice? Foolish question! Life was worth living despite all its problems and dark times. And his marriage was more precious to him than anything else in his life had been, despite the uncertainties and the heartache. And the continued uncertainty and his constant terror for Grace's life and that of their child.

The carriage jolted to a stop before their front door.

"Oh," Grace said before he could kiss her awake, "I have been sleeping. And, Perry, I have been leaning on you and you have nothing against your back. You must be in agony."

"Worn to the bone. A mere shadow of my former self," he said cheerfully, "as I was telling Edmund a little while ago. I will be very glad when this daughter of yours finally puts in an appearance, Grace. Perhaps I will be able to drag myself around again afterward."

"Silly," she said. "Your son will take his own sweet time in arriving, I am sure. Why should he hurry when he has a father who will hold him and his mother so comfortably?"

"Do you want me to throw you both from the carriage?" he asked.

"No thank you," she said. "The servants might think we have quarreled. Get down from here, Perry, if you please, and offer me your hand like the gentleman you pretend to be."

Peregrine laughed and vaulted out onto the cobbled driveway. He had noticed only recently that he could joke with his wife and she could hold her own with ease.

One remembered that it was painful, Grace thought, lying on her side relaxing, waiting for the next onslaught of pain. One remembered that it was worse than any other pain one could imagine. And one knew that as time went on the pains became so frequent and so intense that one hung onto one's sanity by the merest thread.

And yet one did not remember. Not until it happened again. As soon as it did start again, one thought, Oh, oh, here it comes. Yes, this is what it was like. And one knew exactly why it was that nature, or God, arranged matters that women did not really remember.

She did not know what time it was—late afternoon, perhaps? There was still daylight outside. It had been well before daylight when she had finally woken Perry, sure at last that this was no false alarm. She did not know where he was now. He had sat with her, holding her hand and

looking as white as a ghost, until Doctor Hanson had arrived.
Then both the doctor and the housekeeper had urged him
to leave, and he had done so after Grace had smiled at him
and told him that she would feel better without having him
to worry about. He had not even grinned in response.

Would it never be over? The pains had been crashing
through her world at two-minute intervals for several hours,
yet Doctor Hanson still said that she was not fully dilated,
that the child's head was not moving down. He was standing
quietly at the window, looking out. The housekeeper sat in
the chair beside her bed, bathing her face with a cool cloth
every few minutes, chiding her gently every time she bit her
lip, advising her to scream instead.

She could not scream. If she did not hold on to the little
control she had left, she would become demented. Soon now
she would see her son. She must think of that. Soon she
would hold him in her arms. Soon Perry would be able to
come back. Was anyone downstairs with him? Had Lord
Amberley come, as promised? Was Perry calm?

Would it never be over?

She concentrated every power of her mind on not giving
in to panic as she felt the familiar tightening of muscles and
descended into another wave of pain.

"This is ridiculous! Damned ridiculous!" Peregrine
slammed down his billiard cue onto the table. "There are
some concerns that just cannot be drowned out by other
activities, Edmund. It's very kind of you to have spent a
whole day desperately trying to entertain me. I appreciate
it. But it can't be done, you know. I am going out of my
mind."

The Earl of Amberley sighed and laid his cue down beside
the other. "I don't know what else to do, Perry," he said.
"I have no experience at this sort of thing, you know. What
do you want to do?"

"I want to go up there to her," Peregrine said. "Dammit,
Edmund, this is as much my child as it is Grace's. It's not
fair that she should be going through all this alone while I

am downstairs playing billiards, for the love of God.''

"And enjoying yourself enormously,'' his friend said ironically.

"I'm going up,'' Peregrine said. "There must be something I can do.''

"It's not allowed,'' Lord Amberley said. "It's not done.''

"Dammit,'' Perry said. "Would you stay away if it were the countess, Edmund? Grace has been going through this since five o'clock this morning. And that was only when she told me. It must have started long before that. Would you stay away?''

"If it were Alex?'' his friend said quietly. "No. No, Perry, I would not be able to stay away. Do you love Lady Lampman, then? I have often wondered since that nasty occasion when you dealt me a bloody nose. Not that it is any of my business to know, of course.''

"You have doubtless earned my confidence after spending a whole day with me here,'' Peregrine said with the ghost of a smile, "when you have a bride of no more than a week waiting at home. Yes, of course I love her, Edmund. More than my own soul, I sometimes think. What if she dies? God, what if she dies?''

Lord Amberley gripped his shoulder. "She won't die,'' he said. "She's not going to die, Perry. What can we do to take your mind off things? We never lacked for things to do when we were boys, did we?''

"I don't think climbing forbidden cliffs would help at the moment,'' Peregrine said. "I'm going up there, Edmund.''

But even as he said the words, the butler arrived to announce that dinner was served. And Peregrine went to the dining room and even succeeded somehow in swallowing a few mouthfuls of food out of deference to his guest, who ate as little as he did if he had only been alert enough to notice.

She had to push. The need, the purely physical need, was quite irresistible. And a voice was telling her to push. Quite unnecessarily. Her mind was no longer functioning. Only her body. She was pain, racking pain, the only instinct left in her the instinct of survival, the need to rid herself of the pain, rid herself of her burden. She could no longer feel the cool cloth against her face and neck or her husband's hands gripping her own wet ones.

And then finally, mercifully, the pain burst from her and she was free. Free to sink into oblivion, into a pain-free nothingness. She let go of the final instinct to live.

"Grace!" A voice would not let her go. "Grace!" Not that it was a loud voice or a demanding voice. It was quiet and gentle. But it would not let her go. It was a voice that meant something to her, a voice she could not take with her if she went.

"Grace," it said, "we have a daughter. It is a girl. Can you hear me? No, you must not die. I won't let you die. Please!"

There was a baby crying somewhere. It was a sound she could not escape. It would not let her go. And there was a face in her line of vision. She must have her eyes open, then. She did not know who it was. But it was a familiar face. It was a beloved face. She wanted to see it more clearly.

"Perry?" she heard a high, thin voice say a long time later. She closed her eyes with the effort.

"We have a daughter," he said. Her hands were coming back to her. Someone was clasping them. "We have a daughter, Grace. Can you not hear her? She is squawking enough to waken the servants." He grinned.

It was Perry, she thought. He was Perry. "A daughter?" she said, not sure quite where her mouth was or how she formed the words. "She is alive?"

"Very much so," he said. "I don't think she likes being washed, Grace."

Her body was coming back to her. There was another involuntary contraction of muscles and a wave of pain and the soothing voice of the doctor telling her, or telling someone, that it was all over now, that very soon now she would be able to rest.

"Look at her, Grace. Oh, look at her."

But she could not look away from him for the moment. Why was he crying? Was the baby dead? Was she dead?

And then a little bundle of linen was being laid in the arms that did not yet belong to her, and she saw her child, quiet now, red and wrinkled, its face and head distorted from the recent passage of birth. Beautiful. Oh, beautiful beyond description. She could not go. She could not go and leave this child behind. Or that other beloved person. Where was he?

"Perry?"

He was there still beside her, white-faced, smiling, crying.

"A daughter," she said. "She is alive. She is alive, Perry."

"Yes," he said.

It was not him laughing, she realized, but herself. Or was she crying? She could not see him.

"Perry," she said, "hold her. I want to see you hold her."

She could see him enough to know that the smile had disappeared. "I don't think I dare," he said. He reached out and touched one tiny curled hand with his index finger.

"Hold your daughter," she said. "Papa."

The little bundle was gone from her arms. Someone was murmuring gentle endearments. Someone with a familiar, much-loved voice. The baby had stopped crying. She could let herself go. Grace slid down the seductive slope toward an unknown destination that seemed far more desirable at the moment than any of those things or people who had made her laugh and cry and come back to herself a moment ago.

"I am sorry, Alex." The Earl of Amberley lay beneath his wife, her body cradled comfortably on his own, her head nestled on his shoulder, the single blanket, his greatcoat, and her cloak covering her. "I have failed you already and we have been married only a week."

"You have not failed me," she said, turning her head and kissing his chin. "You have just been used all your life to retreating into yourself whenever there is a problem. You cannot easily change the habit of a lifetime just because you have a wife. You told me before we were married that you would have difficulty not excluding me from your life at times. And I told you, once I knew that you loved me, that

I would not let you do so. So I followed you here. I was
not even sure you would be here. I thought perhaps you were
still at Reardon Park.''

They were lying in a small stone hermit's hut a mile or
more from Amberley Court, long a hideaway of the earl's.
It was more than an hour past dawn.

"It was terrible," he said, one hand playing with his wife's
long dark hair, the other over his eyes. "All day yesterday
and then all night after Perry had gone to her. I could not
drag myself away."

"Is she really likely to die?" the countess asked hesitantly.

"She was bleeding a lot," he said. "I am sure Perry's
housekeeper would not have said so much if she had not been
so tired and so worried. And the child was a long time
coming. She is exhausted. And of course she is not a young
woman.''

"But nothing is sure?" she asked. "You did not talk to
the doctor or Perry?"

"No," he said. "Neither of them would leave her. Alex.
Alex, it is a cruel life for women." He hugged her to him.

"I think it is rather sure," she said after a pause. "Will
you mind, Edmund? Will you be very embarrassed?"

He groaned against her hair. "Embarrassed?" he said.
"Oh, Alex, my love."

"But a child after fewer than eight months, Edmund," she
said.

"So," he said, "the world will know that we were lovers
before our nuptials. Shameful indeed! I just wish you had
not raised the subject at this particular time. I'm afraid for
you, Alex.''

Later that same morning the rector's wife met the Misses
Stanhope at the church door with the news that the rector
had been called to Reardon Hall.

"The child?" Miss Letitia asked.

"A girl, and doing well," the rector's wife said.

"Lady Grace." Miss Stanhope's voice broke a silence that
none of the three seemed wishful to fill. Her words were
a statement rather than a question.

"She had a hard time, poor lady," the rector's wife said.

Miss Letitia fumbled for her handkerchief only when a tear dripped from her chin onto the frilled ribbons of her cap. "Poor dear Sir Perry," she said. "He is fond of her."

"She was married from our house," Miss Stanhope said.

The Misses Stanhope paid a call on their friend Mrs. Morton and she on Mrs. Courtney and Mrs. Cartwright and Mrs. Carrington. But they were mournful visits. There was no joy in the afternoon's gossip. Though, as with most gossip, it greatly exaggerated the negative.

Mr. Carrington found his wife in tears.

"Why, Viola?" he said. "What is this? I have not pinched you in a week, is that it? It is just that having passed my fiftieth birthday, I thought perhaps it was time to grow a more dignified image, dear. There was no implied insult to your charms. Dry your eyes now and come and be kissed."

"Don't tease, William," she said without any of her usual outrage. "It is Lady Lampman."

"Oh," he said. "Lost the child?"

"No-o," she wailed. "The child is well. But she is dying, William, or passed on already. The doctor has been at Reardon Park since yesterday morning, and the rector was called there this morning. Oh, the poor dear lady. She has been good for Perry, has she not? Oh, don't just stand there, William. Hold me. Please hold me. Poor dear Lady Lampman."

It was a cold, gray, blustery November day with almost nothing to recommend it to the senses. Two warmly clad figures made their way slowly along the lane leading from Reardon Park, the lady leaning quite heavily on the man.

"It feels so good to be outside again, Perry," Grace said, lifting her face to the cold wind.

"We must turn back soon," he said. "You must not overdo it and exhaust yourself or catch a chill, you know."

"It is so wonderful just to be alive," she said. "Is it not, Perry? Do you not feel it?"

"It is very wonderful to have you alive," he said. "I almost lost you, Grace." He covered her gloved hand with his own.

"No, you didn't," she said. "You kept me alive, Perry. It would have been so much easier at one point to die than to fight back to life. But you would not let me go."

He squeezed her hand.

"Perry," she asked hesitantly, "are you at all disappointed that I did not give you an heir?"

"What?" he said, drawing them to a stop and staring down at her, incredulous. "How could you possibly ask such a thing, Grace? And be without Rose? I would not exchange Rose for a score of sons."

"If I were fifteen years younger," she said, "or ten even, I could give you more children, Perry, and it would not matter that the first was a girl. But I am afraid that perhaps I can give you only this one. I was almost two years married before conceiving her."

"How strange you are sometimes," he said. "You worry a great deal, don't you, Grace? About being ten years older than I. How many times have I told you that it does not matter to me? I would not have you one day younger even if I could. Because I would thereby alter you, and I would not do that for worlds. I love you as you are. Just as you are. And the gift of a daughter that you have given me has filled me so very full of happiness that I am afraid I would have no room in my heart for half a dozen sons. Or even one. I don't want you to have more children, Grace. I cannot take the risk again of losing you."

"Are you happy?" she asked, looking up at him wistfully. "Truly happy, Perry? And do you love me?"

He touched her wind-reddened cheek with his gloved fingers. "I have never said it, have I?" he said. "Why are they the hardest words in the language to say? Yes, I love you, Grace. Oh, of course I do. I love you. Do you believe me, or will you be doubting again tomorrow?"

Her eyes were bright with tears. "I have done so much wrong in my life," she said. "I do not deserve such happiness, Perry. I don't deserve you."

"You have no regrets?" he asked. "You were expecting Rose when . . ." He smiled lamely. "You were expecting Rose."

"Oh, Perry," she said, "I had a great and fortunate escape when I was young. I might have married him. I would be married to him now. And as unhappy with him as I am happy with you. I was dazzled by him, overpowered by his charm as a girl. And frightened by him after you and I were married. I was afraid for a while that I deserved no better and that you deserved a great deal better than me. I thought you deserved a young and beautiful and vibrant girl, Perry."

"Absurd," he said.

"I do love you," she said. "Oh, I do love you, Perry. And together we have made Rose. Life is so very miraculous."

"She knows me already," he said.

"Of course. All women know you," she said. "You have only to smile and they all capitulate. Why should our daughter be any different? I have to confess that she never fails to stop crying when you pick her up."

"She knows that I have a weakness for the female gender," he said. He bent and kissed her lips before turning with her to walk back to the house again. "Especially her mother."

She laid her head against his shoulder. "Everyone has been so kind," she said, "visiting me and sending their good wishes. Did you know that Alexandra is increasing, Perry?"

"No," he said. "So I am to return the favor and pace floors with Edmund, am I?" He shivered. "Ugh! November! What an ugly day. Turn your poet's eye onto this scene, Grace, and make beauty out of it. Quite a challenge even for you, I think."

"Oh, not at all," she said. "Just look around you, Perry, and imagine all the seeds of spring buried and awaiting their chance. They cannot be held back forever, you know. And look at the sky. Those dark and lowering clouds. Why is it daylight nevertheless? Because there is blue sky and sunshine just beyond those clouds, and even the clouds cannot keep out all the warmth or all the light of the sun. And the wind? It is chilly. And it is life. It is not the chill of the grave but the invigorating breath of life. Look. It has made your cheeks and your nose rosy. And mine too, doubtless. It is a beautiful day, Perry. A new day. A new tomorrow."

"You are right," he said with a laugh, hunching his shoulders against the cold. "Whatever would I do without you, Grace? I would still be looking about me in the greatest gloom, counting the months to spring. And since it is such a lovely day, my girl, and you have just proved it to me, you can stand here with me outside our door to be kissed instead of waiting for the greater warmth of your sitting room. Hold your face up to me."

"You expect me to grumble now and beg to be taken indoors for my kiss, don't you?" she said, smiling up into his eyes and putting her arms up around his neck. "I want a good long kiss before you take me inside, sir. And I don't care if the servants see us, either."

The chill of the November wind did not abate as they stood locked in a close embrace on their doorstep. Nor did the clouds part to allow one glimpse of the blue sky and sun Grace had spoken of. But they did not notice and would not have cared if they had. For in each other's arms they found all the warmth and brightness the sunniest day could have brought.

In each other they found the eternal promise of spring.